"BOLD, HONEST, AND INTELLIGENT . . . FOWLER CREATES POWERFUL INTIMACIES."
—The Washington Post

"Strong prose . . . Rings real and authentic."
—*Los Angeles Times*

"A heart-bruising plunge in the wails and scrapes of what it sometimes must have been like to grow up poor in small-town Florida in the mid-1960s . . . Fowler's most honest, penetrating, and therefore most disturbing look at this sometimes unspeakable world."
—*The Miami Herald*

"Achingly real, yet more than real, *Before Women Had Wings* has the authentic ring of truth and myth combined."
—Lee Smith
Author of *Saving Grace*

"Fowler's deeply moving, triumphant third novel brilliantly conveys a child's bewilderment. . . . She sweeps the narrative along with plangent, lyrical prose . . . and establishes herself as a writer of formidable talent."
—*Publishers Weekly* (starred review)

Please turn the page for more reviews. . . .

"STINGING WITH TENDERNESS, THIS IS HER BEST YET."
—AMY TAN

"[Fowler] triumphs. . . . [Her] prose is never less than as sinewy as cypress trees and as rich as Christmas cake. . . . Few writers capture poverty's weird chemistry of aching hope and grinding pessimism like Fowler. . . . This novel will make you hurt in the best way—and make your mind, like Bird's, fly high over pure, paradise seas."

—*Atlanta Journal & Constitution*

"Clearly [this book] ended too soon because weeks after finishing this book I still think about it. That's the hallmark of this writer's work. She makes me care beyond sense what happens to a cast of troubled characters."

—*Southern Living*

"Fowler's real gift is that she manages to present the ponderous problems her characters face with a style and grace that takes your breath away."

—*St. Petersburg Times*

“STUNNING . . .
Establishes [Fowler] once and for all as one of the preeminent voices in current American fiction.”

—*The St. Augustine Record*

“Fowler has made gold out of dross, turned despair toward hope, marked a path out of the dark woods of helplessness where a child who is not cherished inevitably is lost.”

—*The Florida Times-Union*

“A pitch-perfect, bravura performance . . . In *Before Women Had Wings*, the beguiling story of eight-year-old Avocet Abigail Jackson, Connie May Fowler has staked her claim to a part of the southern literary countryside located somewhere between Eudora Welty and Carson McCullers.”

—LAWRENCE THORNTON
Author of *Imagining Argentina*

“A beautifully written book that explores the human gift for survival by clinging to whatever small goods can be found, both real and imaginary.”

—*Tallahassee Democrat*

By Connie May Fowler:

SUGAR CAGE
RIVER OF HIDDEN DREAMS*
BEFORE WOMEN HAD WINGS*

**Published by The Ballantine Publishing Group*

BEFORE WOMEN HAD WINGS

Connie May Fowler

IVY BOOKS • NEW YORK

An Ivy Book
Published by The Ballantine Publishing Group

www.randomhouse.com/BB/

Library of Congress Catalog Card Number: 98-93418

ISBN: 0-8041-1890-6

This edition published by arrangement with G. P. Putnam's Sons.

Manufactured in the United States of America

First Ballantine Books Trade Edition: May 1997
First Mass Market Edition: March 1999

10 9 8 7 6 5 4 3 2 1

FOR FAITH

We will have the wings of eagles
when the fallen angels fly.
—Billy Joe Shaver

I would like to thank my husband, Mika, for helping me face my ghosts. I am indebted to my sister and brother—Deidre Hankins and Jimmy Friend—for allowing me to reopen old wounds and for so graciously sharing with me their childhood memories. I also must thank Joy Harris and Faith Sale—their ever-present strength inspires and sustains me. To my mother and father—Lee and Henry, who passed away before I could ask the questions that mattered—I can only whisper, "I hope I got it right." To Laura Gaines, Carolyn Doty, Kim Seidman, and Col. James Friend, I offer heartfelt and enduring gratitude. And, of course, many thanks to Atticus for standing guard.

BACK IN 1965, on a day so hot that God Almighty should have been writhing with sick-to-the-stomach guilt over driving His children out of the cool green of Eden, my daddy walked into our general store, held a revolver to his head, told my mama that he couldn't take any more and that because of her harsh ways and his many sins he was going to blow his brains out.

Seconds earlier, when it had been just Mama and I in that dusty old store, I'd been thinking about food. Sweets, to be exact. I used to suffer craving spells. Still do when I get to thinking about things. I don't know what spurred the want back then, a want for sugar that was so strong I would grind my teeth flat until my needs were met. Could it be that my deep yearning was caused by a sadness bred in the womb, a dark past we're helpless to undo or make right, a history we have no memory of once we're birthed into this world? Are there events so ancient and awful that our fresh lives are spoiled even before the cord is cut, so we keep craving?

These are questions for which I haven't a single answer. In fact, answers aren't part of my nature. Details are what I'm about—stacks and stacks of details—the bones of my family, calcified vessels, the marrow chock-full of wishes and regrets. In my mind I pick up the bones one by one—a leg bone, a hip, then a spine that looks like a witch's ladder. Before you know it, this skeleton made of memories is rattling me.

I was six years old, dressed in my yellow shorts set—it had white rickrack tacked around the neck—standing in front of the pine bins that were full to overflowing with sweets, trying my hand at whistling in an attempt to get my mama's attention, hoping that she would look up from the black ledger book and its long columns of numbers that evidently foretold our future, wanting her to smile and say it was okay to eat a honey bun—my favorite food in the entire world—betting that she would not snarl at me to get the hell away from the sweet bins because didn't I know it was almost lunchtime, when Daddy staggered in through the front screen door and, without saying hello, proceeded on with that revolver. Held it down by his side and let his arm dangle back and forth, as if the gun were nothing more than a toy, something he might throw across the room.

My mama, whose name was Glory Marie, looked up from her work. Her face slid from distraction to annoyance, and I prayed that my guardian angel, who so far in my life had proven to be an elusive helper, would materialize in front of the counter with its clutter of jars filled with pigs' feet, beef jerky sticks, BC Powder packets, bug spray, pickled eggs. Prayerful words welled up inside me, whirled through my head: *Please, angel, whisk me away. Take me to your house in the clouds, just for a little while, just for today.*

I looked at the black muzzle of the gun and my daddy's

freckled fingers wrapped around its handle like five pale, unsteady snakes. *Come on, angel, come on.*

Mama said something under her breath—probably a curse word, she knew a lot of those. Then she picked up her perfectly sharpened pencil, pointed it at Daddy, dart-like, and said, "Billy, put down the gun. You're scaring the children," although he could not have been scaring my big sister, Phoebe, because Mama had sent her down the road to Mrs. Bryson's to deliver the lard and flour she'd ordered.

My daddy's blue eyes were crazy—thunderhead wild, my mama always called them—you know, that look of madness as if a person's knotted-up, Devil-haunted soul has been forced into the small space inside the sockets, flashing despair, anger, and hurt like a warning light: *Do not enter; do not cross; do not attempt to soothe.*

"Glory, I mean it. I'm sick and tired of trying to make it in this godforsaken world. You and the girls will be happier with me gone." Daddy's voice was loud, trembly. He was crying.

I shut my eyes, and on the backs of my eyelids I saw Mama get up from behind the desk and put her arms around Daddy and coo, "Everything is going to be fine. Yes, baby, I love you. Your daughters love you." If I'd been her, I would have done that.

But my daydream did not come true. When I looked again, Mama was still sitting, thumping that pencil against the coffee-stained pages of the ledger. When she spoke, her words pounded into me as if she were a fancy-footworking prizefighter: "Jesus, Billy, you're behaving like a fool."

A shadow passed over my daddy's eyes. His lips curled into a grimace, then a grin that was all heartache and threat. He looked past my mama at nothing in particular, and I feared he might be staring into the unknowable face of Our Lord and Savior.

Daddy raised the revolver to his temple, and for a split second the gun seemed alive, a blackbird flapping. In a voice too steady for the circumstances, he said, "I swear to sweet Jesus, you're gonna be sorry, Glory Marie."

Then he slipped the weapon into the waistband of his pants—an eerie satisfaction bouncing across his face—and he stormed back out the front screen door.

I expected the door to bang shut, but instead it only whispered because my big sister caught it on her way in. She was sweaty, red-faced, looked as if she'd just stumbled through a mess of stinging nettles—always did when there was trouble at home, which was almost all the time. I heard Daddy's car engine turn over and rev. Phoebe asked, "Mama, where's Daddy going with that gun?"

"Shush, girl," Mama said as she faced the window and watched Daddy peel out of the driveway. She picked up the phone. Its heavy black receiver looked too much like the revolver. Crows outside in the pecan tree started cackling. I ran over to Phoebe and threw my arms around her.

Mama's voice spilled over me: "Yes, Chuck, this is Glory Marie. Billy's got a gun. Says he's going to shoot himself. Can you send an officer after him? He's headed north, toward town. Try Moccasin Branch. He's threatened before that if he ever killed himself it would be by the river. And can you please send a cruiser over for the girls and me?"

After a series of okay's and I think so's, she hung up the

phone, gathered her pocketbook and cigarettes, and told us to go outside and wait for the police. But I couldn't move. My muscles and bones turned to rubber. So I stayed put, clinging to Phoebe. She wasn't going anywhere either.

Mama was a pretty woman. I didn't look a thing like her. She had black hair and black eyes, and I figured her to have been Indian although she never confessed to such a thing. I was redheaded-near-to-blonde, with my daddy's thunderhead-blue eyes, and I'd blister under the sun before you could say squat. Phoebe looked like Mama's child with all that darkness—skin and hair and eyes and all—but even shared looks didn't make the two of them close. No, she wasn't a woman you could get close to on a regular basis.

Mama pushed her chair away from the desk, smoothed her dress as she stood, then walked over to the counter. She took a wad of folding money out of the cash drawer.

I squeezed Phoebe's arm tight as I watched Mama run her thumb over the stacked corners of the paper money, silently adding. Then she glanced up, saw us standing there like a couple of stunned deer. "I said go out there, now! I've got to shut things down."

Phoebe took me by the hand and steered us toward the door.

Mama called to me as she locked the cash drawer, "Quit that foolish crying, Bird."

I wasn't crying, but her scolding words pushed me over the edge. Phoebe hustled me outside, where we stood in the glare of the noontime summer heat. The sun, the sandy road, and the palmetto scrub leading to palm trees and oaks blurred into a smear of bright light tinged in greens and browns as my tears broke loose and freely flowed. I cried because my mama had told me not to. I cried because I didn't know what else to do.

Mama walked out onto the porch and locked the door. Her thin and lovely hands shook as she lit a cigarette with a lighter Daddy had given her on her birthday just three weeks before. The lid was cherry red, but the bottom part was crystal clear so that you could see the lady in a pink swimsuit skiing in a sea of fire-triggering fluid.

We uttered not a word. Just stared into the scorched distance. A fear grew inside me that maybe Daddy was already dead. I tried to reason away the rising doom: Nothing was kicking me down to my liver, no angelic voices screeching, "He's in heaven." *That's right,* I thought, *I'll hear the revolver fire. I'll feel the bullet ripping through my own cheekbones when Daddy's life slips into that boiling sky.*

"Where in the hell is the cruiser?" Mama's voice broke our silence, and as she spoke a dust devil appeared far in the distance on the unpaved Prince of Peace Citrus Highway, the road our store was on.

"That must be him," Mama said. She tossed her cigarette on the ground and smashed it with the pointed toe of her gray pumps. Mama dressed nice when she worked in the store, but didn't go in for fads—no miniskirts, no sunglasses the color of limes.

The policeman stopped the car so fast it bucked. A skinny man with an Adam's apple nearly the size of my fist, he got out and nodded at Mama, his long face scraping the humid air.

If Mama's heart was turning itself inside out with worry, she did not show it. With hands on hips, that pocketbook dangling off her arm, she looked like a woman determined not to become unhinged. "Hello, Jack. Thanks for picking us up."

"No problem at all, Glory Marie." He opened the backseat door for us. His arms were so long, looked like they'd been stretched in a torture chamber.

"Get in, girls," Mama ordered.

Jack touched Mama on the shoulder. "Glory," he said in a concerned tone, "everything is going to be all right. Chester Smith is on his way to Moccasin Branch Bridge right now."

Mama nodded, her lipsticked mouth sealed like a knife slash across her dark face. Phoebe was already in the car, but I resisted. If people saw me speeding by in a copmobile, they would think that I was going to jail. "No!" I screamed.

"Goddamn it, Bird, get in the goddamn car," Mama yelled.

I wanted to zip past her and into the store and run my hands over piles of penny candy in their cellophane wrappers, candy so pretty they looked like glass. I took a quick step in the direction of the front door, but Officer Stringbean Jack blocked my way, spurring in me a different idea: I would stand my ground by turning as still and unmovable as a garden statue.

But my mama, she would have none of that. She grabbed my arm, right where I'd been vaccinated, her face flying in a thousand directions, and she shook me. "What's wrong with you, you little hellion!"

I opened my mouth, tried to explain, but fear and panic snatched my words, ferried them to a place I could not go.

Mama shoved me into the cagelike backseat, and as she

did she banged my head hard into the car door. "Ow!" I screamed. *Please don't hurt me.*

"Get in there, you bitch. Don't you dare fight me!"

She did not say sorry or check if I was bleeding, which I wasn't. But if I'd been that statue, my gray face would have been dropping into the dirt, a thousand broken pieces.

I scooted over next to Phoebe, and Mama got in next to me, her hands clutching that pocketbook as if she might start slugging me with it. I buried my face in my sister's lap. It was a good way to sit—Mama couldn't hit me full in the face, and nobody would see me as we sped toward Lily, a town named in praise of the resurrection of Jesus, and the river that marked its edge.

For the next few minutes, I attempted to hide and to hear beyond the siren and to hold my breath because the back of the police car smelled like piss. I gritted my teeth, readying myself for the sound of a gunshot or a sudden pain inside my head caused by Daddy's passing. I thought about my angel who never came and I cursed her: *God-damn you, angel, straight to hell.*

My whole body turned hot, then ice-block cold. I thought I might throw up or pass out. Did I feel sick because of my breath-holding, the bump on my head, my blood connection to Daddy? I didn't know, but I needed air bad, so I sat up, looked at Phoebe, studied her nettled face. Figured she could use some kind words. So I leaned into her: "He ain't dead."

Then I scrunched down in the seat, but not so low that I couldn't see out. The countryside whipped by fast. It felt like I was watching a moving picture. We streaked past farms and groves and signs that touted fresh citrus and the power of God. As we neared Moccasin Branch Bridge, I grew amazed, for it appeared as if every man, woman, child, and dog in Lily had gathered along the western bank. How they knew to be there, how they knew Billy Jackson was going to attempt to take his life right there on the slim white shoreline of that brown-water river, was a mystery to me. I hadn't yet learned that in a small town everybody knows everything instantly.

I eyed those busybody folks and was seized by a funny thought: *It would be a good time to rob the bank.* Then my heart stumbled a beat, as if it had gotten caught on one of the cypress snags in Moccasin Branch, and I searched that crowd for my daddy. But I did not see him. I looked to Phoebe, whose cinnamon skin was flushed and clammy. Her dark eyes were dry, which was a terrible thing to see. My mama always said the Devil steals tears—keeps them in a box with your name on it so that when you go to hell you will spend eternity crying the stored-up teardrops of a lifetime.

Mama struggled and cursed as she tried to get out of the police cruiser, but you can't open the back door of a cop car if you're on the inside, so the three of us were trapped. I felt a fit coming on, one of those leg-kicking, arm-flailing, wailing fits, when Mama had one of her own. She let loose with a string of cussing so potent it caused Jack the policeman, who was standing outside talking with another of his own kind, to blush.

He opened the door and said, "Sorry, Glory, I just needed to make sure what was what. We've got Billy in custody. He's okay."

Jack nodded in the direction of another police car, and I craned my neck to see, but there were so many people milling about that my view was blocked. "You want that we take him in, or that you carry him home?"

Mama stared straight ahead, her eyes hard as steel. She said, "Take the son-of-a-bitch in."

Then she gathered her pocketbook into the crook of her arm and took me by the hand. I slipped my other one in Phoebe's. Pretending we were women of grace, wearing our pride like long black veils, we slipped out of the cruiser and threaded our way through the gawking crowd—friends and acquaintances all. Some said, "Glory, can we help?" but my mama responded to no one. She fixed her granite gaze on the storm clouds rising upon the horizon and pulled us right along behind her.

We got in Daddy's white Impala. Under the sun's glare not yet shadowed by the approaching clouds, the Impala seemed only a glimmer, a ghost car that would ramble through the Florida scrub toward a future thick with questions and grief.

Mama drove us home. She kept her lips sealed, and through instinct and experience, Phoebe and I knew to keep our own traps shut.

We had a shotgun house on a lake no one had ever bothered to name, in the middle of a citrus grove owned by Mr. Bailey T. Watson, a rich man who lived a lifetime north of us in a mansion that overlooked Lake Panasoffkee. We rented our house from him, and it was okay. The grove was a good place to hide.

As we walked up the front porch steps, Mama, who looked whipped but stubborn, said, "You girls play Chinese checkers or something. Do anything but fight."

My sister said, "Can we have a Co'-Cola?"

"Yes, you may, but don't drink too much."

Then Mama and Phoebe went into the kitchen, and I stayed on the porch and looked through the cracks in the wooden floor slats and said, "Here, kitty, kitty," because there was a wild cat that sometimes stayed under there and I wanted to tame her, thought that would be a fun thing to do.

Phoebe tried to catch the screen door with her foot as she came out with two Co'-Colas, but she wasn't fast enough. It made a popgun sound. From somewhere inside the house Mama yelled, "Damn you, young'uns!"

I took my cold drink. "Why do you think she's making Daddy stay in jail?"

Phoebe ran her finger down the long crest of her nose. "Try to teach him a lesson, I guess."

I took three big swallows, and as the soothing fluid rushed down my throat I wondered what kind of lesson could he possibly learn—not to play with guns, not to make Mama angry, not to do anything to attract attention? That must be it—I acted poorly whenever I desired sweet attention. Maybe all my daddy needed, more than anything in this world, was for my mama to be Jesus-like, all-forgiving, and gentle to little animals.

Phoebe looked out toward the grove. Its straight, orderly rows of citrus trees were shady and often cool. She swatted a fly off her forehead and said, "I wish the rain would come soon."

"Me too."

I liked the way I sounded when I agreed with her. I thought I came off as grown up, trying on my big sister's words and ideas rather than my mama's high heels and beads, which always landed me in trouble. I blew on the lip of the Co'-Cola bottle, coaxing from it a long, sad whistle. Daddy could whistle like nobody's business. Was he in that jail cell all alone, or had they thrown him in with a bunch of robbers and murderers? Was he wearing one of those striped prison outfits? Was he safe? I didn't have any answers. "Sister." I patted her leg. "Will you play me one game?"

Phoebe looked down at me as if I was a pest, but then her sharp black eyes softened and she said, "Yeah, Bird, I'll play you a game."

We sat on the porch, Indian-style, placing the marbles on the Chinese checkers board. Mama came out, pocketbook on arm, paper sack in hand. She'd put on fresh makeup and had changed out of that nice linen dress and high heels she'd been wearing earlier and into a blue wraparound skirt, a white cotton blouse, and flats. Despite the dark circles under her eyes, she looked comfortable, newly scrubbed.

"There's egg salad in the refrigerator," she said. "Phoebe, fix you and your sister a sandwich while I'm gone."

Phoebe didn't look at Mama, just kept on with those marbles, glaring at them as if they were being unruly and she was trying to make them obey. "Where you going?" she asked.

"To take your daddy something to eat." Mama bit down on her bottom lip. I saw her whole face start to tremble and then pull itself back together. She took a deep breath, stared over our heads, and in a justifying tone of voice—as if we were accusing her of something—she said, "He's probably hungry by now."

"I guess so," Phoebe said.

A mockingbird started singing, and in some faraway field a tractor droned to life. A wisp of hair fell in Mama's eyes. "I've got to go," she said. Then she hurried down the steps, settled into the car, fiddled with the keys. Had to try three times before that heap of wheels and metal would start, but once she got it going, she hollered, "You two behave while I'm away. Bird, don't give your sister a hard time. If your head hurts, put some ice on it."

Then Mama was gone, disappeared down the road in the white Impala. A clap of thunder cracked the heavens, and a flock of sparrows flew from the live oak that overhung our tin roof, taking cover in the grove.

Phoebe seemed unmoved by the rumbling sky. Just kept her eyes on the Chinese checkers game board and its perfect triangles filled with marbles of such luscious colors I wanted to eat them. But they wouldn't be sweet, no they wouldn't. Sister, she looked beautiful, staring down at the board, her face framed in shadows and cloud-spangled light. I thought, *She would make the most perfect angel.*

I watched as she stretched over the board to flick off a fallen leaf. Underneath her thin cotton shell, I saw how fragile the bones in her back were, far too sliver-prone, far too light to support a pair of wings.

Something tickled my arm. I looked down; a ladybug walked among my many freckles. My hairs must have seemed like a forest to a creature so small. I brought my arm close to my lips and softly blew, my breath a gust of wind to send the ladybug on her way. She flew off to another world, maybe a blade of grass, maybe a flower with a pool of water cupped in its petals. I wiped the sweat out of my eyes, stared into the heat. "Do you think she's gonna yell at Daddy; do you think he still has that gun?"

My wingless sister moved a red marble. I thought I heard the cartilage holding her skeleton together snap as she said, "Who cares, Bird. Who the hell really cares."

MY TRUE NAME is Avocet. Avocet Abigail Jackson. But because Mama couldn't find anyone who thought Avocet was a fine name for a child, she called me Bird. Which is okay by me. She named both her girl children after birds, her logic being that if we were named for something with wings then maybe we'd be able to fly above the shit in our lives.

I don't believe Mama realized that she named my big sister for a bird that's known for wagging its tail feathers and me for one that's been near to shot out several times and is currently hanging on to existence by the thinnest of threads. No, when she was pregnant with us, Mama simply visited the bookmobile, thumbed through a *Peterson's Field Guide*, and picked a sound she thought was pretty, never bothering to read up on our namesakes.

When I was old enough to think about such things, I asked Mama why she hadn't bird-named my big brother, Hank, so that he, too, could fly above the horrors of life. Without even pausing to look up from the chicken she was butchering, Mama said, "Child, men *make* the shit in this world. Let them wallow in it." Then, using nothing but her bare hands, she broke off a wing right at the shoulder joint and tossed it onto a fleshy pile of chicken parts.

Despite her awful comment, I know Mama loved Hank

as much as she loved the rest of us. But her love was obscured by a mean streak that showed itself at random.

Hank was her son from a soldier she was married to before she met Daddy. So really Hank was only our half-brother, but he was raised by my daddy because his got killed in a paratrooping accident. And I never thought of him as half or incomplete in any way, since he had personality to spare.

I don't remember a time when Hank actually lived at home. That's because he was born thirteen years before my mama and daddy did anything about the spark in their eyes that would become me. When we had the house in the grove, Hank lived up north. He was putting himself through college in a dry county in Kentucky. Despite the teetotaling nature of the town, Hank drank and was, my mama said, "hopped-up on pills." Each week she sent him a portion of the grocery allowance Daddy gave her. She told me that if Daddy ever found out why "the grocery money doesn't buy as much as it used to," he would have a fit.

Our secrets, though, they traveled down a two-way street. Mama made Phoebe and me swear not to tell Hank about Daddy's hell-raising ways or about how much the two of them fought. She warned us that if Hank knew, he might kill Daddy and that he almost did kill him before I was born. Hank had come home from school and discovered Daddy beating on Mama. I don't know the details, just that Hank used his fists to calm Daddy down. Mama said Hank and Daddy never did speak much to each other after that. But Daddy didn't beat her again, not for a while. That was her story, anyway.

I was both glad and frightened that Mama had gone to

visit Daddy the day he tried to kill himself. Glad because it meant she was being nice. Frightened because I thought she might lose her temper and be thrown behind bars, too. But during that long, hot afternoon while our parents chased their pain, Phoebe and I didn't place any bets on the outcome of Mama's trip to the county jail. We tried to stay busy, tried not to pin our hopes and fears to our shirtsleeves.

After Phoebe whipped my butt in Chinese checkers, and after we gobbled down some of that egg salad, she brought the phone out on the porch and called her friend Becky Sue. Phoebe giggled and gossiped and never once let on that Daddy was in jail, even though Becky Sue most surely knew. I guess they stayed friends by not asking dicey questions. Still, I didn't like that girl, because when she was around, my sister ignored me.

I bided my time by looking for the wild cat, and then by pretending I was José Gaspar, a pirate who lived during a time when people walked around with gold nuggets in their pockets. José pillaged Florida's west coast and took over Tampa, a big city south of here. My mama told me, however, that José Gaspar never existed. He was an excuse, she said, for Tampa's business community and politicians to run through the streets behaving like rapists and thieves.

Every February I watched the pirate parade—Gasparilla, they called it—on TV, and at first I had a difficult time understanding that during the rest of the year those drunk, bloodthirsty pirates were businessmen, attorneys, city council members. As I got older, though, it made perfect sense.

Believing in the pirate was way more fun than believing

my mama. So while Phoebe gabbed on the phone, I play-acted as if I were José himself, swiping a Spanish bayonet leaf through the sweltering air and fencing with a make-believe swashbuckling foe. I ignored Phoebe's repeated order, which she yelled into the phone receiver so Becky Sue's eardrums must have been sore, to "put down that Spanish bayonet before you poke your eye out."

After skewering invisible enemies and capturing all of coastal Florida, I became bored, so I stuck my bayonet in the dust and wandered down to the water. The storm clouds that had been building all day circled our grove and nameless lake as if they were jewels in a heavenly necklace.

I closed my eyes and willed it to rain. Thought about people who were God-powered, like Moses, who could part the sea. I looked around and spied a long, knobby stick nestled in the mud at the edge of the saw grass. I picked up the stick and held it over the lake, which reflected the sky's gray face. "Part, you moccasin-infested water," I shouted. "In the name of Jesus, part!"

The water lapped at my toes and the wind gusted and I do believe I might have started a miracle had Phoebe not shouted at me to get inside the house, didn't I know it didn't have to be raining for lightning to strike, and I'd better get my butt in gear and help her wash the dishes. Even though she was only thirteen, she'd already mastered the fine art of pushing me around.

Several days' worth of dishes were stacked in the sink like a house of cards. Phoebe washed while I dried. That is, when we weren't squealing and dropping plates and bowls because of the cockroaches eating off them.

Phoebe was telling me that Becky Sue's parents were

going to buy a boat and that maybe she'd let us take a ride in it across Panther Lake, when the Impala roared down the dirt lane. The car radio was on full blast, tuned to the country station so loud as to irritate the neighbors—if we'd had any. The car engine gurgled as though it could not stop sucking gas, and then it fell silent, as did the music. Two doors creaked open, slammed shut. Then Mama's laughter crawled through the heat and into the house. She sounded breathless: "Billy, stop that! The girls will see!"

"She brought him home!" I said to Phoebe, delighted.

My sister tossed the sponge into the dirty dishwater and said, "So? It won't last."

"It will, too!" I shot back.

"No it won't," she said as she shoved me.

I could feel my fist balling up all on its own.

Phoebe looked at me and laughed. "What are you going to do, hit me, two-pint? Go ahead. Ohhhh, it will hurt so bad," she mocked.

The bells Mama had hung from the front screen door softly tolled as my parents walked into the house. "Girls, where are my precious angels?" Daddy yelled. "I'm home!"

I ran out of the kitchen and into the living room. Daddy was an ox of a man, six feet plus, more muscle than fat. His face was long and big-boned, and his blue eyes seemed to be forever on fire. He had a bottle of whiskey in one hand and a bucket of fried chicken in the other.

"Come here, sunshine," he said. He handed the chicken to Mama, who seemed happy, if unsteady. I went to him, and he picked me up, kissed my cheek, and asked, "How's Daddy's little girl?"

"Fine," I said.

He put me down and looked at Phoebe—she was a challenge, stiff and stubborn.

"Sweetness, it's good to see you." He put a hand on her shoulder. "Now listen to me. I've been overworked about some things lately. Adult things you don't need to worry about. But do Daddy a favor: Act like a big girl and forget today's foolishness. Hear me? Agreed?"

Phoebe nodded, but I could tell she'd locked away her heart.

Daddy smiled. He pinched her nose.

Mama shifted the bucket of chicken from one hip to another as if she were wrestling a fat, squalling baby. "Billy," she said, "I could sure use a drink."

"You hear your mama?" Daddy asked. "Sounds like she's aiming to tie one on."

"Don't talk like that in front of the girls," Mama scolded. Daddy didn't smart off, but as he walked into the kitchen I saw him silently mimicking Mama. She ignored him.

I went in, sensing I'd best walk softly, and sat at the table. Daddy's eyes still shone too bright, Mama's too dull. *Poor Mama,* I thought, *she probably spent the entire drive into town cussing Daddy and trying to gut-tie her willpower so as not to bail him out.* But my daddy was a seasoned sweet-talker. We all knew that. I bet the second Mama stuck the egg salad sandwich through those jail-cell bars, Daddy was whispering sweet nothings to her: "Call Lou Miller, honey, he'll put up the bond."

Phoebe helped Mama set out supper. This involved laying down newspaper on the kitchen table, end to end, because the house wasn't the only thing that belonged to

Mr. Bailey T. Watson. He also owned every stitch of furniture, a fact Mama never let us forget. She was forever warning us not to scuff or scratch anything that wasn't ours. So we never ate a meal, not even Thanksgiving or Christmas, where we couldn't also read about the events of the day and look at ads for items we could not afford. That's how I learned to read, during mealtimes, Mama pointing out word after word until the letters that were lined up in neat, newspaper rows began to make sense.

With Daddy threatening to shoot himself and Mama having him arrested, I guess you could say we'd all had a bad day. But even so, supper was a feast. Kentucky Fried Chicken, mashed potatoes and gravy, corn on the cob. Daddy made drinks for him and Mama in no time flat. My parents, they weren't hungry at first. While us girls ate, Mama and Daddy drank. Daddy gave Phoebe and me a sip of his whiskey, and we both soured our faces and almost died. It tasted like gasoline. I had no idea how he and Mama tossed one glassful after another down their throats.

Mama said, "Billy, don't you give the children any liquor," but she was laughing, so we knew she didn't really mind.

I gnawed on the end of a chicken bone—I liked the gristle—and Daddy looked up from his drink and said that we were the two most beautiful girls in the world, next to our mama, of course. And Phoebe told him that Becky Sue's daddy was buying a boat.

"Is that right? Mike Baggett is getting himself a boat. Well, what do you know," Daddy said. Then he put his hand over Mama's and told her that he'd been thinking about turning a part of the store into a lunch deli. He believed he could do a fair business selling salami sandwiches, potato salad, and an array of pickles and cheeses and such. He said, "Glory Marie, I want only the best for you and the girls. It hurts like hell when I can't give you everything you deserve."

"Oh, Billy," Mama said as her face stumbled from happy to sad to the verge of angry, "let's talk about it later."

I saw a fragile haze of well-being slip away from my family and hover above us like a cloud of empty promises. I thought Daddy was going to push about his ability to be a good provider. But instead he took his hand off Mama's, picked out all the dark meat chicken from the bucket, and piled the pieces on his plate. Mama shoved the mashed potato container over to him, and I helped by offering the corn. Daddy then proceeded to eat so much that halfway through supper he had to unbutton his pants. When he was finished, he pushed away his plate, with its every-which-a-way pile of chicken bones and naked corncobs, and said, "Ooooweee, that was gooood food."

When supper was over, Phoebe and I threw the scraps in the garbage and wiped off the table, while Mama and Daddy drank and listened to WSUN, Country Music Radio. Mama kept putting ice in her glass and saying, "God, it's hot." My daddy drank his whiskey neat, and the steamy weather did not appear to bother him.

Little Jimmy Dickens came on the radio singing my favorite new song, "May the Bird of Paradise Fly Up Your Nose." I sang along, badly, as loud as I could. Daddy beamed. He said, "Atta girl."

Phoebe slopped dishwater on me and said I was nothing but a show-off.

After we finished cleaning the kitchen—we even had to

sweep the floor—Mama touched Daddy's blond hair as though it were a wide ribbon of gold. "You girls kiss your daddy good night and then go on to bed," she said.

Daddy kissed us both, first on the forehead, next on the cheek. "Sleep tight, pumpkins. Don't let the bedbugs bite," he said.

Mama lit a cigarette and then, over her shoulder, warned, "I'll be in to check on you in a minute."

We weren't being told to take baths, which pleased me no end. I hated baths. But once we were in our bedroom, Phoebe told me to brush my teeth. "You're not my mama. You can't tell me what to do," I sassed.

"Bird, do as your sister says," Mama called.

So I did. And even though I acted as if it pained me, I actually liked the feel of clean teeth, the smooth enamel against a peppermint tongue.

Our bathroom—even the walls—was covered in dingy baby-blue linoleum that bore the dirt of Mr. Bailey T. Watson's many former renters. Didn't matter how hard Mama scrubbed, the dirt wouldn't go away. All the fixtures leaked. There was a hole in the floor by the toilet. When I was four, on a cold December night, I went in to pee before going to bed and a rat with a long tail and everything squeezed in through that hole, just as if it were the entryway to a Holiday Inn. I came right up off the toilet. Screamed so loud I scared my mama, my daddy, my sister, myself, and the rat.

But there weren't any rats in the bathroom right then. Just me, brushing my teeth and touching the goose egg on the side of my head that Mama had put there when she shoved me in the cop car. A deep purple-and-scarlet bruise was spreading from my hairline to my eye socket. Daddy hadn't even noticed. Since I was on summer vacation, at least I wouldn't have to make up a lie to tell my teacher, not like the one I told in first grade about how a woodpecker had pecked me because I'd gotten too close to its nest, when in actuality Mama had seen fit to take a high heel to my face. A couple of days after that particular beating, she explained that my smart mouth made her miserable.

Standing on my tiptoes so I could see in the medicine cabinet mirror, I finished brushing my teeth and then smiled at my reflection. An imaginary sparkle lit off my gleaming, picture-perfect grin, just like in the Pepsodent ad.

I put the cap on the toothpaste, wiped my mouth on the closest towel, went back into the bedroom, and said, "It's your turn."

Phoebe didn't respond, just walked out. I heard her in there, though. She brushed her teeth hard.

I rummaged through our chest of drawers, found my pajamas, and put them on. From beneath the bed I pulled out the heart-of-pine treasure chest Daddy had made for me two years before. Twice the size of a shoebox, with a hinged lid and my initials burned into the top, the chest contained bits of spring, nature's own charms that I gathered for safekeeping: the first flowers of the Confederate rose that were shaken off the limb by May thunderstorms and then dusted the ground like powder puffs (the blossoms start out pink and then turn white—the bleeding heart of the Confederacy, my mama told me), scattered and broken bird eggs, fallen nests that had been attacked by 'coons and squirrels, dragonflies dead from only God knows what, baby lizards frozen by late frosts—stiff and brittle as crystal.

Sitting on the floor, sifting though my petrified garden, I thought about what a pretty time of year spring was. I loved the sight of cypress trees suddenly bright with feathery green needles, and azaleas so heavy with shocking pink and blistering white blooms it seemed as if God had taken out a paintbrush and gone hog wild. But springtime was also a season of sadness because so much of nature's young glory didn't live long enough to see me through the heat of summer.

When I first started bringing dead pieces of spring into the house, Mama threatened to throw out everything, even my beautiful lifeless butterflies. That's why Daddy made me the treasure chest, so Mama wouldn't feel compelled to make good on her threat. "Sunshine, put all your heart's desires in here. That way, they'll stay out of harm's way," Daddy said the day he gave me the chest. His words brought to my mind the Devil's teardrop box, and I realized my daddy had a knack for understanding the ways of this world *and* the next.

In the dim light of the bedroom, I picked up a dragonfly and studied its sheer, blue wings. Unbendable and still, the wings reminded me of tiny fishing nets, tightly woven, fashioned to catch the wind. "Fly, fly away," I sang as I waved the dragonfly through the air. But right then Phoebe barged in, shut the door, and ordered, "Bird, put that stuff up and go to bed before you get us both in trouble."

I made a monster face at her, nestled the dragonfly back into the petals of an old blossom, whispered, "Sweet dreams," and closed the lid.

Phoebe and I slept in the same bed, which was fine with

me because I was scared of the dark and of the trolls who owned the night. We kept the fan in the window and aimed it straight at us, so all through our sleep we were wrapped in a thick, billowing heat wave.

While my sister brushed her hair, black as a buzzard's butt, I plumped my pillow and tried to stake out some territory because Phoebe was bad about taking more space than was her share. When she was done with that mane of hers, she flipped off the light and told me to move over some.

"*You* move over some," I countered.

"Bird, don't act like a baby." She flopped onto the mattress, belly-down. She kicked the sheet to the footboard.

I nudged her and then rested my leg on hers.

"Get off, Bird, it's too hot for you to be lying on me."

I moved my leg but said, "You hate me."

"I do not hate you. It's just too hot. Go to sleep."

"Phoebe?"

"What?" she said, as if the word were full of rocks.

"Tell me a story."

"I'm tired. Leave me alone."

"Please, Sister. You ain't that tired."

"Damn, Bird, if I tell you one story will you shut up and go to sleep?"

"Yes," I said, "I will." Because of my propensity for believing in ghosts and trolls, leprechauns and angels, madmen and saints, I was forever pestering my big sister to tell me a bedtime ghost story or a human-gone-over-the-edge tale. And even though the stories were often reruns, I never tired of hearing them. I turned my face to the fan and settled in to listen. As heat lightning fired the darkness, Phoebe spun a plot I knew by heart: A teenage girl and her boyfriend are making out in the woods when they're hacked to death by an escapee from Chattahoochee, Florida's insane asylum. Phoebe was good on the details—the sound of fallen leaves being crushed by the madman's feet, the boyfriend's heavy breathing, and the girlfriend's slow realization that his wasn't the only breath against her skin.

Being scared by make-believe was always fun, but there was more to Phoebe's stories than the cheap thrill of a good fear. Her words made me feel tingly between my legs and in my heart. I would fall asleep thinking about a stranger touching me in places my mama said were private.

As Phoebe spoke, I concentrated on the pictures her words drew in my mind. The radio blared through the thin walls, and Mama's and Daddy's rhythmic steps echoed on the pine floor as they danced in the living room to some barroom dirge. Then slowly, and strangely on cue, Phoebe's voice wavered and the music and my parents' slow two-step faltered under the rising tide of Mama's accusing words.

"What did you do with yesterday's receipts, buy the gun with them? That's just like you. The money could have bought your daughters new shoes. We could have paid the light bill. But no, Mr. Big Shot goes out and buys himself a gun and then comes in the store and waves it around in the faces of his two girls."

"Jesus Christ, Glory, I've had the gun for six months. I didn't tell you because I knew you'd flip your lid. I bought it to keep in the store, for protection. I didn't steal any money from you or the girls. I didn't take anything away from you."

"I could name all the things you've taken from me. My peace of mind, my hopes for a decent future, my good health, my—"

"Listen here, I'm doing the best I can, woman. You know that. But I'm sick and tired of trying to please you. You are always on my back. Nothing I do is good enough for you, Glory Marie, nothing! Not a damn thing. But I'll keep trying right down to my last drop of blood."

"Trying, like hell! You son-of-a-bitch, when was the last time you tried anything that turned out right!"

"Get off my goddamn back, Glory. Why can't you ever get off my back? Who pays the bills around here? Who keeps us in groceries and your feet in those pretty high heels you love? I do, woman!"

"You think you're so smart. Listen to me, Billy Jackson, you've brought me nothing but pain and worry. I keep the books. I do the ordering. I try to make ends meet, ends that at a touch turn to dust. Then you come in here spouting your big ideas about a deli. Bullshit. What you're good for is staying out with your friends all night, drinking, and hanging with whores. You're no good, Billy Jackson, you're no damn good!"

Mama was screaming and slurring her words, and I thought I heard her pounding on him. I grabbed Phoebe's hand and held it. I wanted them to stop yelling and I wanted my mama's meanness to dry up. I wanted to understand why she told us to obey our daddy if he was no damn good. Why did I love him if he was as bad as she said?

Something hit the wall and crashed to the floor. The front door slammed open and shut. I heard the Impala's engine turn over and the car speed down the dirt road into the night.

Then the music was suddenly gone, and moments later the bedroom door swung open. I hung on to a lock of Phoebe's hair, scared that we'd done something to earn a beating.

"You two all right?" Mama asked gruffly.

Phoebe and I played possum, not answering, not even breathing.

Mama said, "If you're awake, you'd better say so. Your son-of-a-bitch father just about wrecked the place."

We didn't move or make a peep. Mama shut the door. Phoebe whispered "bitch" into her pillow.

As for me, I felt as if I were tumbling through a black and empty space. When sleep finally came, I dreamed I took to the skies on dragonfly wings.

But as morning forced open my eyelids, I knew that notions of flight were nothing more than dreamtime whimsies, because Mama was in the bed with us, one arm over her eyes and the other flung across my chest, holding me down, keeping me still. Daddy must not have come home. I eased her arm off me and tried to sneak out of bed, but she woke up and so did Phoebe. I blinked slowly, put on a groggy face, pretended to be falling back asleep because the last thing I wanted was for Mama to start in on us. But she surprised me. With crusted tears rimming her eyes, she hugged Phoebe and me, kissed us each on the tops of our heads, and said, "I love you girls so much. I really do."

AND SO IT went. Thunderstorms blazed and rumbled all around us, but the grove and our little house and the lake that I tried to part remained untouched by cooling rain. And every night my parents fought. Most times, the fights weren't preceded by anything so spectacular as Daddy holding a gun to his head. No, the twin evils that fueled their anger were moonrise and liquor. My mama's voice would grow loud and hateful. My daddy would start counting, tossing paper money on Mr. Bailey T. Watson's kitchen table—"fifty, seventy-five, a hundred"—trying to prove that we weren't utterly destitute, that he hadn't spent our living on worthless women.

Mama remained righteously unconvinced. She would holler and badger, shove and throw things, until finally Daddy would speed away in that white Impala. Once he was gone, she would call him names or cry all night, wailing that she missed him. "Please, Billy, come back," she'd scream. It was a bad kind of love.

Some nights I would put my pillow over my head, trying to block out the sound of their arguing. And I would pray to Jesus. I would say, "Dear sweet Jesus, give me angel wings so I can fly away from here."

But beyond my prayers, I would lie in the hot darkness and try to lose myself in Phoebe's hopscotching tales. There were gaps and pauses in her stories as she stopped to listen to the fighting. She was monitoring Mama and Daddy, making sure they didn't kill each other. But me, I just wanted to pretend my parents did not exist. No damnations, no dishes crashing against bloodstained walls, no vengeful tears filling up the silence of a broken-off, mid-holler brawl. Every time Phoebe stopped talking, every time the sound of the fighting grew too awful, I would pat her on the arm or head and try to goad her on. "More stories, Sister," I would whisper. "Please, more stories."

THREE WEEKS AFTER Daddy tried to shoot himself, I discovered that Phoebe was taking instruction in order to become a bride of Christ. That's how my mama explained Phoebe's twice-weekly meetings at Immaculate Conception Catholic Church in Lily.

This revelation threw me into a tizzy because, as far as I knew, I was the one who wanted Jesus, not Phoebe. When nobody was around I would lie on my bed and stare at the Woolworth's picture of Our Savior that hung beside a plastic crucifix Mama nailed up one morning after Daddy had walked into the kitchen and announced that he'd just seen his dead mama in the medicine cabinet mirror and she told him that his children were in need.

Even though Daddy's words spooked me, I liked having that religious stuff nailed to the wall. Through the sacredness of the Woolworth's picture, Jesus and I would talk, and my mind would wander all over Him. He was skinny, but I bet He was strong. I loved His silky, long brown hair. Wished mine looked silky instead of like a dried rat's nest. That lamb He cuddled was proof to me that He was a sweet, gentle Savior. And His eyes! They looked out upon the whole world with a loving, wise light, and I knew that they saw me in particular. He watched everything I did, knew my deepest thoughts. Even saw my unclean deeds when I touched myself in that place Mama said was named Filthy. In my daydreams, Jesus and I would walk off into a blazing sunset, holding hands. I may have been nothing but a kid, but in that gauzy dream, I was gorgeous. There we were, Him with his Prell-perfect hair, and me sporting a good figure. In my heart of hearts, Jesus was my first boyfriend. And I was dead certain He loved me special—no matter what hocus-pocus words Phoebe learned to say in that big-assed church.

I did not know how to stop Phoebe from becoming a bride of Christ, but I did know how to bother people to distraction. So I vexed Phoebe and Mama endlessly, asking questions my mama said were foolish, such as, "Have you seen Him yet?" "Does He take instruction, too?" "Does He teach the class?"

The sudden concern over my sister's soul seemed all the crueler to me because my mama and daddy were not religious people. Not in a day-to-day, let's-go-to-Bible-meeting sense, anyway.

Daddy claimed to be a nonattending Southern Baptist. He'd get tears in his eyes when he watched TV preachers on Sunday mornings. But points he earned in heaven for that did not stick, because after sitting through a boob-tube sermon and three or four beers, he'd start making fun of those sweating, jowl-shaking, Bible-thumping preacher men.

The Catholic in the house was Mama. She kept rosary beads in her pocketbook, and they'd fall down to the bottom and get dusty and pasty from the tobacco that also ended up in the far reaches of her bag. We ate fish on Fridays. Once a year on a Wednesday, Mama would go to church by herself and then return a few hours later with a smudge of ash on her forehead, which I found embarrassing because it looked as if she'd forgotten to wash her face. Other than that, she seemed not to have too much use for God, either.

Mama occasionally talked about religion, though. She told us stories about growing up in South Carolina shoeless, foodless, homeless, and hopeless until Catholic missionaries came and saved them. Mama was careful never to mention much about her relatives other than that they were all dead and that they'd been heathens before they became Catholics. Except once she slipped up and revealed that her mother's name was Sky. Sometimes I'd pretend Grandmama Sky lived with us and that she had a wide, soft lap and welcoming arms, all of which she put to good use holding and spoiling me. And Jesus loved her almost as much as He loved me.

Mama was busting with pride over Phoebe's confirmation. Talked about it at supper, talked about it at lunch, talked about it, I bet, even in her sleep. Made me sick. After days of letting righteous jealousy eat me up, I gathered my nerve and told Mama that I didn't think it was fair for Phoebe to be allowed to become Jesus' bride and that I wanted to marry Him, too.

We were sitting on our front porch. Phoebe was inside

changing into shorts, having just come home from instruction. Mama was snapping beans and drinking sweet iced tea with bourbon, one of her favorite daytime drinks. I was slathering Mercurochrome on the deep scratches that striped my arms and hands. Seemed that wild cat I'd been trying to tame wasn't ready to settle down. So I was painting myself and blowing on the scratches because they stung and expressing my religious desires when Mama dropped the bombshell.

"Well, Bird, I'm afraid that's impossible," she said in response to my bride-of-Jesus inquiry.

"No it ain't. Phoebe's gonna be. So can I."

"Pay attention, girl," Mama said. She leaned toward me, and her black hair, which was held back in a tail, spilled over her shoulder. "When you were born, your daddy and I decided: I'd get Phoebe. He'd get you. You're a Baptist. Like him."

The fact that my religious destiny had evidently been bartered away at birth didn't immediately sink in. "If I'm a Baptist, that means I can't be Jesus' bride?"

Mama paused from her bean snapping, thought for a minute, and then smiled at me. "That's right, Bird, the Baptists don't go in for all that horseshit."

"But, Mama—" I started.

" 'But, Mama' nothing," she interrupted. "You don't have any say in this, Bird. You don't even know what it's all about. So just get used to it." Then she said to the beans, "Your daddy wanted a little Baptist. He's got one."

She certainly didn't seem to have much use for Baptists. She might as well have been calling them and me a dirty name. I put the cap back on the Mercurochrome and then patted Mama's leg. "Do you love Daddy?" I asked.

Mama shot me an ugly glare, her faintly wrinkled skin tightening as if anger were a drawstring attached to her angles and bones. My impulse was to pull back because Mama could slap you silly right out of nowhere. But before I could get away, her face softened and her black eyes went misty. She set aside the colander, pulled me onto her lap, hugged me so hard it hurt. Mama smelled like the orange blossom perfume we sold at the store to poor country people and tourists. I loved the smell. It was almost as good as the real thing, only sweeter. I sniffed as deeply as I could. She brushed my bangs off my forehead and said, "Bird, I love your daddy with all my heart. His intentions are pure, like yours. But he doesn't always know how to keep them that way. That's why I worry so much about you. You're just like your daddy." I knew she was crying because her voice was quivering.

"But, Mama, I'm not bad," I said. "Am I?"

She leaned away and looked me in the face. I wanted to wipe off her cold tears, but I was afraid to. "It's not about being bad or good. It's about dreaming too much. Listen to me," she said, and she pinched my leg. "When your daddy was a young man he wanted to be a star. A country music hotshot. Hank Williams himself. And you know, baby, he did have talent. Just through the sheer loneliness in his voice, he could make you laugh and cry in a single phrase. But, Bird, your daddy never knew when to stop dreaming. He didn't see that there were other singers who were equally talented but who showed up at the clubs and recording sessions sober and on time. He was blinded by his own star, his own furious, terrible light. Honey, he squandered his chance at education, he squandered money, he squandered years that might have been spent leading to something we could count on. And now look at us," Mama said with a bitter laugh. She squeezed her eyes shut and wiped off her face with the back of her hand. Then she put her cheek to mine and warned, "I've seen you get that same faraway look in your blue eyes. It's as if you're not even with us, as if you're in some sort of dreamland. Listen to me, Bird, dreaming is for fools, and I don't ever want to be accused of raising up a little fool."

Mama kissed my forehead and patted my fanny. But I was not comforted. I had no earthly idea how to avoid being a Baptist or a fool. Evidently both roles had been woven into my soul at birth. I was weighed down by the burden of being two things my mother wished I was not and by the fruitlessness of trying to overcome what must have been my basic nature.

"Be a big girl, sweetheart, and run some cold water over these for Mama," she said, handing me the colander filled with bits of emerald green.

I stood at the sink on a small step stool Mama had bought at a garage sale just for me, watching the clear, cool water rush over the beans, and I imagined that I really was handling emeralds and that the glistening bubbles of water that rolled across the beans were diamonds. I dreamed we were rich folks and Daddy was a man Mama was proud of.

Then I dug my nails into my palms and their web of red-swabbed scratches. I dug as hard as I could, until my fists went white and the scratches bled. Pain was exceeded only by fury. Jesus may have been my boyfriend, but at that moment it didn't matter. I wanted God to rot in hell for making me a dreamer.

THE DAY OF my sister's confirmation, I escaped into the grove. It was no longer a working grove—that is, misery-swaddled migrant workers did not descend in rusted buses and pluck the yellow and orange globes for slave wages. The trees still produced fruit, but Mr. Bailey T. Watson wasn't interested in harvesting the bounty, since he had so many other methods of making money, the details of which eluded me.

When people stepped into the grove, they usually caught their breath because the sweet scent of ripening fruit mingled with the stench of rotting oranges, lemons, and grapefruits that pimpled the ground like dung heaps. I didn't mind the competing smells. In fact, I liked the mess: the bad with the good, the living with the dying, made sense to me.

I didn't have permission to go into the grove. In my mama's worldview, disobeying this rule was equal to committing a federal offense. Her instructions were clear: Never was I to enter the grove alone, and never were Phoebe and I to go unless Mama said we could. Bad behavior earned attention—at least, it always worked for Daddy. I longed for Mama to understand that I was deeply unhappy.

How could my parents be so stupid and blind, I simmered as I roamed through a stand of lemon and grapefruit trees, as to minister to Phoebe's religious failings while ignoring my aspirations? Not only were they taking my big sister from me in some very real sense, but they were also sacrificing me to the Baptists—before I'd even stepped into one of their ugly, plain churches.

Maybe my parents didn't like me, maybe they wished I'd never been born. Probably so. Why, they wouldn't even let me visit classmates who lived in Lily. "Too far to drive," Mama would say with hammer-blow finality.

In a few weeks school would start, and I'd bet all the money in the world that my best friend from last year would not want anything to do with me. After all, we'd spent the entire summer without seeing each other. Julia Mae Wescott was a skinny girl with stringy brown hair her mother forced into braids. We had become fast friends during art because we both drew pictures of grimacing parents and screaming children. Our teacher, Mrs. Stepp, scolded us for it and refused to thumbtack our drawings to the bulletin board alongside everyone else's. Also, we had to stand in the corner more often than anybody in our class, Julia Mae for whispering funny stories to me, and me for laughing too loud. Julia Mae said that her mama slept till noon almost every day, as she was a barmaid at the Orange Blossom Tavern, and that she refused to cart Julia Mae out to the country just so she could act the fool with me.

So I was spending the whole blasted summer without anyone to play with save a sister who was getting religion and a wild cat who would let me pick her up just so she could cut me to ribbons. I decided to stay in the grove until dark. Find a comfortable spot, make sure it was free of snakes, and revel in the heartache my absence would cause my parents. I kicked a deflated grapefruit and imagined the night closing in, my mama's cries—"Bird, where are you? My sweet child, where in heaven's name have you gone?"—and my daddy's flashlight piercing the darkness, casting light on the fruit-burdened trees.

A hot wind tangled my hair, the citrus leaves rustled, and I wove between the shadows, zigzagging, until I ran up on the grapefruit and kicked it again, this timer harder. That thick-skinned fruit rolled in a wobbly arc, coming to rest behind an old smote pot. I started to walk on—the farthest reaches of the grove my intent—but in the blink of an eye everything changed: the grapefruit rolled back, the air filled with the smell of snakes, my heart buckled and stopped. Then out from behind the smote pot jumped a little coal-eyed boy.

"Don't be afraid," he said. "It's just me."

"Who are you, and what are you doing in my grove?" I asked, trying to sound braver than I felt.

"This isn't your grove, smart-ass. You don't own it," he said, and he giggled. He was shorter than me. But his teeth were big, as if they were full-grown and he needed to catch up with them.

"Do *you* own it?" I asked, thinking that maybe he was Mr. Bailey T. Watson's son.

He snorted—reminded me of a horse—and waved away my question. "It doesn't matter. My name's Larry. What's yours?" He picked a golden ripe orange off the tree he was standing next to and tossed it in the air, catching it without even looking. *He must play baseball,* I thought.

"My name is Bird," I said.

"Bird!" He started laughing. He laughed so hard he

doubled over. "What kind of fucking name is Bird!" he spewed.

I pulled some leaves off a tree and threw them at him. "Don't say the F word, and don't laugh at my name."

He kept laughing.

"Stop it! Stop it!" I screamed.

I ran toward him and pushed him down, and he dropped the orange. He was wearing denim overalls without a shirt and he wasn't sweating, which seemed impossible given the ninety-degree weather. I stood over him, ready to fight if he laughed anymore.

His hair was the color of my mother's, but his fell in messy curls. His eyes seemed all-knowing, but cold, not at all like Jesus'. Ideas shot through my brain: I imagined burning heat billowing through his nostrils, and I could bet that he'd seen dead people.

Something smooth and cool wrapped around my ankle. I screamed, sure it was a snake. In my banshee dance to get away, my feet went out from under me. I fell down, flat on my back. Larry slithered on top of me. His breath was hot and smelled like the grove—spoiled sweetness. He ground his hips into my belly and bones and he said, "This is what girls want. You want it, don't you?"

He brought his face so close that all I could see was darkness. "Leave me alone!" I said.

"Fuck you. I ain't finished." He snickered and then smashed his slobbery lips against my mouth. His teeth knocked into mine, and it hurt.

My stomach turned inside out. I thought I was going to puke. *Press yourself into the earth. Let the dirt swallow you whole.*

Larry sat up. "You taste like shit," he said. Then he

pinned my arms to my sides and sang, "You little whore. You little whore. You little whore. You little—"

"Get off me!" I shouted, and he laughed again. He reached for the orange that he had dropped earlier. He gripped it as if it were a fastball and then began stuffing it in my mouth.

I groaned. Clawed at his back. Felt my lips rip as he forced the orange between them. My tongue rolled back and lodged against my windpipe. I was suffocating. I was going to die. Larry's face was bright and shiny. He was having fun. I looked up through the citrus branches. An egret flying, a white arrow slicing the blue. I wanted to be that bird. Then I heard screams. Familiar and certain. Phoebe's voice wailed through the grove and surrounded us. I shut my eyes and—because I knew I had to or die—I shoved away my fear.

"No!" I yelled in my gut. I threw Larry off. He tumbled through the dirt, blackening as he rolled. I scrambled to my feet. Running toward the house, I unwedged the orange and dropped it. Fresh oxygen burned my throat. I thought I heard rattles hissing. It seemed as if I was running for hours, as if the grove would never end, but finally I bounded into the blinding light of midday. Phoebe's screams were bright and clear, edging on song.

I flew up the steps and into the house. Mama grabbed me by the shoulders. "Where have you been?" she demanded.

"In, in, in the grove," I stammered.

"Who gave you permission? Tell me. Now!" She was shaking me, and her eyes were wild, the same wildness that colored my daddy's the day he tried to shoot himself, thunderhead wild.

"N-n-nobody," I cried.

"Didn't you hear us calling you?"

"No, ma'am," I managed.

"Listen to that." Mama pointed to her bedroom door. I heard the hollow airy whine and then the whack as my daddy's belt met my sister's bare flesh. "She's getting a beating 'cause of you. We told her to keep an eye on you. We told her Daddy had things to do in the store this morning and I was busy in the kitchen. Today is her confirmation, and because you can't keep your fat ass where it belongs, she's getting her behind ripped raw. You're next," Mama said.

She whirled me around and marched me toward the closed door. "Billy." Mama rapped at the door before busting in. "Here she is."

Daddy towered over my sister, belt in hand, his white undershirt soaked. Phoebe was leaned over a chair, her butt striped red. I looked away, embarrassed, tears welling.

"Phoebe, pull up your panties and turn around," Mama said, disgusted. "Bird, apologize to your sister."

I kept my gaze on my feet. "I'm sorry, Sister."

"Phoebe, go get washed off. When you're ready, I'll help you dress." Mama looked at me and said what she always did before a beating: "This hurts your daddy and me a helluva lot more than it hurts you."

Then she walked out of her bedroom and slammed the door shut.

I stared at the needlepoint blue jay Mama had finished last winter. Framed in cheap black plastic, it sat on Mr. Bailey T. Watson's pine chest of drawers.

Daddy said, "You know the routine, Bird."

I pulled down my shorts and panties, laid myself over

the seat of the chair. The pine still held Phoebe's heat. I noticed a cluster of tiny scales under the fingernails of my right hand. Dear Jesus, maybe they were snake scales. Maybe Larry wasn't a little boy at all but an evil, spell-casting serpent. I closed my eyes and listened to that airy whine. *You little whore. You little whore.* I held in a grunt as I took the hit. Everything would be okay. Yes, it would. Daddy never beat me as hard as he did Phoebe.

LYING BELLY-DOWN on the bed, I watched Mama take care of Phoebe's belt welts. She knew how because before she met my daddy, she'd been a nursing student. She Vaselined the welts and then told her to put on a clean pair of panties and a nice outfit, maybe the blue number with the bib collar she got for her birthday. Phoebe rolled her eyes. My sister had already complained to me that the other girls in her confirmation class were wearing special dresses—creations of satin and lace that were tantamount to wedding gowns. "They're all going to make fun of me," Phoebe had said. I knew I should have responded, "Don't worry, you'll be gorgeous in the eyes of God." But I did not. Jealousy was turning me mean.

Mama wanted to know what was wrong with my lips. I said I must have tripped and fallen as I ran home. She tossed me the Vaseline. "Put this on them. You need any on your fanny?"

"No."

I had to bite my tongue in order not to stick it out at her. She kissed Phoebe on the forehead and said, "You wait right here. I've got a surprise for you."

Phoebe changed her underwear and then stood in front of the vanity mirror. Feeling too ashamed to speak, I kept quiet but watched her study herself. She slid down her panties, fingered a belt welt, then pulled them back up. She looked distant, as if Daddy had beaten the spirit out of her or maybe her spirit had escaped and would reclaim her some sweet day when our lives were better.

She walked over to the chest of drawers and reached for the honeysuckle perfume—an Avon product, a present from some Christmas past. She sprayed it on the pulse points of her wrists, and I was struck by how much I envied her dark skin, her black hair. She held her wrists to the light and gazed at them as if they weren't hers.

Her titties were sprouting and were newly bandaged in what Mama and she called a training bra. A few months before, when I had asked what they were being trained for, Mama and Phoebe had fallen all over each other in fever-pitched laughing spasms.

I watched Phoebe close her eyes and sniff her wrists. *Forget it, Sister,* I thought, *ain't no amount of Avon going to turn you into a happy girl; you ought to be downright grateful that despite your caul of sadness, you're a skinny-minny and pretty to boot.* I looked down at my chubby fingers. Cat-scratched. Each nail spoiled by crescent moons made of dirt and God only knows what else. Wasn't no boy in all the world going to put a wedding ring on these chunky stubs. Suddenly I wanted, more than anything in my life, to look like Phoebe—minus the despair. But maybe there was no hope, and maybe I, too, would turn old before my time. As Phoebe sprayed behind her ears with that sugar-and-spice perfume, I sent up a silent prayer: *Dear Jesus, don't let this hard life take away her pretty face.*

Mama cracked open the door and said, "Phoebe, child, shut your eyes." My sister did, and then Mama walked into the room, backward, clutching something to her chest. Mama spun around, a genuine, good-hearted smile lighting her face, and said, "Ta-daaa!"

She held a dress of white lace and silk. If that dress could have talked, it would have screamed, "Virgin."

I gasped. "Ain't it the most beautiful thing!"

Phoebe opened her eyes, and for a minute her sadness lifted. She smiled and said, "I can't believe it! I just can't believe it!"

I couldn't either. Torn between envy and relief, I told myself what-for: *Phoebe deserves this gift. She deserves to feel like a queen, like a bride of Jesus.*

"Do you like it?" Mama asked.

"Yes, Mama, I do." Phoebe touched the scalloped neckline.

"Your daddy and I had to do some serious penny-pinching, but we wanted this day to be special."

"Thank you, Mama," Phoebe said, and the two of them hugged.

I was wowed by this gown that shimmered and softly crackled, reminding me of the sound of falling rice, as Mama helped Phoebe into it.

"Mrs. Crenshaw sewed it. I do believe she took care with each stitch," Mama said, examining the hem. She tugged and straightened and then zipped up the back. Phoebe winced. Mama and I acted as if we didn't notice.

"Here, sweetheart, I also bought you these." Mama retrieved a box she had set outside on the floor in the hallway. "You can't be confirmed barefoot," she said.

Phoebe ripped away the gift wrap, which was pastel pink with silver crosses. She lifted the lid, and even though she didn't clap her hands or bounce on her toes—as I would have been tempted to do—her eyes shone. The box contained a pair of white patent leather shoes crowned by stiff satin bows. Underneath the shoes were sheer lace gloves with pearl buttons that fastened at the wrist. Below the gloves, thin white ankle socks edged in lace. Phoebe held the socks to her face, feeling their softness.

Then she said, "Oh, Mama," as she pulled out a lace-and-seed-pearl shoulder-length veil. Later, the veil would fall in graceful folds against Phoebe's black hair. And it would rise like wings testing the wind when she walked out the front door.

At the very bottom of the box lay a small Bible bound in white leather. It zippered shut, which made it all the more special. Phoebe's name was inscribed in gold letters on the front.

I knew Phoebe and I were thinking the same thing: This stuff must have cost a fortune. I watched a few drops of happiness slide down Phoebe's face. Then I looked away.

BY THE TIME the four of us piled into the Impala to drive Phoebe to her confirmation, it was six in the evening and hotter than Hades. Phoebe sat in the front seat between our parents. I could tell she was keeping her butt slightly lifted off the seat. Me, I didn't care if my behind was torn raw, I'd never let them know I was hurting.

Mama wore a gray dress with white piping around the neckline and each sleeve. Before we left the house, I saw Mama tuck into her pocketbook her own veil—a circle of black lace—and a brand-new sky-blue rosary. She spent the entire thirty-minute trip spouting instructions as to window height, car speed, wind velocity, in a sorry attempt to ward off the heat and car-induced gales.

"We don't want to blow the poor child to hell and back before we get her to the church," Mama snapped. "Billy, roll up your window just a smidge further. Open the fly. No, more. It's still not right."

Mama's window was cracked about an inch or so, and she held her cigarette out the passenger fly, which was her habit.

Exactly like an old hound, I pressed my face to the window and prayed for wind. *You taste like shit.* I put my hands to my ears. "Go away!" I whispered, and then started humming a nonsense tune, hoping the sound of my voice would erase the boy's evil words.

Mama glanced over her shoulder. "Bird, sit up straight and can the noise. You're acting like a goddamn savage," she said.

I threw myself against the backseat and huffed, my discontent spewing like rain.

The air inside the car was sweltering, and I thought, *So what if Sister gets blown to hell and back, at least we'll be alive.* I decided to roll down my window just a tad because, truly, I was sweating to death. But the window was loose and it jiggled lower than I meant for it to. A loud swoosh was followed by a draft that tugged on Mama's cigarette, almost pulling off its ash and snuffing it out.

"Put up the damn window back there, Bird!" Mama yelled. Then she bitched, "You're so stupid, there are days I can't believe you're my own flesh and blood."

"My, Phoebe sure looks beautiful," Daddy crooned.

He and I were not allowed to attend the confirmation. Mama said it was because we didn't know how to behave. After we dropped them off at Immaculate Conception, Daddy was to take me to Beckett's Soda Fountain and Pharmacy, where, per Mama's instruction, he was to buy me any sort of ice cream confection my heart desired.

As we neared the church, Mama took her veil out of her pocketbook and began fitfully pinning it to her head.

Daddy shot her a cockeyed gaze and said, "You look real nice, Glory Marie. I could marry you all over again. What do you think, Phoebe, will your mama be my bride? Will she walk with me down that fancy aisle and tell the preacher man she loves me with her whole heart?"

Phoebe looked down at her lap and mumbled, "Yeah. Yes, sir."

Daddy laughed. "Damn straight she'll say yes!"

"Billy, please," Mama groaned.

The church's parking lot was full. Mama said Phoebe was being confirmed with six other girls and she hadn't expected so many people to attend.

"That's nice," Daddy said absentmindedly as he thumped the steering wheel and looked for a spot to drop them off. He wiped sweat out of his eyes and then pulled into the circular driveway in front of the church.

He stopped behind a blue Chevy pickup. Mary Jane Parker's big sister, who weighed a whole lot more than she should have and was dressed like a velveteen cupcake, struggled out of the truck. She was wearing a crinoline, which I found amazing because it gave her a party rather than a bridal air. Her mama, who was matchstick skinny, stood beside the truck, beaming, peacock proud, as if her daughter were the most beautiful girl in the world.

Maybe, I mused, this confirmation business was actually a thinly disguised beauty contest. And we were certainly wild for those.

I watched Mr. Parker lean over toward the passenger door. He shouted to his wife as if she were deaf, "Sweetheart, I'll park the truck and be right in"; then to the girl, "Don't give in to the jitters, doll. You'll be just fine. You look so perty." He was talking to his daughter in the same singsong voice people use with small dogs and babies.

"Jess Parker, move that truck right along," Daddy said, obviously amused. Then he turned to Phoebe and said, "Do good in there, girl." He kissed the top of her head, veil and all.

Mama told him to come back in two hours, they were having cookies and punch afterward, and he said okay. Then she and Phoebe got out of the car. Mama blew

Daddy a kiss, told me not to get on Daddy's nerves, then blew me one. Daddy started driving away, and I turned around to wave at them—I hadn't even told Phoebe good luck—but they were already walking into the church, arms linked. It was as if the afternoon had never happened.

I sat back against the seat and bit back tears. I was figuring out I had a tendency for easy crying. But being a crybaby might not be so bad, could mean the Devil would never be able to fill that box in hell with my name on it.

Daddy said, "Bird, scramble on up here with me."

I brightened at the invitation. I crawled over the front seat, an action that would have earned me at least a smack from Mama. Immediately I rolled down my window. Daddy did the same. Then I fiddled with the glove compartment latch. Sometimes there were dollar bills in there. "Are you gonna get me that ice cream?"

"Is Daddy's girl going to give him a smooch?"

I slid over, causing my hurt bottom to make itself known, and kissed his cheek. His skin smelled like Mama, orange blossoms and sweat.

"That's some gooood sugar," he said. Then he flipped on the radio and whistled through his teeth. He reached under the front seat. The car swerved, but he found what he wanted and brought us straight before we hit anything. "Take the lid off for Daddy," he said as he handed me the dented and scratched flask.

I couldn't count how many times I'd seen Mama hurl that flask at Daddy. She usually missed. I unscrewed the lid and gave the flask back. Daddy took a long swig. The whiskey's earthy smell mushroomed through the Impala.

We drove past the elementary school, and Daddy made a right on Main. Most of Lily was built of wood, cypress, and pine. But not Beckett's. It was in a row of brick buildings, a row we called downtown. Washington palms lined the street, and even though most people in Lily made only enough money to stay two steps ahead of the bill collector, the towering slender-trunked palms and those red-brick stores could have caused a stranger to think Lily was a moneyed town.

Beckett's was one of my favorite places on earth. You could buy anything there, corn plasters to pineapple parfaits. It was air conditioned, so even on the hottest mid-August day you could walk in Beckett's and begin to believe the cool winds of fall might actually arrive. The pharmacy was at the back of the store. Behind the drug-ordering window was a long shelf that stretched the length of the building. Giant glass vials of sapphire- and ruby-colored fluid sat alongside mortars and pestles big enough to powder Jack and the Beanstalk–sized pills. On the wall above the shelf was a sign that read BECKETT'S PHARMACY, SERVING LILY THE VERY BEST SINCE 1885.

When I was real small, maybe three or four, I had gone into Beckett's with my sister so she could buy some sanitary napkins for Mama, and I had asked her to read me the sign. She did. I was impressed.

Pictures of hot dogs, fudge sundaes, and banana splits hung from the ceiling above the chrome gadgetry of the soda fountain. These weren't just pictures but posters cut into the shapes of the actual delicious items. They swayed up there, stirred by the air-conditioning. Their effect on me was the same as a mobile's over a baby's crib. I would watch the posters pirouette on the invisible currents, and a temporary calm would seep over my bones.

Daddy snagged a great parking space, right by Beckett's

front doors. Once inside, we headed straight for the soda fountain. I climbed on a stool and started spinning. Daddy asked me what I wanted.

"Root beer float." It's what I always ordered.

"One root beer float to go," Daddy told the soda jerk, a pimply boy a few years older than Phoebe.

"Noooo!" I said as the room twirled by. I wanted to stay at Beckett's and enjoy the cool air, the waltzing posters. Daddy slapped his hand on the stool and the spinning stopped. He tousled my hair. "I thought you and me would take a ride, sugar foot. A Sunday ride on Wednesday," he said, referring to our on-and-off habit of tearing down the highway on Sunday, Daddy driving thirty miles and more over the speed limit, Mama and he sharing the flask—sometimes fighting and sometimes not—stopping at a pig stand near Bushnell, eating barbecue and getting sauce all over us, Mama rubbing our faces clean with her spit, and then heading back home in the dark at the speed of light. Usually it was a bang-up time.

Daddy handed me the float, paid the boy, winked as he guided me toward the door, and said, "Now don't go telling your mama."

We didn't speed until we got out of the city limits. WSUN blared. Daddy sang along with almost every song. He did have a good voice, and when Johnny Cash came on singing "Ring of Fire," I joined in, chortling like a sick cow because I couldn't carry a tune any farther than a house sparrow could carry a tree. Didn't matter. Daddy liked it when I sang with him. He was happy, speeding and singing, and I felt I understood his dream to be a music star. He should be making records and appearing at the Grand Ole Opry, women should be blowing him kisses and throwing him their scarves. Mama was wrong to be mad at him. Maybe it was her fault he failed. You never knew, you just never did. We drove so fast that my eyes teared and I had to hold on tight to my float.

We traveled deep into the middle of nowhere, pell-mell down a narrow, ditch-lined dirt road. The ride was bumpy, and I knew Mama would have rapidly screamed for him to "slow down, goddamn it, if we hit the ditch we'll flip." We passed a farmer on his tractor who angrily shook his hat at us. Daddy simply honked the horn. I waved. Fear was part of the fun of these hell-bent rides, and so were the dour expressions that darkened people's faces as we sped by in our cloud of dust.

Daddy took a couple of turns and finally slowed down, stopping in a field under a lone oak. Its canopy was wide and perfect, and I was in awe. How could anything be that lovely all on its own? About fifty yards back, built close to the road, was one of those Pentecostal shack churches. A dozen or so rattletrap cars and trucks were parked outside. Looked like a full house for Wednesday-night Bible meeting. I could hear the churchgoers in there singing, but I couldn't make out any words.

Daddy sipped from his flask, and I finished the float, wiping my mouth with the back of my hand. The early evening sky was an inky wash of gold, orange, yellow. The colors reminded me of the fruit abandoned in the grove. "Daddy," I asked, "do you believe in the Devil?"

"Hell yeah, I believe in that son-of-a-bitch," he said as he caught a glimpse of himself in the rearview mirror and ran his hand over his blond waves. "I've looked him straight in the face and spit in it."

"You did! What did he do?"

"Ran off like some scared jackrabbit. The Devil ain't nothing but a bully. And you know what a bully is, don't you, Bird?"

"What?"

Daddy leaned into me, spoke real low: "A sissy in wolf clothes." Then he grabbed his pack of Lucky Strikes off the dash, fished in his shirt pocket for a lighter.

"A bully, Daddy, is not a sissy," I said, floored by his lack of understanding.

He lit his cigarette, looked at me through the smoke. "Yes, little girl, he is. The very worst kind, the sort that's always making threats, causing you problems and pain, that is until you figure out that if you breathe on him hard he'll turn tail, screaming and hollering like a damn woman."

"So I shouldn't be scared of the Devil?"

"Sunshine, you shouldn't be scared of nothing. 'Cause I'll always be here for you, Bird. I ain't gonna let nobody hurt you. Ever. I know I spank you now and again, but that's for your own good. You know that. But the Devil," Daddy made a face as if he was talking about some spineless runt, "he ain't gonna bother you as long as I'm around, or my name ain't Billy Jackson."

The wind blew, carrying the tattered noise of those church people. Sounded to me as if their religion had hold of them by their privates and wouldn't let go.

Daddy turned and looked in the direction of the church, listening. Then he faced forward again, his eyes breaking into a smile before his mouth did.

"What's that racket, Daddy?"

"Jesus H. Christ," he said, fingering the lip of the flask,

"I didn't know anybody out here still did that. Bird, how would you like to indulge in some snooping?"

Before I could even answer, Daddy had the Impala bouncing along in reverse, the flask squeezed between his tree-stump thighs.

"Where are we going?"

"To church," he said, his blue eyes glittering like a neon sign. "Yes, sir, to church."

He drove willy-nilly, backward through the field, and jolted us to a stop on the west side of the Written in Heaven Pentecostal Holiness House of God. Well, let me tell you, God's house was a mess, a clapboard shack sorely in need of tending. Daddy laughed as he read the name of the church, which was scrawled in peeling black paint on a warped piece of wood that was leaned against a huge limestone boulder. I looked to the sky. Against that pretty sunset, a gaunt cross was perched like a cheerless crow on top of a simple, boxy steeple. Both steeple and cross leaned to the east. In fact, everything about this place leaned, even the roof. As for the yard—no flowers, no trees, just some patches of stickers and a desert's worth of sand.

In a flash, my mind was made up. "I don't want to go in there, Daddy."

"We ain't going in, Bird," he explained as if I was the stupidest child on earth. "We're going snooping, like I said."

With blue eyes afire, he got out of the car. I scrambled out on his side and stayed close, because worse than barging into a church that looked like a haunted house was staying alone and spooking myself to death. As we walked, I smoothed my yellow cotton shirt, straightened the legs of my Bermuda shorts. I wasn't dressed for church. Daddy headed straight for the sole window. Without even asking me if I wanted to see in, he picked me up. Good sense told me to keep my eyes fixed over Daddy's shoulder and on the car. But curiosity killed the cat. I turned my head. Just a peek, just one quick glance. Pow! A spell was thrown on me. I could not look away. Could not move. Was forced to gaze upon a frightening sight. A dozen or so folks, poor crackers all, jerked, twirled, moaned, groaned. "Dance for the Lord!" an old voice raged. On the far wall someone had scrawled a Bible verse in red paint: "They shall take up serpents—Mark 16 : 18."

Daddy whispered in my ear, "Lookie, Bird, over there."

Maybe Daddy was under a spell, too. Or maybe he simply liked to view the scary side of life. All I know for sure is that I was compelled to follow the line of his finger.

Near the front of the church, three stubble-faced men danced jigs—and not in rhythm to any music I'd ever heard before or since, but that's because they were keeping time to the music of snakes, snakes that they handled, caressed, taunted. I choked back a scream as one of the men grabbed a serpent by its head and then put his mouth on that diamond-backed creature.

The grove, the coal-eyed boy, the scales under my fingernails—suddenly they made sense, and suddenly I knew my daddy was wrong. He could not protect me. He wasn't powerful enough. And I dared not tell him the awful truth. I dared not confess that that very morning, lying on the ground in the dirt and darkness, surrounded by fallen fruit, I had been kissed by the Devil himself. Kissed even as my daddy did the Devil's evil bidding by beating my sister.

Oh, dear God, this was surely bad. Maybe that kiss had sealed my fate. Maybe like Mama sometimes said, I *was* the Devil's child, an easy mark for the spells he cast all around. I started crying, gasping for breath, drowning in the notion that I was hell-bound in a handbasket.

Daddy hugged me close and carried me back to the car. He smiled gently, the light in his eyes flickering as he tried to wipe away my tears. "Don't worry, baby, no, please don't cry," he said, "those people was just playing."

THE SNAKE HANDLERS and the Devil may have been playing, but it didn't matter because the spell stuck. Two years passed after my run-in with that fork-tailed boy, and even though I never again ventured into the grove, the memory of his wicked kiss kept the hex alive. How do I know this? you might ask. The answer is simple: By our deeds.

I continued to fancy myself as special to Jesus—it was the only way for me to take the sting out of the Devil's claim. My sister was devoutly unaffected by her confirmation. Never a churchgoer, never given to prayer, she was no more a bride of Christ than I was. Mama and Daddy still drank and fought. Daddy kept on with other women. Mama threatened day and night to kill him. Phoebe and I suffered beatings as frequently as some children were showered with hugs. "We're trying to make decent humans out of you," Mama would explain.

After enduring a beating, I'd stomp into my bedroom and stare at the Woolworth's picture of Jesus and I'd ask, "Why have you forsaken me?"

A voice in my head would answer. It would say, "Because ain't love the damnedest thing. Ain't love mean."

Then I'd flop down on my bed, look out the window, and wonder if guardian angels really existed. Or if there were children in the world who, at that very moment, were being doted on by fat grandmamas. Or little girls whose hair was being brushed out of their eyes as their honey-tempered mamas whispered, "You're such a good child."

My mama, she wasn't capable of whispering such sweet words. For her, kind comments were nothing more than fireflies trapped in a jar: they were pretty for the short while they lasted. Then they died and you had to throw them out.

And as loving words shriveled into wistful dreams, Mama grew ever better at conjuring blue moods. She began to walk around Lily wearing her unhappiness as if it were a ruby brooch that might, without warning, drip blood down the front of her white cotton blouse.

Now I've heard it said that change is inevitable. I guess it's true. That's why none of us should have been surprised when my mama broke her own mold. I saw it all—the way luck crept up on her and made her smile, and the way life stole the silver ring of happiness right out of her hands.

It was the summer of 1967, and one, two, three, these things happened: Mama bought a secondhand Plymouth; my wild cat birthed babies underneath the front porch;

my brother, Hank, roared into the grove in a cherry-red ragtop MG.

Other than for timing, these events were unrelated. But then again, Daddy always said that timing in life was everything.

Mama's Plymouth was angel's-wing blue, the color of air, and she insisted the ride was so smooth that driving it was like swiping your finger through a cloud of whipped cream.

She'd been desiring a car of her own for as far into the past as I could see. "I can't even go into town without asking you for permission," she'd say to Daddy. "And what happens when you don't come home for days? The girls and I are stuck in this godforsaken hole. I can't even open the store, so we end up being more broke than the day you left. And what if one of us gets sick and you're not home? I need my own transportation. Why can't you understand?"

Mama repeated this so many times we knew it by heart. I can only guess at what spurred Daddy to finally give in. Perhaps after listening to her plead like a pitiful child for years on end, he either grew tired and bored or decided she was old enough that the freedom a set of wheels could give her wouldn't be the sort of freedom that might threaten him.

Well, regret can be a potent poison. Mama had no sooner gotten behind the wheel of that angel-blue Plymouth, when other people and places started calling her name. Who they were or where she went, I could not say. But I felt as if Mr. Bailey T. Watson's cracker shack was suddenly overrun by a herd of giant, dangling question marks. And Mama did absolutely nothing to erase them.

She'd waltz home past suppertime and laugh at Daddy when he asked her where the hell she'd been. She didn't push him into a fight or beg for forgiveness or say she was sorry. No, there was only laughter. And a shadow of happiness, blowing like a tumbleweed across those high cheekbones and defiant black eyes.

Phoebe took care of us. She cooked. We ate a lot of hot dogs and macaroni and cheese poured out of a box rather than Mama's homemade noodle and cheddar recipe that was chock-full of ham. Almost every night, Daddy brought home honey buns from our store and we ate them for dessert. My butt got bigger with every bite. I had my moments of being happy that Mama was stepping out and doing whatever ladies do when they smell a better life around the corner. During her brief stints at home, she was not her usual harsh self. She smiled more often and didn't yell about every little thing, like when we slammed the screen door behind us.

And I was deep-down glad that a wholesale fight didn't break out when Daddy accused her of seeing someone named Jack. The only Jack I could think of was the policeman who drove us to Moccasin Branch Bridge the day Daddy tried to shoot himself. When I asked Phoebe if Daddy's suspicions were on the money, she said, "How am I supposed to know? Why don't you shut up?" I did.

But my mind worked overtime. What would it be like to be the daughter of Jack the cop? My imaginings ran from him being a devoted daddy who tried to buy our love with toys, to him policing our every move and not allowing us to visit with our real daddy. But mostly I settled on him having mountains of cash that we greedily spent on movies, games, and a big red-brick Yankee house with a swimming pool. In the make-believe world, Jack brought me home honey buns but I never got fat off them, and when I lounged around Jack's pool in my sinful polka-dot bikini, I was as skinny as those pretty girls in my sister's beauty magazines.

Of course, it takes a special person to live in a make-believe world twenty-four hours a day. I wasn't cut out for it. Circumstances kept kicking me, bouncing me back to real life. Truth of the matter was, when Mama was out of the house, we lost all sense of direction. For instance, without Mama's continual bossing, Daddy barely knew how to put one foot in front of the other. It was as if he lived for her praise and disgust, just like Phoebe and me. His eyes changed. Only in my dreams were they thunderhead wild. The rest of the time they were gray-blue and flat. They had lost their light. When Daddy looked at us girls, I could swear he was seeing not his two doll-babies but two walking, talking worries.

My favorite thing in the whole world to do with my daddy was for us on Sunday mornings to sit on our front porch—him in his boxer shorts and me in whatever I felt like wearing—and for him to pick up his six-string guitar and sing to me.

But there wasn't any singing while Mama was sowing her oats. And there wasn't any parenting—bad-tempered or otherwise. It was as if we were those fireflies trapped in a jelly jar and it was getting damn hard to breathe, damn hard to spark the night. So even though when Mama *was* home that summer she was gentler than her normal self, her paltry doses of kindness amounted to too little, too late. My family had fallen to the bottom of the jar, and every time one of us succeeded in loosening the lid, a sudden wind came along and blew us farther asunder.

TOWARD THE END of Mama's nod at freedom, she and Daddy called an end to their truce by waging a doozy of a fight in the general store. I'd gone to work with Daddy—he promised to pay me if I worked hard. Mama breezed in about three o'clock, her hair stylishly clipped—short at the neck with gentle wisps framing her face. She looked so pretty.

Daddy, who'd been rearranging the canned goods aisle with my help—we moved the syrupy pears and peaches right up front, stuck the sauerkraut down at the end—snapped at Mama the second she walked through the door. "So look who it is. The queen of Lily graces us with her royal presence. Is it within your high-and-mighty grasp to tell me where you've been?"

"No place in particular. Just out. Why?" Mama seemed to enjoy Daddy's discontent. She patted her new hairdo. I liked the yellow dress she was wearing. I'd never seen it before. It gave her skin a tinge of gold.

Daddy banged a can of peas on the shelf and walked over to her. He'd had enough. "The whole town is talking about you, Glory Marie," Daddy said, wiping his hands on his shirt even though they weren't dirty. "I've been quiet for a long time, but no more. You're bringing shame down on this family. I ought to just quit you. The goddamn children need their mother. I need you. Oh shit—I'll forgive everything, won't ask any more questions, if you'll just straighten up. That's all I ask, Glory Marie. Straighten up!"

Mama tossed back her head, a crooked grin spreading like a snake across her face. "Oh yeah, Mr. Big Shot? Sounds like you're calling the kettle black. What makes you think I'm doing anything wrong? Anything to be ashamed of? Maybe I'm just driving around. Maybe I'm running up and down the highway, thinking, getting my life worked out in my head. Why is that so impossible for you to believe? And furthermore," she spread her feet apart as if she knew what was coming, as if she was preparing not to be knocked on her ass, "when was the last time you acted like a father to your girls instead of like a useless drunk?"

Daddy inhaled, swung his arm as if it were a bat. Then his breath crashed across his lips as he backhanded Mama smack in the mouth. A thread of bright red blood trickled down her chin. I ran to her, but she pushed me into the sweet bins, marched out the door, tucked herself into the Plymouth, and flew away.

At home, I sat on the edge of my parents' bed and watched the pea-green hands of Mama's Big Ben alarm clock go around and around. As if it were a genie bottle, I rubbed the clock's face and softly sang, "Come home, Mama, come home."

That night, I tried to wait up for her. I wanted to hold her hand, put some Mercurochrome on her busted lip. For a long time, Daddy and I sat on the couch, watching TV. Phoebe hid out in our room, reading those glamour magazines she was so fond of. I grew drowsy and, to stay awake, I pinched my thighs and cracked my knuckles. But somewhere along the way—after the eleven o'clock news and before Johnny Carson introduced his guests—I conked out.

I was faintly aware of Daddy picking me up and putting me to bed and also, all night, even as I dreamed, I knew Mama was wandering the blue yonder. This shook me. I needed Mama. I needed to hear her careful laugh when I said funny or silly things. I needed to have a bowl of cereal waiting for me on the kitchen table every morning of my life. I needed for her to worry over me when I had a fever, and to kiss my forehead before I went to bed, and to every now and again murmur those rare words, "Bird, you're my little buttercup." Beatings, damnations, threats, they all shriveled up like dying leaves each precious time my mama behaved kindly. Was she ever going to come home? Was it my fault she left? Was Jesus paying me back for those times Mama had beat me and I wished her dead?

Even as I tumbled through nightmares and prayers, I felt as if something big was happening, something awful: I was disappearing. I could feel my skin, cell by cell, evaporate into the warm night air. Desperately, I tried to rise out of Sandman Land, as Mama called it, but I remained until there was nothing left, not a toenail, not a hair on my head. Finally, come morning, a blackbird in the live oak outside my bedroom window started flapping her wings so hard that she swept away my sleep. When I woke up, I could not speak.

I kicked off the sheet that was tangled around my legs and called for Mama. But my voice did not work. I got out of bed and looked out the window. Mama's car was still gone. The Impala was missing, too. I put on shorts and a cotton shell, went into the living room. The top of my head felt as if it was going to blow off. Phoebe was sitting on the couch watching "Teen Beat," a local copycat of "American Bandstand" that aired out of Tampa. As I walked by, she didn't say good morning or anything. I asked, "Do you know where Mama is?" but she couldn't hear me.

So I went outside to find the blackbird who, I was sure, stole my voice. The sun was at the ten o'clock angle, burning a white brightness into the grove and the dust beneath my feet. I shaded my eyes and searched the oak branches. The blackbird was hidden from sight, but I heard her, cackling up a storm, spending my whole lifetime supply of words as if speeches and phrases were free.

"Shut up!" I tried to yell. "Give me back my voice. Where are you?" But she didn't stop squawking, nor did she show herself.

As I walked back to the porch, wondering what in the world I was going to do, I saw my wild cat stroll out of the grove.

"Here, kitty, kitty," I sang, and she trotted straight at me, mewing. And that's when I knew animals could hear me, but nobody else.

The wild cat was solid black with gold eyes and black claws, except for one that was white. I was sure it was the white claw, distinct and eerie, that was so good at razor-slitting my flesh. As she came closer, I saw that she sported a new figure. Her middle was as round as the souvenir liquor cask my brother had sent me from Kentucky for my last birthday. How wonderful, she was going to have kittens! Maybe the babies wouldn't be as wild as their mama. Maybe they'd let me hold them and care for them as if they were my very own. What fun it would be to walk back into the grove at last, the kittens following at my heels, fear fleeing from my nature no matter who or what I came across—a rattlesnake, the Devil, or God Almighty!

The wild cat stopped at my feet, mewed, then rubbed against my legs. I said, "Hey, Big Mama, I'm going to get you some milk. How's that?"

I ran into the house and told my sister that Big Mama was going to have babies, but the words flew from my mouth and rose to the ceiling, where they stayed stuck like helpless bats.

On TV, a commercial for Maybelline mascara was full of glamorous girls with long black lashes being gazed at adoringly by boys who probably had nasty thoughts on their minds. Phoebe watched intently. I went into the kitchen, poured the wild cat a bowl of milk, and took it out to her. As I stood on the porch steps watching her drink, I heard a car. The muffler wasn't loud so it couldn't be the Plymouth, and the radio wasn't blasting so I doubted that it was the Impala. I watched the road uneasily. Mama had instilled in us an abiding fear of strangers.

But as soon as I caught sight of that sporty red MG and who was driving, my uneasiness turned into outright glee. I yelled at Phoebe that Hank had come home, but my words refused to budge from the back of my throat. I ran to the living room window and pounded on it, which provoked a slit-eyed glare out of Phoebe, and then I raced for the yard, where I tumbled into my big brother's arms.

Hank didn't visit often, and when he did it was always unannounced. To me, that made his homecomings all the sweeter, but Mama cursed him behind his back for being an ungrateful son who didn't even have the common courtesy to call her and say he was coming so she could fix something special, like blackberry cobbler. But while he was in our presence—all smiles and good news—Mama would sing a different tune. She'd cry and hold his hand and say how good it was to see him.

Out in the bright light and dust, Hank hugged me so good that if I'd been a glass figurine I would have broken into sharp and shiny pieces. He tweaked my nose. My brother was built like a welterweight boxer—he wasn't real tall but was well-muscled and handsome. "How're you doing, tiger?" he asked.

I said, "Fine," but, of course, he couldn't hear me.

"What? Has the cat got your tongue?"

I shook my head "yes" just because I couldn't explain that it was a bird, not the cat, and he said, "Well, let's go find that little bugger. Here, kitty, give my beautiful little sister her tongue back!"

An unbroken stream of giggles flowed out of my mouth, and it was a good feeling to know that I could at least make noise when I laughed. Hank's silliness thrilled me. He was my partner in fun and in bringing home stray animals. When he was visiting, even if for only a few days, we could be certain that he'd drag into the house some mangy, good-natured dog or a gentle, fleabag cat who needed love. Hank always told me that he would shelter me from all harm. And even though I'd never seen any real evidence of it, I believed him with my whole heart.

I took my brother's hand and led him into the house. "This is good, this is *so* good," a voice sang inside me—with Hank in town, Mama would have to come home.

PHOEBE DID NOT spill the beans and tell Hank that, evidently, Mama had run away. Instead she straightaway picked up the phone and said, "I'll call Mama at the store and give her the good news."

She said this so naturally, I thought that maybe Mama wasn't missing and that she and Daddy had made up and were working side by side, two little bumblebees whose stingers were bent beyond repair so they couldn't hurt each other anymore. But there wasn't an answer at the store. Phoebe's brow furrowed as she said, "I let it ring fifteen times."

Hank flashed a grin that stretched from his ear to China, which was his manner, and told her not to worry. "They'll be home," he said, and he looked over her head and into the heat as if he'd just said something important. He was always doing that, voicing simple ideas in such a way that you're convinced down to your underwear that he's teeming with secrets. And because life is better if you think positively, I decided Hank was right—Mama and Daddy would be home soon, and maybe a miracle would happen and everybody would get along.

My brother brought with him a bottle of vodka and a big can of tomato juice. Health food, he called it. He fixed himself a water glass of health food, showed us a picture he kept in his wallet of a pretty dark-haired girl named

Ana, and said that during the past year he'd so successfully juggled work and school that he'd saved enough money to buy the MG *and* take the summer off.

"Yes sirree, I'm going to see some countryside. Thought I'd drive west, tour Wyoming, maybe Montana, rope me some cows." Then he laughed, poked my belly, and leaned against the kitchen counter. "Bird, you want to go catch some cows with your big brother? You and Phoebe, pull on your cowgirl boots and let's go!"

Even though I knew he was joking, I couldn't help but imagine what fun it would be for the three of us to travel to places where there were real, live cowboys. Why, I'd learn how to perform rodeo tricks. I'd seen that once on TV, a golden-haired girl standing on the back of a galloping pony, the crowd wildly cheering as if she were the hottest thing in town.

Hank finished his drink, rinsed the glass, set it in the sink, said, "The house looks good," and then started nosing around. He went in all the rooms, paying special attention to Mama and Daddy's. He whispered questions to Phoebe and she whispered back and that made me mad, them acting like I wasn't old enough to be let in on the what-fors of life. I stomped into the living room, plopped down in front of the TV, and watched "Let's Make a Deal."

Just as Monty Hall was telling a woman who was dressed like a pumpkin that he'd give her a fifty-dollar bill if she had a bobby pin, Band-Aid, and whistle in her pocketbook, my brother and sister came in and joined me. I let go of my hurt feelings because I didn't want to spoil Hank's visit. But the fact that I could not talk kept tangling the afternoon. My brain was full of interesting tidbits I wanted to share with Hank. Did he know how old I was? Did he know I could recite the alphabet backward? Did he know that people who are double-jointed will probably never bear children? Did he know that deadly coral snakes have such small jaws that you practically have to stick your pinkie right in their faces and insult them before they'll bite you? When Hank asked, "Is there a *TV Guide* in this house?" I moved my mouth to answer, but only silent words tumbled out. Hank laughed as if I were the funniest child on earth, and Phoebe said, "Stop this dumb game of yours, Bird. It's irritating." I hated her when she talked like Mama.

Hank was on his third vodka and tomato juice when I sat next to him on Mr. Bailey T. Watson's couch and reached for an oval of silver that hung around his neck. "That's St. Christopher," Hank said. "The patron saint of travelers. Figured I could use a little protection on my trip west. I'm telling you something important here—my good buddy St. Christopher is one damn fine saint. You girls want a St. Christopher medal?"

I nodded, and Hank gulped his drink. Maybe all I needed for the world to be right again—for the grove to be a safe place, for Mama to stay home, for bad spells to catch the next gust of wind out of here—was a piece of silver and a saint's name.

Phoebe fixed us bologna and cheese sandwiches; she even toasted the bread. And when Hank asked her if Mama and Daddy still drank too much, Phoebe did not betray them. "I don't think they're drinking as much as they used to," she said so casually I looked at her twice.

After lunch Hank yawned and said, "God, I'm tired. I think I'm going to take a nap." Then he stretched out on the couch, fell immediately into a deep sleep, and snored so loud I got out my sister's tape player and recorded him.

When Phoebe saw what I was doing, she started laughing. "Bird," she said, "you are crazy." Then she reached for the phone and dialed—I thought she was calling one of her girlfriends, but instead her eyes darkened into a scowl. "Damn it, why aren't they answering!"

I thought to myself, *Now I've got you, Phoebe—you said "damn it" right into the tape recorder, and the next time you're mean to me, I'll just play the tape for Mama.*

As Phoebe hung up the phone, we heard cars in the distance. I snapped off the tape player and set it on the floor beside the couch. Then I ran onto the porch. First Mama pulled in, then Daddy, but he wasn't alone. Some stranger was with him.

They got out of the cars. Mama looked at me and waved. She seemed happy, swollen lip and all. The three of them walked over to the MG and admired it. The stranger, who wore a patch over his left eye, said that maybe it belonged to one of Mama's secret beaus. "Bird, whose car is this?" Mama called.

I raised my hands to the sky as if I did not know and then I ran inside, patted Hank's chest to wake him. Phoebe stood in the middle of the living room like a frozen doll. Mama walked into the house, laid her eyes on Hank, and burst into tears. Hank went to her and they hugged each other for so long I had to look away. I didn't want to bawl in front of my big brother.

Mama pulled back and said, "Sweetheart, it's good to see you. Are you in trouble? Why are you home?"

Hank laughed too loudly and kissed her forehead. He and Mama and Phoebe shared the same dark good looks, except Hank's eyes were lit up with something other than life. Even I could see that. Hank touched Mama's lip and said, "What happened here?"

"Oh, nothing, just a silly accident," she said as she pulled away and covered her mouth with a shaking hand. *Liar, liar, pants on fire,* I thought, and a flood of anger rushed through me. Why hadn't Mama come home last night? Where'd my parents been all day? Who was this stranger with an eye patch? Why were they playacting as if everything were hunky-dory? I looked at my big brother. He must have sensed my upset because he pulled me to him and held on.

Daddy and the stranger came into the house. "Billy," Hank said without a hint of friendliness as Daddy brushed past him.

"Hank," Daddy responded. "What brings you here?"

"Just come to see my mother and sisters," Hank said, managing to sound threatening.

"This is Mr. John Macon, Hank," Mama tried to chatter lightly, "an old friend of Billy's. He lives in Tampa. They haven't seen each other in years, and just by accident, while I was in Lily on an errand, Mr. Macon stopped in the store, not realizing Billy owned it."

"What errand was that, Glory?" Daddy asked as he walked into the kitchen and got himself and Mr. Macon a beer.

"Me, too, please," Mama told Daddy, and when he came back, he tossed her a can, which she dropped.

Hank glared at Daddy, then down at the floor, then at Mr. Macon. "Nice to meet you," Hank said. "You have business in Lily?"

"No. Just passing through." Mr. Macon's voice was

deep, and I didn't like him but I was fascinated with his eye patch. Did he play pirate during the Gasparilla parade? Was anything really wrong with his eye, or was that patch for show, or did his eye get put out by somebody during a barroom brawl? The broken-off neck of a beer bottle could be dangerous, yes it could. I figured him to be in his early forties, like Mama and Daddy, but that patch turned his whole face into a puzzle.

"How long you here for, Hank?" my daddy asked.

"Don't worry. Not long."

Mama laughed and nervously pulled at her short hair. "What a nice surprise, a really, really nice surprise," she jabbered, and I could tell she'd been drinking. Then Phoebe told Mama I was acting like a baby, refusing to speak, and Mama told her to leave me alone.

Mr. Macon cast his one good eye on Mama as if he liked what he saw, and Hank looked disgusted with the whole damn lot of them. Daddy turned on the hi-fi and told Mr. Macon he ought to dance with Mama.

"Dance! What a good idea, I'd love to dance!" Mama said. I didn't want Mama to dance with Mr. Macon. *Daddy must be drunker than a coot,* I thought, *to suggest such a thing.*

"Jesus Christ," Hank whispered. "Mama, why don't we sit on the porch and talk awhile. It's not like I'm home every day."

"Boy, let your mama dance and have some fun if she wants to. Don't walk in my house thinking you can call the shots."

"Now, Billy, Hank was just saying—"

"Forget it, Mama, we'll talk later. Looks like you're busy." He grabbed his keys off Mr. Bailey T. Watson's coffee table and asked, "How would you girls like to go for a ride in the MG?"

I turned my face hopeful, and Phoebe said, "Sure."

"Hank, no, please don't go," Mama said. "Stay and we can—"

Daddy interrupted. "Hell, yeah, the girls could use a nice long ride. Why not cruise through town and then toward the coast? You won't recognize the place. Buildings going up faster than a frog on the Fourth of July. Now don't short-change yourself on our account. Take your time. Lots of new construction to see, you'll be surprised."

I couldn't figure out Daddy's sudden friendly tone, but it didn't matter because I was getting my way.

Hank tossed the keys in the air and grabbed them—midair—as if he were snaring a fly. "Come on, girls," he said.

That MG was a tiny car. Phoebe got in first, and I sat on her lap. She bitched that I was breaking her legs, so just to be nasty I shifted my weight.

Daddy, Mr. Macon, and Mama came out on the front porch. Hank joked that there was room for everybody if they wanted to come.

"Have a good time," Mama called. "Don't be gone too long. I think I'll fry some chicken for supper."

"That sounds good, Mama," Hank said.

I watched Daddy hand Mr. Macon something when Mama wasn't looking—money, I thought—and then he said he was going to the store to get some more beer, that they were almost out. He told Mr. Macon to take care of Mama while he was gone, and the three of them laughed. Mama yelled at Hank to drive carefully. I waved good-bye to Daddy and Mama as my big brother fired up the MG.

He tooted the horn and then zoomed down the road before Daddy had even stepped one foot off the worn and sagging porch.

My brother, even though he wasn't blood-related to my daddy, took after him in this one respect: he drove like a speed demon, and in that little car you could feel all the curves and bumps. My long hair blew in my eyes and mouth, and I knew I'd have a bad time brushing out the tangles, but I didn't care. We were having fun. Phoebe was actually giggling, and Hank sang along to Beatles songs that blared from the radio.

He drove around Lily, and I hoped we'd stop at Beckett's and get something good to eat—at least a box of Red Hots—but we didn't. We cruised past the high school and then by Rhonda Louise Kiefer's white house with the red-striped aluminum awnings. Hank said he'd been sweet on her for about three weeks when they were seniors. But he didn't stop to see her. Instead he headed north, out of town, away from the coast, away from our house. I was settling in, enjoying the speed and eager to see whatever we might pass. But before we got very far, Hank slowed down and yelled above the radio racket, "You know, I don't trust that son-of-a-bitch Macon."

Phoebe yelled back, "Me neither."

"Do you think we ought to go home?"

"I don't know, Hank. Maybe we should stay gone for a while. Daddy didn't seem very happy to see you."

"Naw. Something else was eating him. I've got a bad feeling. He wanted us out of that house. He sure did."

Hank slammed on the brakes and I thought, *No, no, no!* I wanted to stay in that MG and drive forever. I wanted to end up in some big city—maybe Atlanta, maybe Raleigh.

Lead a trouble-free life. Mama and Daddy would come find us and they'd be different. They'd behave like TV parents. But before I could even try to muster up my lost voice and convince Hank to keep driving, he made a U-turn in the middle of the highway. My heart sank as we headed away from the big cities I'd probably never see. But then I told myself, *At least Mama is home; that's what you wanted, now quit complaining.*

Hank drove down Prince of Peace Citrus Highway, past our general store. He slowed the MG, peering at the place, looking for something. Daddy wasn't there. Nobody was, and there weren't any lights left on inside. Every night before closing, Mama and Daddy turned on the lights by the front door and over in the back by the fertilizers so that the whole place was lit up and you could see in from the road real easy. Such was their security system.

"Looks like Billy went someplace else to get that beer," Hank said. "Not even any fresh tire tracks." Then he gunned the engine.

This is what I remember most about arriving back home: the silence. No laughter. No radio or hi-fi noise drifting out to the yard and into the far netherworld of the grove. Not even that blackbird cackling my useless words into the twilight air. The Impala was gone, and the Plymouth was where Mama had parked it when she came home earlier. Hank started toward the house and told Phoebe and me to wait in the yard.

We tagged along behind him. He spun around and said, "I mean it, you girls stay out here."

This is stupid, I thought, *there isn't anything wrong in that house.* We waited until Hank was inside, and then Phoebe and I edged our way to the porch. From there we could hear the scratchy sound of the hi-fi, the needle stuck at the end of the record.

"I'm going in," Phoebe said.

She walked up the steps. I started to follow her, but Hank kicked open the screen door and stepped onto the porch, a limp Mama in his arms. There was blood on my brother's face and shirt, blood matted in Mama's new hairdo, smeared like jam on her yellow dress. "Son-of-a-bitch," Hank said. "Goddamn son-of-a-bitch. I've got to get her to the hospital."

He took a step, and Mama's face rolled lifelessly from his chest to his arm. I saw everything so clearly and wished I hadn't. Her face was pummeled into ground beef. Her nose was no longer in the middle of her face. I wasn't sure where it was. Her black-and-blue eyes were swollen shut.

"I think her ribs are broken," Hank said, rushing past us. "Phoebe, where are the keys to Mama's car?"

"In the ignition, she keeps them there," Phoebe said, her eyes wide and dry.

Hank somehow managed to open the car door and lay Mama in the backseat without dropping her. I remember thinking, *Mama might be dead.* I started to run to the car. Phoebe grabbed my arm.

"I'll call you from the hospital," Hank yelled as he got in the car. Then he sped away.

In my head I shouted, *Let go of me!* But my sister pulled me close and held on.

"She'll be okay," Phoebe whispered, "I promise, she'll be okay," and as the words rolled off Phoebe's tongue, a chill swept through me. A northern wind pounded my bones. It was a furious wind—the kind that cuts through folks as if the air is full of peril, silent razors made of ice. Summer crashed to pieces all around my feet.

"Come on, Bird, let's get inside before the mosquitoes start eating us. I mean it, Mama will be okay."

My teeth were chattering. I followed my sister. The house smelled like blood. In one glance, I saw it everywhere—on the floor, couch, tape recorder, lamp shade, beer cans.

"Go draw your bathwater," Phoebe said, her face hard, her tears piling up in the Devil's box. "I'll clean up the mess."

For once, I did as I was told. I filled the tub with dish liquid and water so hot it should have scalded me but did not. I sank into the suds, turned the faucet back on, then drank as much hot water as my body could hold. *I'll burn these cold winds out of me,* I thought.

But that water, it turned to poison. My stomach somersaulted. I vomited a hellish mix, and as I did the wind howled, the blackbird cawed.

HANK TOLD US Mr. Macon had beat Mama, that he kicked in her teeth, smashed her face, crushed her nose, and cracked four ribs. Said that our daddy had hired him to "hurt her bad" so that she would stop straying so far from home. Hank learned this from Mr. Macon. He tracked down that horrible man after dropping off Mama at the hospital. Phoebe asked if he turned in Mr. Macon to the police, and Hank said no, not to worry about it, that he'd handled matters in his own way. I knew what that meant because I saw the bruises on Hank's hands.

There was no doubt in my mind that Mama wouldn't tell the police. Nor would she contact one of those groups that were becoming a fad—doctors and such who try to help ladies who get beaten by their husbands—because Mama was always saying that people need to handle their own problems, that she didn't want any outside interference.

As for Daddy doing something this awful to my mama, I couldn't think about it. I made pretend as if Daddy was simply away on a drunk, that he'd not been anywhere near Mama or the grove the afternoon of her beating, that I'd never met anyone named Mr. Macon, that Daddy didn't have those sorts of mean bones. It was easy to behave as if I'd never seen my mama's blood smeared across the living room wall, because the truth was too terrible to believe.

Mama was in the hospital for three weeks. Hank, unaware that I preferred my make-believe world, took us to visit her twice. I wasn't allowed in the room because of my age, so Hank parked the MG in the visitors' lot that faced her window. Then he hoisted me onto his shoulders, and Mama and I waved to each other. I was thankful that there was a big pane of glass, some shrubbery, and a few yards of asphalt separating us. I was afraid that if I got too close to Mama, her anger and sadness would rub off on me and make it even tougher to get rid of the cold wind that swirled in my veins. So when I waved, I tried to appear as if I was looking at her. But I wasn't.

During Mama's hospital stay, Phoebe and I mainly raised ourselves. Where Daddy was, nobody knew. Hank, who came home about every other day to sleep, said he was looking for him. My brother was good to us. He bought groceries and, before Phoebe and I went to bed, he would hold us close and say that everything was going to be all right. He swore that he couldn't say what he was up to, that it was between him and his God—as if he had his own private Lord and Savior none of the rest of us could talk with—and that even though Billy Jackson had done a bad thing to our mama, Daddy was crazy for us girls and we were never to forget it. "Do you understand your big brother?" Hank would ask in his important tone.

Phoebe would answer for us, "Yes, we do understand. Thank you." Hank would brandish his giant smile and then plant a kiss on our foreheads. I loved the smell of his aftershave and I wondered if Ana, whose picture he carted around in his wallet, loved my brother and if she, too, was scared by his haunted eyes or if she even noticed.

One night when Hank was home for supper, Phoebe stared at her plate and said, "Hank, somebody must be looking out for us. If you hadn't come down here when you did, Mama might be dead. Bird and I wouldn't have known what to do. You saved Mama's life." Phoebe put her hands over her eyes like people sometimes do when they are crying. But she didn't spill tears, she simply moaned as if her pain was so deep it was kicking her in the gut.

Hank reached across the table, took her hands off her face, and squeezed them. "Come on now. Hang in there with me. Your mama and your sister need you. Sweetheart, I don't know if the big man upstairs was responsible for me being here, or if it was purely chance. But I will tell you this: Your daddy is not going to harm Mama again. I promise you. And you know what they say, every cloud has a silver lining. I bet ours is that this family is finally going to get its act together."

"I sure hope so. That would be nice," Phoebe said.

Of course it would be nice, I thought, *but maybe we're not supposed to be a sweet family. Maybe Jesus has other plans for us.* I grabbed hold of my fork and stabbed it into the fat part of my palm. The tines left four red dots. Mama being made to suffer in order to purify my family seemed like a dirty deal to me.

WHILE MY MAMA was in the hospital, I discovered that the wild cat had birthed her babies. They were living underneath the porch. I spent many hours lying on the wooden slats, peering with one eye down into their little cat den. The babies hungrily sucked on their mama's titties, and Big Mama seemed content, as if the kittens' constant mewing was music to her ears. There were four kittens total. One was solid black, identical to Big Mama. Two of them had wide splotches of black and white, and one was orange. She was my favorite, I guess because she was the oddball of the litter and I identified with that.

When I showed Hank the babies, he said they were fine cats, indeed, and that if he wasn't going to be leaving soon, he'd take one for himself. I furiously shook my head no, and he said, "It's okay, Bird, I'll leave all the kittens with you. You'll take good care of them, I know."

But that's not what I'd meant. I put my hands on his face, felt his beard stubble, his broad nose, his rugged cheekbones. I pressed as hard as possible, and he pulled away, laughing. Then I flashed my Pepsodent smile, even though I felt like screaming. I smiled because I wanted to please him, because I wanted him never, ever to leave, and because if Jesus had hurt Mama for a reason, Hank needed to stick around and make sure that in this game of devils and saints, the hateful did not win.

MAMA TOOK A cab home. I was in the front yard playing with the kittens—I'd succeeded in taming them—when Mr. Anderson drove his rickety yellow cab—he owned the only one in town—through the smoky dust leading to our front door.

I did not run to Mama and throw my arms around her. What if the beating had made her more short-tempered? What if she blamed Daddy's meanness on me? Maybe she hurt too much for me to hug her.

She got out of the cab, carrying a pink overnight case that Phoebe had taken to her on our first hospital visit, handed Mr. Anderson some cash, then turned around and said, "Hello, Bird. What do you have there?"

I pointed at the kittens, and she smiled. Mama's nose looked like a cauliflower, her face was puffed and bruised, and she had three black holes in her mouth where teeth used to be. "Come here and give Mama a hug," she said.

I did, but I wondered where her teeth were. When Mr. Macon kicked her in the mouth, had she swallowed them? I pictured a small row of chompers sitting in her belly, dutifully chewing on mouthfuls of spit-moist food. My anger flared, but it had no direction, just flopped all over the place: the yard, inside my head, my silent throat.

Mama said, "Let's go inside and I'll see what kind of snack I can fix you." She put her arm around my shoulders and moved slowly up the steps. "Has your daddy been around?" she asked.

I shook my head no, and she said, "Bird, why aren't you talking?"

Quickly, I looked around for the blackbird, but she was nowhere to be seen, so I just shrugged.

Mama opened the front screen door, and as she did, Phoebe walked into the living room, clutching one of her glamour magazines. Phoebe must not have heard the cab pull up, because her mouth dropped open, forming a silent O. Then she burst into tears—a rare sight, indeed.

Mama set down her overnight case and walked over to Phoebe with her arms outstretched. She said, "Goddamn it, baby, please don't cry." Then she hugged Sister, and I saw that Mama was crying, too.

I dug my nails into my wrists, and as the sting pushed back my tears, an awful notion struck me. It would be years before I could pin all the right words to the sickening feeling in the pit of my stomach, but this is what I felt: My family, we needed to get the hell out of this roach-infested shack stuck in the middle of the Devil's grove. If we didn't, we'd never be decent people with happy lives. No.

We'd continue to be tiny chickens suffocating at the bottom of the heap. Bewildered folks—the sort moneyed people make fun of and never give jobs to. Dumb-assed crackers who drink till dawn in a sorry attempt to forget about all the things they will never have, never become. But there's no forgetting when you're white trash—smirks, stares, stolen glances remind you at every turn that you're not worth squat. So the men, raging drunk, bullshit each other into believing that bruised fists and broken noses will act as charms, paving their way to heaven. And we females—girls and women alike—can't find enough strength in our battered souls to escape, so we birth our boys into legendary scoundrels, characters made better in the crosshairs of half-truths. Yes, smiles break out all around as we cast daddies, brothers, husbands into near-respectable village idiots in the stories we spin over bowls of homegrown, freshly snapped peas, clotheslines draped with bleach-scented, bloodstained damp sheets, sinks filled with suds and supper-crusted dishes. And after all that, we still aren't decent. We're still trapped.

Mama, Phoebe, and I waded through the dark fear that flooded our house. We wandered into the kitchen, and I watched my mama and sister search the cupboards for something sweet to eat. They slid aside bags of flour, boxes of macaroni, cans of pork and beans as if they were drug addicts, as if sugar would stave off the desperation to come. Finally Mama said, "Bird, I think all I can figure is some sugar-and-cinnamon toast. How's that?"

I nodded yes and patted her hand because I loved sugar-and-cinnamon toast, and I reminded myself to be careful not to let the hot sugar-scabbed butter scald the roof of my mouth, which it often did because I'd forget to blow on the broiled treat before devouring it.

Mama spoke quietly to Phoebe as she tossed squares of white bread on the cookie sheet like someone dealing a hand of cards. She wanted to know when was the last time we'd seen Hank.

"Two days ago."

"And Daddy?"

"He's not been home at all."

"I'm scared of what Hank is going to do to your father if he finds him."

"Maybe he won't find him. Maybe he's already headed west."

Mama looked at me to see if I was listening and understanding. Then she looked at Phoebe, and I could read the words in her black eyes. They said, "No, he's still in town. This bad spell ain't over yet."

That evening the blackbird visited my dreams again. She cackled all night long, and I knew that each time she opened her mouth, my words flew out of her gleaming night-colored throat and tumbled through eternity. I wondered if they were falling toward heaven or hell. I saw Jesus standing at the pearly gates with a butterfly net in His hands, ready to snare my words and take care of their frail sounds and meanings until I could find my way home to them. Then I saw that little boy from the grove standing at the fiery entrance to hell. He brandished a baseball glove and was laughing and singing, "You ain't never gonna see your words again, they gonna burn in hell, just like you, just like you, they gonna burn in hell."

Come morning, I slowly floated up through layers of dreamtime, feeling a rush of wings against my skin, growing exhausted with the sound of flapping. I reached over to Phoebe's side of the bed, but she wasn't there.

I went into the bathroom, pulled down my underwear, sat on the toilet seat, and peed, wondering what it would be like to pee like a man, standing up and aiming. It was probably fun. I wiped myself from front to back, as Mama had taught me. I flushed and watched my pee swirl down and away and thought, *Maybe that's what's happening to my words, they are swirling into some unknown dark place I will never reach.* I pulled up my underwear, got some shorts and a T-shirt out of the clean-clothes basket, and put them on. Then I walked out of the bathroom and into the kitchen, glad that this morning, unlike the past three weeks of mornings, Mama was home.

But I stopped dead in my tracks. Mama sat at the kitchen table, her eyes wild and red-rimmed from tears; Jack the cop, in his uniform, stared into a cup of coffee and said he was sincerely sorry; and Phoebe stood by the sink and peered at the linoleum as if in its geometric patterns of brown and yellow she could view all the world.

Mama looked up and saw me. But her gaze drifted away to Jack, then Phoebe, then she put her hand to her mouth and said, "Oh my God, what am I gonna do with my little baby?"

I knew she meant me even though I wasn't a little baby anymore. And I didn't like her question; it made me feel guilty just for existing.

Jack the cop grabbed his hat, which was on the table beside his coffee cup, and said, "Glory Marie, I think I'll be going now. If you need me for anything, feel free to call. I'll keep an eye out for Hank."

Mama's face fumbled through a haze of tears, and she stammered, "Thank you."

Then Jack made his own way out the door, and Mama said, "Come here, Bird, I need to talk to you."

She touched my cheek, gently hugged me, then pulled away and held my face in her tear-wet hands. "Bird, I don't know how to say this easy, so I'll just say it hard. Your daddy was found this morning by the police. He was in his car. At Moccasin Branch. And, well, he had such a tough time with life, he couldn't handle it no more, honey. Bird, your daddy, he's gone to heaven."

I could barely hear her for the blackbird cackling in my head. I wanted to know how it happened, why nobody had taken him by the hand and walked him away from the darkness that called, why he didn't love us enough to stay on this side of heaven. But my words came out as meaningless, garbled noises. I tried with all my might to make sounds they would understand, but the alphabet danced a crazy jig at the entrance to my voice box, refusing to line up in the order of words. So I wailed and kicked and hit. My bones snapped like ice.

Mama screamed, "Bird, stop. Stop acting this way. Damn it, I can't take it. Dear God, don't do this to me."

THERE WASN'T A funeral. We didn't have any money, and the priest wouldn't agree to a service because

Daddy wasn't a Catholic and he'd killed himself, so they said, and that was a sin in their church.

I missed my daddy so bad that my skin and my hair and my innards ached. If I closed my eyes for more than a few seconds, his face would form behind my lids and I'd see him the way he looked right before he pulled the trigger: a man so riddled with despair that he couldn't imagine a future, couldn't imagine Phoebe graduating from college or me becoming somebody respectable. But there was more, I saw it all: His thunderhead-blue eyes turned creamy white, and the voice deep inside him that gave him hope froze into a mass of silent, untouchable dreams. The other voice—the one that loved to screech, "You're no damn good"—took over, erasing from his mind any chance for forgiveness. He looked out at the river and saw only the slow, unending ripples of his sins. With me far out of his thoughts, he pressed the barrel to his temple and took the bullet. Then his face was gone, replaced by empty blackness. Then I'd open my own eyes and try for a while to not even blink.

There were moments when I blamed Hank, whose whereabouts were unknown. Maybe Hank had found Daddy in the hours before his death and had pushed him too hard, cracked his spirit, showed him too well the beauty of the Grim Reaper—that tricky ghost Daddy had flirted with at least once before. But then I thought, *No, Hank wouldn't do that. Hank wouldn't take my daddy away from me.*

I returned to the rosy world of my make-believe family. Daddy didn't pay Mr. Macon to beat Mama—that was an ugly rumor spread by the Devil. My daddy had been solely sweet-hearted. The ferociousness of Mama's mourning—she wailed and worried, wore nothing but black, ate only rice—caused me to believe Mama also had decided to remember Daddy's good-natured side and nothing else. All other ways of thinking were simply too hurtful, like walking barefoot down a long road of jagged glass.

And something else is true: Daddy's death didn't seem final to me. He could not be gone forever, he just couldn't. If his death was temporary, it meant I didn't have to mourn. Yes, I wailed and kicked when Mama first told me that Daddy was dead, but after that—nothing. I could not have squeezed out a tear if someone had hit me with a hammer. My emotions were tied in a hard knot. With each breath, I felt weight banging against the trip wire of my spine.

It wasn't just my imagination that helped me to believe that death was an open door a soul could walk in and out of. The day after Daddy died, at about five-thirty in the evening, I thought I heard the Impala roar down the lane, just as if Daddy was arriving home from the store. I was in my room, lying on the bed, staring at the ceiling, having a vision of myself as a singing star who made Daddy proud as he gazed down upon me from heaven. And a few minutes after I heard the car pull up, the bells on the front door rang, and then Daddy's voice clearly traveled down the hall and into my room: "I'm home, sunshine!"

Hearing his voice did not scare me. I just thought, *It's about time.* I got up from the bed, opened the door, and walked into the living room, positive that Daddy was going to be standing there with his arms wide open, ready to hug me. But damn it, nobody was in that room. I peered out the window, didn't even see so much as an ant crawl by. Something must have happened, the Devil must have scared Daddy off. I kicked the wall as hard as I could, and Mama, who was in the kitchen with Phoebe, yelled, "Bird, what are you doing?"

In my mind I whispered, *Goddamn you, Devil, you're the one who has been drowning my family in sorrow. And you're the one who is going to get the hell out of here.* I rushed into my bedroom, snatched the crucifix off the wall, stuck it under my shirt, and hurried out into the stillness of the dying day. As I walked toward the grove, I looked over my shoulder to make sure Mama wasn't watching. I dared not actually enter the grove, but I did hover at its very edge. Dragonflies flew all around, but they, too, stayed in the light, veering clear of the darkness and the stink of fallen fruit. *That's the smell of death,* I thought. I glared into the shadows, raised the crucifix over my head, tried to force my voice, but all that came out were grunts. That was okay—I knew what the grunts meant, and the Devil did, too. "Get on out of here, you nasty son-of-a-bitch. Leave my family alone. Go somewhere else with your evil spells. It ain't me kicking you out. It's Jesus Christ, the Son of God. And while you're at it, get your dirty paws off my daddy."

"Bird, what in the hell do you think you're doing?" Mama's words bellowed past me. I could see her voice, red and smoky, curling through the grove's smelly air and then disappearing in a stand of orange trees. I lowered the crucifix and turned around. Mama was stomping down the stairs, heading straight at me. Her fists were balled up, and her teeth clenched. I stood very still and was calm. I didn't care what she might do. Mama wore an old, faded pink dress that was too big for her, and one of its sleeves was ripped. She looked like a ragamuffin.

"Maybe I ought to send you to the juvenile home, maybe that will straighten you out!" Mama yelled when she was within striking distance. She grabbed the crucifix, waved it in front of my face, and shouted, "This is not a toy, goddamn it!" Then she spun around and marched back into the house.

I slapped a mosquito off my arm, spit into the dirt, and asked Jesus, *So now what?*

THE FRUSTRATION I first felt when the blackbird stole my voice was, after my daddy's death, replaced with satisfaction. Because I couldn't talk and because the wild emotions that used to send me bouncing were tied up and floundering, I was able to keep Mama and Phoebe at a distance, and that's just how I liked it. The living seemed a horrible bother. But the dead were another matter. The dead seemed safe to me. I could tell them anything.

On the afternoon that county workers buried my daddy, I sat by myself on our front porch swing, and next thing I knew, Daddy was beside me, picking out a tune on his six-string guitar. He asked if there was anything I wanted to talk about.

I said, *Yes, sir*—I was positive the dead could hear me. *Did you know Phoebe sometimes calls Mama a bitch?*

He chuckled and said, "Honey, that's just her temper talking."

So then I told him what I really needed to. I said that even though he shot himself and that was a sin to most folks, it wasn't a sin if he didn't mean any harm by it. And if Hank had anything to do with the shooting, Daddy should forgive him because we'd all been under the Devil's influence and nobody was thinking straight. And then I said, *I love you,* and he disappeared.

I was just as up-front with Jesus. Four days after Daddy passed on, as Phoebe and I sat at the kitchen table trying to eat a breakfast that neither of us wanted, Mama refilled her coffee cup and said that when we got some extra money she was going to take me to a doctor to see if he could fix me. Well, Queen Phoebe put in her two cents' worth. She stirred her cereal and said maybe there was nothing wrong with me that a spanking wouldn't cure. So I turned around in my chair, looked at Jesus, who was standing by the door—I felt His presence—and I said, *Don't you dare let Mama whip my voice back into me. You'll be sorry if you do.*

That afternoon Mama sold Daddy's white Impala to Jack the cop, who planned to give it to his son. I couldn't believe it, selling Daddy's car just wasn't right. He loved that car, it was part of him. But Mama thought otherwise. She sold it for a cool hundred, which seemed to me like an awful lot of money, but then Mama said to Phoebe, "I know I sold the car too cheap, but I couldn't look at it again. I just wanted the god-awful thing out of my life." Then she started crying and asked, "Where the hell is my son? I wish he was here. I need to talk to my son."

That very night she got her wish because Hank showed

up while we were eating supper. Mama had made rice with gravy, and I was just poking at it—even the smell made me sick—when we heard the unbroken growl of the MG. I kept my face aimed at my plate. I actually felt a pinch of happiness, but I didn't know what to do with it.

"Well, it's about time," Mama said. "Ungrateful bastard." But when she got up from the table she was smiling, a smile I hated to look upon, with its gaping holes. "You two stay out of this." She grabbed her ashtray and cigarettes and was out the door.

Phoebe rolled her eyes and stabbed at her food as if it were a plate of wiggling worms. I wiped my mouth with the back of my hand.

"Where are your manners? You know Mama doesn't like it when you use your arm instead of a napkin," Phoebe said.

Go to hell, I thought, and then I picked up my glass of milk and poured some onto her plate.

"You little shit," Phoebe said, but then she shut up because we heard Mama wading in on Hank:

"Where the hell have you been? I've been worried sick," Mama said. "What kind of son leaves his widowed mother alone? Didn't you think your sisters might need you?"

"Look, Mama, I'm sorry you're mad. But I had to get away. I couldn't think straight in this two-bit town."

"What makes you so much better than the rest of us?"

"It's not that, Mama. Don't twist my words. Look, my sisters know I love them. And before you jump to conclusions, despite what Billy Jackson did to you, I loved that lousy son-of-a-bitch. God only knows why."

Then they barged into the kitchen. Hank was holding two sacks of groceries, which I'm sure pleased Mama.

"Hey, dolls," he said. "How are my pretty sisters?"

"Fine," Phoebe said.

"You hungry?" Mama asked.

"Me? Yeah, I'm always hungry," he said, and he laughed. He patted my head and then pulled a prescription bottle out of the breast pocket of his cotton shirt. "Boy, I tell you, my sinuses have been giving me a fit."

He rummaged through one of the grocery sacks, came up with a six-pack, handed Mama a beer, cracked one open for himself, and popped two pills.

I looked at Mama, who was scowling at Hank. She said, "Girls, go find something to do in the living room. Your brother and I need to talk."

"I'm not done eating," Phoebe sassed.

Mama hit her with her open palm on the back of the head. "Do as I say."

My big sister and I skulked into the living room. I thought about turning on the TV but decided against it. Phoebe went into the bedroom and came back with an emery board. I grabbed for it. "Go get your own, pest!" she said.

So I did. And then the two of us sat on the couch and bent our ears to hear what was going on in the next room. We couldn't catch it all, and at one point Phoebe got bold enough to stand by the kitchen door. I stuck right beside her.

Through the Sheetrock and pine, we heard Hank swear he didn't have anything to do with Daddy's death. Yes, he saw him. Yes, he talked to him. "I tried to reason with the man—told him he was never going to hurt you or my sisters again. When he wouldn't listen to reason, I gave him choices," Hank said.

"You shouldn't have done that. He was sick. He needed our help." Mama spit the words.

"Why are you taking up for him? You always take up for him. The man beat you, for Christ's sake. And when he thought he couldn't beat you hard enough, he hired somebody to do it for him. What's wrong with you, Mama?"

Mama murmured that she didn't know, she just didn't know. Then she said, "I don't think I can stay here. There's so much to figure out. I've got to decide what's best for the girls. Oh, God, how am I going to raise two girls all by myself?"

"I'm here for you, Mama. I'll always be here for you. Please don't doubt me."

Hank's words stabbed my heart. I knew Mama wanted Hank to behave like the man of the house, to provide for us and never wander. But my brother had things to do, places to go. He was running from his own demons. Mama had said so a thousand times. I believed it. I'd heard him cry out in his sleep. And I knew he hurt all the time, it was there in those eyes. Most of his sorrow was seeded in the years before I was born, when Mama and Daddy were younger and even wilder, after Hank's daddy died and mine raised him as his own.

I pictured him in a cowboy bar out west, telling men with big belt buckles and sunburned faces about his wonderful mama and two beautiful smart sisters. I saw him drinking his liquor and weaving his charm and painting us in the most immaculate light.

In the years to come, I'd realize Hank wouldn't be there for us in an ordinary sense, but in ways far-flung and wonderful.

I heard Mama whisper that she wanted to die, and Hank

mumbled, "There, there, Mama, life's going to be better now," and I imagined the Silver Spur Saloon full of burly men in ten-gallon hats, and Hank's big smile sweetened by tender memories, and I thought, *At least somewhere on this earth, wherever my brother makes friends for the night, I will be a perfect child, my mama a sinless woman.*

THAT NIGHT THE blackbird once again scattered my dreams and stole more of my words. She lit upon my windowsill and then flew into the room, lifted me by my shoulders, and carried me out of my house, far above the treetops and then across the star-tossed sky. Wind rushed past my face, and I saw the earth the way angels must see it: a ball of light, blue and clear, where nothing is still or certain.

Come morning, I could barely wake up, and when Phoebe told me to brush my hair, that I looked like Phyllis Diller, I grabbed the brush and threw it at her.

Hank had stayed the night and was still sleeping on the couch when I came out of the bedroom and headed outside to check on my cats. I stood on the porch and was delighted because the kittens and Big Mama were in the yard playing.

But a noise broke the morning calm, and the entire yard was suddenly a jumble of shadows and sound. The kittens cowered, and Big Mama hissed. I looked up. Five vultures circled.

I remembered my daddy arguing with one of his buddies who hung out at the store about whether vultures ate live prey or not. Daddy swore they did. "If it's an easy kill they do it," Daddy said, and he seemed so upset his buddy quit arguing with him.

Convinced that the vultures could hear me, I screamed, *Go away, you evil bastards.* I ran into the yard, flapped my arms, stomped my feet. I heard *swoosh, swoosh, swoosh.* I screamed louder, banshee-danced harder. Wings clouded the air. The orange, oddball kitten was blanketed by a tumbling vulture. There was screeching, so much screeching, as the buzzard's massive claws and beak slashed open the kitten's throat. Big Mama cat-howled, her cries echoed across the grove. The blackbird cackled. I looked at the live oak. The bird was in the branches, watching me, the cats, the vultures.

Mama and Hank ran onto the porch, both wanting to know what in the hell the racket was. Mama gasped and Hank said, "Jesus fucking Christ!"

Mama said, "Hank, do something!"

He ran barefoot into the yard and to his car. He opened his glove compartment and pulled out a gun. He aimed at the birds. But it was too late. One-two-three-four. Right before my very eyes, a buzzard chose a cat. Even Big Mama, who was making the most ungodly sounds I'd ever heard as she struggled to get free and save her babies, was no match for these killers. The kittens squirmed and yowled and the vultures looked at us as if to say, "Just try and stop us."

The blackbird was flinging my words into the air as if

they were nothing but tiny turds. I put my hands to my ears. Wailed as loud as I could.

Mama slapped me.

Hank said, "What, baby, what do you want?"

I pointed at the blackbird and wailed again, and Hank somehow understood. He read my mind or heard my words in the bird's raking voice. He lifted his gun, he zeroed in, he shot the blackbird. She fell out of the live oak, heavy as an anvil, and landed in the dust with a leaden thud. Mama turned me away from the vultures and my kittens, away from the dead blackbird, and then I heard myself in a clear and certain voice: "I want to go away from here. Please, Mama, take me away!"

WE LEFT THE grove, never to look back, on an intensely hot and silent summer day. Mama didn't tell Mr. Bailey T. Watson we were leaving. Saying he'd figure it out eventually, she tossed the house keys on the kitchen table and made a crack about how he sure loved to receive the rent check on time.

Hank headed down the road two days before we did. I hated to see that MG disappearing into the distance. It seemed to me that my big brother was the only safety net I had. And he was full of holes, so go figure. Before he drove away, the four of us sat on the front porch steps—not a single sign of carnage was left in the yard—and he tossed us pearls of wisdom. He warned about the temptation of spending money foolishly, told Mama to let the priest at Immaculate Conception know where we were so that we could be found, told Phoebe and me to take care of our mama because she was going to need our help, cautioned us to beware of strangers, and asked that we never stop believing in "good old Hank." Then he kissed us good-bye, promised he'd see us soon, and roared away to destinations that I knew about solely through watching Channel Thirteen's Weekend Cowboy Matinee.

On our final morning in Mr. Bailey T. Watson's house, I watched Mama pull down from the cupboard a slim, rectangular package that I thought was a box of cooking chocolate. Suddenly my sweet tooth was throbbing for some of her homemade thick and luscious hot chocolate. It didn't matter that it was the end of summer and I should have been desiring a cold drink—Mama's was full of good stuff like butter and milk and sometimes cinnamon.

When she set the package on the counter, I picked it up. Spelled out in blue chunky letters was the word "Gulfwax." That certainly didn't sound like anything I could eat or drink. On the box were pictures—they looked like crayon drawings—of candles and home-canned goods. Mama turned on the faucet and snapped, "Leave that alone. Just go away."

I set the package back down and, with my feelings hurt, walked out of the kitchen. Mama's back was to me, so I stuck out my tongue at her. "Don't you talk back to me, you little hellion," she said, giving credence to her occasional claim that she had eyes in the back of her head.

Curiosity would not allow me to stray too far. I stood at the doorway on the living room side, spying on her. She unwrapped the wax, held a square of it under the hot tap water, gritted her back teeth, and then quietly cussed as she shaped and reshaped the white nugget. After about three minutes, she leaned over the sink, opened her mouth, and jammed the wax into one of the gaps where a tooth used to be. She repeated the procedure twice more, and I heard her breathe hard each time a homemade tooth touched her raw gum line, so I knew it hurt.

Later that morning, when she told me to stop dawdling and to help my big sister load the car, I carefully studied her mouth. Her wax teeth weren't perfect, but they could fool you at a few yards out.

We packed the angel-blue Plymouth with our few possessions: the crucifix and Jesus picture, the little pine chest Daddy had made me along with its pieces of spring, a box of dog-eared family photos, some oddball dishes she insisted were ours even though I was fairly positive they belonged to Mr. Bailey T. Watson, and a big ugly black suitcase—now filled with our clothes—that she bought for five cents at the church thrift sale. As for the general store, we didn't own the building, the land, or most any of the merchandise, as Daddy had stretched his credit far more than such things should be stretched, so Mama just walked away from everything.

It was early afternoon when we got in the Plymouth, me in the backseat, Mama and Phoebe up front. A strange feeling soured my stomach, as if change, turmoil, and dead daddies were looking for a place to permanently roost.

Mama said, "Well, it's just the three of us now. You girls sure you want to leave?"

"Yep," said Phoebe.

I cracked my knuckles. "Drive fast, Mama."

She let loose with a startled laugh, then cranked the Plymouth. As we bumped along that rutted, dusty drive, I waved good-bye to the grove, prayed we were leaving the Devil behind, imagined his spell was coming off each one of us—festered fleeces tossed to the wind, three little snakes slipping their skins. Once on the open road, we'd be reborn, and the many strangers along our path would say, "Now there goes a trio of sparkling treasures." And, I decided, Daddy's ghost was riding the wind, following his family, giving us a dose of protection. Phoebe stared straight ahead, and while I didn't know what she was thinking, I hoped she, too, was conjuring a kinder future.

We knew where we were going but had not a clue as to what we'd do once we got there. We'd decided to move to Tampa. Mama said there'd be more opportunity in a big city. "I think they have good schools, and there are lots of Cubans so you'll be exposed to different ways."

The only thing I knew about Cubans was I Love Lucy's husband—I watched that show sometimes in the morning—so I imagined a city teeming with men who spoke broken English and were mad for redheads, which was good for me. Then I thought that maybe Mama should dye her hair red so that she'd nab us a new daddy. We'd live in a clean apartment, and I'd learn to play the maracas. Sister would sing in the band. And then I thought that really I didn't want another daddy, that we'd probably be better off just us females.

Mama took Prince of Peace to Highway 41, a long and lonely blacktop truck route that began so far up north our map didn't even say where. Just showed it meandering south out of Georgia, then through Florida backwater towns, the big-city lights of Tampa, and beyond to south

Florida, a land I'd never seen but I'd heard a lot of tales, all of them having to do with crocodiles and crime.

I studied the map, which we did not need because once we were on 41 there was no way we could get lost. I was fascinated with the land south of Tampa. From the looks of things, it was a watery world filled with exotic, magical places. I whispered the names of towns as if the map's black trail of letters would lead me to salvation: Ruskin, Rubonia, Osprey, Laurel, Nokomis, Naples. Stretching west and south of Naples was the Everglades. That's where I wanted to go! River of grass, land of Seminoles, and more birds than even God could count. I bet there were thousands of avocets in that south Florida swamp. I said to Mama, "Once we get to Tampa, do you think we could take a trip to the Everglades? Maybe see us some Indians and birds?"

"We went there not long after you were born. Just a bunch of mosquitoes. You don't want to go there, Bird."

Mama, she sure knew how to burst a bubble. I tossed aside the map, started clicking my tongue against the roof of my mouth, stared out the window. Occasionally a semi blasted past, sometimes honking its horn, which caused us to giggle. Mama would flash her lights. When I inquired what for, she answered that she was being courteous, alerting the drivers that it was safe to get back in our lane. Said that truckers were known to be good Samaritans. I didn't know what that meant, and she explained they would help us if we had trouble on the road, and I asked, "You mean like guardian angels?"

"Well, yeah, Bird, sort of like that."

From then on, I'd wave whenever a trucker drove by, hoping he'd notice me in particular, praying that he really was an angel and that as he sped by he would shower us with invisible good-luck dust. Yep, truckers, they had an ideal job, sitting high up near to heaven in brightly colored cabs that were outfitted with horns and lights and shiny chrome and windshields big enough to cradle the whole damn sky.

I wanted to eat pie and drink milk at one of the truck stops along our way, but Mama said Tampa wasn't that far and we'd eat once we got to where we were going. Next door to most of the truck stops were citrus stands proclaiming that they sold the juiciest, best-tasting Indian River oranges and grapefruits in the state. Most of them also sold straw hats, rubber 'gators, flip-flops, and Georgia pecans. I know this because the merchandise hung in net sacks from signs, beams, awnings—everything just whipping and twirling in the breeze. When I asked if we could stop and maybe buy something, Mama snapped that such places were tourist traps and she wouldn't be caught dead at one.

All in all, the three of us were feeling better than we had in a long time. Mama, who was not as pretty as she used to be, not with those wax teeth and a nose that refused to settle into its pre-busted shape, talked about the future. She said a new city meant we each had a chance for a fresh start. And even though there was a hole in our lives caused by Daddy's death, our hearts were still beating. We had to go on.

As we passed three teenage boys riding horses, I waved, and one of them gave me the finger. Mama didn't see the boy or his obscene gesture. She was looking dead ahead and jabbering, "I want the two of you to make me proud.

Don't ever use your daddy's death as an excuse not to excel."

Phoebe set down the crossword puzzle she was working on and said that she was scared to meet a brand-new group of kids. "What if they don't like me?" she asked. "What if they think I'm too backward or too, you know, poor?"

"You are just as good as anybody else," Mama said as she pressed the gas and passed a red Beetle driven by a boy with long, frizzy hair. "Phoebe, I don't want you to worry. You're going to be so popular. I just know it. You've got a good personality. People are naturally drawn to you."

"That's right," I piped up from the back. "You do have a good personality."

"The key," Mama said as she pushed in the cigarette lighter and then tapped out a Salem on the dashboard, "is to project your personality and to do so without risking your reputation." Mama sounded like an expert.

"What does that mean, 'reputation'?" I asked as I pushed my feet against the back of Phoebe's seat.

Mama took a deep drag off her cigarette and said, "Explain it to her, Phoebe."

Sister turned and faced me. She screwed up her lips in concentration and then said, "It's how people think about you. If you behave right, you'll have a good reputation. And if you don't, well, then you'll have a bad one."

"But like what? What sorts of things do you have to do for people to think you're bad?"

"Jesus, Bird," Mama snapped, "things like lying, stealing, running with boys."

"Oh," I said. "Now I get it. So if Phoebe started dating a

boy who smoked and drove a fast car and maybe played in a rock band, she'd get a bad reputation."

"Yes," Mama said.

"Good." And then I said, "Phoebe, I bet you get a boyfriend as soon as school starts."

"Over my dead body," Mama said as she slowed down to take a curve. "Phoebe has other things on her mind. Like making good grades, something you could stand to do, Miss Priss."

"I bet I will make good grades in Tampa, Mama," I said. "I bet I'll do okay."

"Let's hope so. Oh, look at that lake. Isn't it beautiful!" Mama pointed with her cigarette off to the right.

"Look at them ducks!" I said.

"*Those* ducks," Phoebe corrected me. "*Those,* not *them.*"

"Don't tell me how to talk."

"But you sound stupid."

"Who are you calling stupid?"

"Stop bickering right this second," Mama ordered, and we did shut up. But when Mama stopped at a roadside store to pee and get a cup of coffee, Phoebe and I stayed in the car and I pinched my sister.

"Ow! What was that for?"

"For calling me stupid."

"I did not call you stupid. I said you sound stupid when you don't talk correctly."

"Well, I don't care. I didn't like it."

"Okay, let's just forget it. Mama has a lot on her mind. We shouldn't do anything to upset her." Phoebe reached over the seat and offered me her pinkie. "Friends?"

"Yeah, I guess so," and we pinkie-shook.

When Mama got back to the car she said, "The rest

room is clean. Phoebe, take your sister in there and you two go. You'll have to ask for the key."

"Mama, I don't have to pee," I said.

"Bird, don't lie to me. Now get on in there."

Phoebe and I did as we were told, but I wasn't happy about it. I hated peeing in public rest rooms. I'd rather go in the woods and risk getting eaten by a bear. But it ended up not being too bad. And when we were finished, Phoebe bought us a whole handful of bubble gum. The old man working the cash register said, "Your mother told me you three are heading to Tampa. Be careful there, young ladies. Things go on in that town that don't even get reported in the papers."

"Yes, sir," Phoebe said. "Thank you."

When we got back in the car we told Mama what he said, and she started laughing. "Old goat. If the terrible events don't get reported, how does he know they occur?"

"Yeah," Phoebe said, "that doesn't make any sense."

"It sure don't," I said. Phoebe turned around and glared, a correction on the tip of her tongue. But I pointed at Mama, shook my head, and mouthed the words: "Don't upset her."

Phoebe turned back around, picked up her crossword puzzle book, and every once in a while read us a clue. That's how the rest of our drive went: Mama pointing out pretty scenery, Phoebe saying things such as, "I need a seven-letter word that means *alien* or *anonymous*," and then the three of us stumbling through our entire language as we tried to fill in those little white squares in Phoebe's book. It was a nice ride.

During late afternoon, we crossed Tampa's northern border. Here, Highway 41 became Nebraska Avenue, and it was a strange mix of gas stations, motels, bars, minimarts, virgin land, and clear-cut lots. Everything seemed haphazard, accidental, as if yesterday that 7-Eleven had been a cow-grazed pasture and everyone was surprised that the grass and wildflowers had gone away and an ugly building with plate-glass windows plastered with advertisements had sprouted in their place.

"This city sure is growing," Mama said as she tried to drive and sightsee at the same time.

"I'm hungry!" I moaned.

"We'll stop soon," Mama promised as we passed a stubble-faced drunk who was sitting on a bus-stop bench, brown-paper-bagged bottle in hand. "There's your first real wino, girls," Mama said, and I laughed because I thought wino was a funny word.

We passed Triumphant Fellowship Church. A colored boy and a lady I figured to be his mama were in the front yard, on their knees, pulling weeds. I wondered if the two of them kissed snakes.

Ahead of us on the right was a large neon sign. In orange and green it announced itself to be The Travelers Motel. Phoebe said, "Look, Mama, that motel is sort of cute."

The place looked like a little village. Small red-brick cottages, shaded by oaks and nestled among azaleas, were scattered about what must have been a city block or more. The cottages had turquoise shutters with sailboat cutouts in the middle of each one. Right out front was a swimming pool. White neon burned brightly: VACANCY. I checked the sky—didn't see a single vulture.

"I don't know," Mama said. "I guess we could stop and ask the price. What do you think?"

Phoebe shrugged her shoulders, and I bellowed, "Yes," because I liked the looks of that swimming pool. Mama made a U-turn in front of May Ellen's Cafe and Truck Stop—a place where truckers could take showers for free and tourists could buy two boxes of oranges for the price of one—and we crossed back over to the motel. Mama parked in front of the office, under an oak. She grabbed her pocketbook, looked at herself in the rearview, fluffed her hair, and then said, "Wait here. I'll go in and try to get us a room."

The oak provided shade but not much respite from the heat. In the far distance, a lawn mower droned. Nearby, a dog barked. Across the street, a diesel engine sputtered and died. I heard a flutter of wings and a hollow cry of doves. Opera music wafted from the office, as did a sudden scent of garlic. Phoebe waved away a fly and huffed, a sure display of boredom. Minutes ticked past as I sweated and wondered what was taking Mama so long.

I said, "It's too hot, I'm suffocating."

Phoebe said something that sounded like agreement, and then I asked, "You want to sing?"

"I guess so."

Singing had been one of the mainstays of our Sunday-afternoon hell-bent rides with Mama and Daddy. It was also one of the few things Phoebe and I did together that didn't end up in a sister fight, except when she started correcting my words, as in the song "Sweet Chariot." She made fun of me for singing "Georgia" instead of "Jordan," but how was I to know the right word was a Bible town when Georgia was right across the Florida state line?

Phoebe stretched out on the front seat, her back against the door, and said, "But let me pick the song." She chewed on a fingernail, thought for a few seconds, and then, in a soft, sweet voice, she started: "Michael rowed the boat ashore . . ."

And I joined in: "Alleluia!"—trying to sound as angelic as was humanly possible. I imagined we were members of the Christy Minstrels, spreading goodwill and cheer with our simple yet inspiring singing style. We had started in on a rousing chorus of "Sister helped to trim the sail"—I could hear that tambourine shimmering with silver-tipped wings along the edges of our voices—when a boy who appeared to be just about Phoebe's age walked out of the office, a three-legged collie hobbling beside him. The boy was darkly handsome and must have been one of those Cubans Mama had told us about. He was holding a wrench and paid us no mind. His hair was jet black and he was shirtless, and even I liked the muscles that rippled as he walked. He and the three-legged dog strode slowly past our car as if they owned the whole world, and then they disappeared into a shed near the end of the dirt road lined with cottages.

Phoebe and I, we stopped our foolish singing as soon as we laid eyes on him. Phoebe took the hairbrush out of the glove compartment, looked at herself in the rearview, and went to work trying to get the tangles out of her pretty black hair.

I said, "That sure was a sweet-looking dog."

"Bird, that dog only had three legs."

"I know that. He was still sweet-looking. A dog don't have to have all its legs to be beautiful. Besides, beauty is in the eye of the beholder."

"Well, that's excellent news for you. Good luck finding a beholder." Then she laughed at her own sassy remark.

"Phoebe, you're just a snotty . . ." I started, but stopped because Mama walked out of the office.

She ducked her head in the car window and said tersely, "Listen, this won't take long. Stay in the car." Then a short, bald man, who had the same complexion as the boy who'd walked by minutes earlier, came out of the office, and Mama and he walked away, down a dirt road that angled off to the right.

"Where's she going?" I asked.

"How do I know? I guess she's looking at our room." Phoebe studied her reflection in the mirror, searching her face for blackheads and then checking out the road.

"You're looking for that boy," I said.

"I am not."

"You are too."

"Shut up, Bird. You don't know what you're talking about."

"He's probably got cooties," I said. And when that didn't get a rise out of her, I just let my mouth run: "I wonder what Mama is doing. She's taking too long. My stomach is growling. I'm hungry."

"Quit complaining," Phoebe said. "You don't hear me crying 'I'm hungry,' " she mocked, "and I've had just as little to eat as you have."

I remembered the pimento cheese sandwiches Mama had made us before we left the grove. I wished we had brought some with us. And I wished I had an RC Cola. That would be just perfect—a pimento cheese sandwich and an RC. "Do you think we'll eat out tonight?"

"Damn, Bird, all you can think about is food."

"I'm gonna tell Mama you cussed." She didn't respond. I gazed at the road. There was a lot of traffic on Nebraska

Avenue. It would be a difficult street to cross. "I think we should take a walk by the pool."

"Go ahead, if you want to get a beating."

Phoebe was being such a smart aleck I decided not to talk to her anymore. She fiddled with her hair, and I fiddled with whatever I could find in the backseat. I was snapping the ashtray lid open and closed when the air turned salty and faintly familiar, like an old memory that's fuzzy around the edges but clear and potent enough to push aside the qualms of the here and now. I looked up from the ashtray, and on the road Mama had gone down stood an old, black woman. She was dressed in men's clothes—dungarees, a short-sleeved workaday shirt, and a hat that cast a half-moon shadow across her face. It seemed to me she was staring right at us with eyes that even from afar appeared more yellow than brown. Again, I heard a gentle flutter of wings, and then she quickly disappeared down a path overgrown with wildflowers and thorns. The smell of the sea skittered off as well.

I was about to ask, "Did you see that old colored woman?" but right then Mama and the man rounded the corner. When they reached the Plymouth, the bald man said in an accent that I couldn't quite place, "And who do we have here?"

"Phoebe, Bird." Mama coated our names in sugar. "Say hello to Mr. Ippolito."

We dutifully mumbled our greetings.

"Beautiful, beautiful daughters," he said.

Mama thanked him and asked if she needed to sign anything.

"No, no! You and your daughters settle in, relax a little.

We can take care of our business after that. Maybe in the morning you come see me."

"All right, I will, first thing tomorrow," Mama said as she opened the car door and gracefully slid behind the wheel.

He said, "Don't forget about that pilot light. It's a tricky."

"I won't. Thank you. Thank you very much."

"My pleasure." Then Mr. Ippolito turned around, waved his hand in the air in a backward good-bye, and disappeared into the office.

As Mama put the Plymouth in gear, she said, as if she could not believe it, "Girls, I think we've got us a new home."

MR. IPPOLITO WAS a divorcé. And a Yankee, having moved to Tampa from New York after his divorce. But more than a Yankee, he was Italian. He could cook and sing to prove it, too. He had three incredibly good-looking sons who moved down here with him and who, he said, helped him run the motel: Joe, Manny, and Louis Junior. But Joe and Manny were hardly ever around. For the first few weeks we lived there, I thought they might be ghost sons. Louis Junior—he was the boy who walked by with the three-legged dog—cleaned the pool every morning, wearing nothing but his swimming trunks.

Of course, in my imagination I made Mr. Ippolito and my mama a couple, but then I broke them up because the two of them together didn't fit.

We did not move into one of the cottages, as I would have liked. Mr. Ippolito rented us a broken-down travel trailer abandoned on the far northern end of the motel grounds. Once pink, the trailer had faded under the intense central Florida sun into a shade reminiscent of a blister.

We were fairly isolated, surrounded by fields and trees on two sides. The motel driveway ran in front of the trailer. Across the street were more cottages, and in front of them was the pool. Our postage-stamp yard of weeds and sand faced a tin-roofed, wall-less double garage that was stacked to high heaven with trash: rusting tools, a fender off an old truck, worn-out ovens and toilets, mangled bed frames, bald tires, leftover rolls of linoleum, busted light fixtures, empty Valvoline motor oil cans, lawn mowers that hadn't cut a blade of grass in ages, cracked-mirrored medicine cabinets, file bins filled with mouse nests, bits and pieces of no longer recognizable objects.

Mr. Ippolito said he had a difficult time throwing things away and that the decrepit hunks of metal, glass, plastic were part of the history of the motel and, besides, you never knew when one of those pieces of junk might come in handy. Mama always laughed when he said this, but I knew what she was thinking. Behind her black eyes floated the words: "You crazy son-of-a-bitch."

The arrangement Mama had made in the motel office while Phoebe and I sweated and sang and fiddled in the Plymouth was that we'd pay seventy-five dollars a month for the trailer, water included, and Mama would work days handling the front office plus some light book-keeping. For her labors, Mama would be paid the sum of fifteen dollars a week. But she would be paid under the table because Daddy's passing had put us on public assistance, and if she claimed real wages, whatever she earned would be subtracted from our monthly seventy-dollar government check. And she wasn't earning enough to afford the subtraction. I heard her tell Phoebe that she was getting older and losing her looks, that there weren't a lot of businesses that would hire a woman hurtling headlong into her fifties, especially not one with wax teeth in her mouth. Said she was real lucky to be getting work from Mr. Ippolito because, besides being paid in cash, she was, essentially, at home so she could keep an eye on us.

The trailer was small, hot, and paneled with fake dark wood warped from water damage—the ceiling leaked in heavy rains. We had jalousie windows, and from noon until dusk the reflection of those rectangular slices of glass fell across the walls like bars. Phoebe and I shared the only bedroom. Mama slept on the couch. She said she preferred it that way since she no longer had our daddy to hold on to. We lived with an infestation of roaches and giant gray tree spiders. The spiders, in particular, scared Phoebe and me to death. Mama would say, "Jesus Christ, you two are behaving like a couple of little fools."

She'd pick up a shoe or a newspaper, her face would turn to granite, she'd smash the spider into oblivion, and her hard expression would crack into a thousand twitches. When she swept the crumpled corpses into the dustpan and carried them into the bathroom to flush them down the toilet, she held the pan as far away from her as her arm would stretch. See, she was as scared of the spiders as we were. But she was our only parent. It was her job, hiding that fear.

We moved into the trailer on a Saturday. Ten days later, school would start. That barely gave me enough time to get used to my new home. But I did my best. Phoebe and I spent our mornings by the swimming pool. That's where Louis Junior first said hello and where he sat down beside Phoebe's lounge chair and asked, "What did you say your name was?" I spent long afternoons investigating. I counted the cottages, thirty-six total, and peeked into the windows of ones that were vacant. They were all just alike, neat as a pin, double beds, small living rooms, dollhouse-sized stoves and ovens—kitchenettes, my mama called them. I made friends with the gimp dog and set out peanuts along the rail that ran the length of the garage for the squirrels. It didn't take long at all for those creatures to find the peanuts, and within three days, one of them ate out of my hands. I discovered an oak tree that was home to a family of woodpeckers. I picked up lizards that were sunning themselves on the steps outside the trailer, held their mouths to my earlobes. They would grab hold of me with their little lizard jaws and it did not hurt. I walked around The Travelers wearing live lizard earrings. Phoebe said I was sick. Everywhere, I looked for signs of Daddy's ghost: in the Spanish moss that hung from the tree branches, in the shadows cast by passing clouds upon the surface of the pool's water, in the steam rising off Mama's morning coffee. I never did see him. And even though I looked, I did not run into that old woman I'd seen hurrying down the overgrown path. To be honest, I have to say that I suspected that she, too, was a ghost.

The day before school started, Mama told us to sit down

on the couch and listen. She told us we had to try our hardest to make good grades. We were poor, poor people, she explained, and worse than that, we were females. We would have to scratch and fight if we were ever going to succeed. That made me think of Big Mama and how all her scratching and fighting had been for naught because those vultures still killed her and her babies. But I couldn't say that to Mama because, before I could, she started crying and damned Daddy to hell for leaving us in such a predicament. Then she looked to the stained, sagging trailer ceiling and said, "I wish God would strike me dead this instant."

Phoebe and I didn't know what to say. This was the first blue mood Mama had suffered since we left the grove. It was awful; I felt like she was stuffing us back into the firefly jar. My sister and I, we shifted our weight on that scratchy, uncomfortable, mothball-smelling couch until she got to her point.

"You two are going to go to college, you hear me? We might not have a pot to pee in, but the both of you are going to work hard and make straight A's. Do as I say and you'll have a chance to win college scholarships. Education and hard work—that's the only way this family is ever going to get ahead. From this day on, use your heads. Not your hearts. And if I catch either one of you not living up to your potential, whichever one it is will have hell to pay. Understand?"

We both said, "Yes, ma'am," and I do believe we fully intended to make Mama proud of us. But it was difficult. Right away, within the first few weeks of school, the other kids made sure Phoebe and I felt like a couple of toads among a pond of beauty queens. We couldn't afford new school clothes, so Phoebe and I just wore our homemade outfits we brought with us from Lily, and when the kids wanted to upset me, they'd call me Rags. My classmates snickered at me on Savings Bond Day because the teacher, Mrs. Ritly, said that by purchasing savings bonds we were displaying our patriotism. But no matter how much of a fit I pitched, Mama wouldn't give me money to spend on bonds. She said it was a waste of hard-earned cash, and besides, we were broke. I think Phoebe and I were the only people with a dead parent—and not having a daddy was just one more wart in a mountainous pile. I guess the topper was that we lived in a motel. My classmates made it perfectly clear that they and their parents believed that anyone staying at The Travelers had to be white trash, and that spelled trouble. So nobody was allowed to visit me after school, even though we had that great swimming pool with a slide *and* a diving board.

Despite what the other kids put us through, Phoebe kept her wits about her and made straight A's. Me, I tried. But I couldn't do math. No matter how hard I struggled and fought, those numbers and formulas remained a foreign language to me. I might as well have been trying to speak French. And Mrs. Ritly was harsh, harsh to the point that when she called on me, I'd get all worked up—just as if my teacher had somehow become my screaming mama—and I'd respond in exactly the same way I did when I was in trouble at home: I'd stutter. And that caused the girl who sat beside me, Patty Hill, to whisper loud enough that I could hear, "The only people who stutter are liars." But Mrs. Ritly never heard Patty. Saying practice makes perfect, my teacher made me do math drills on the blackboard. In front of twenty-five gloating faces I trembled, got all the answers wrong, and silently prayed for help from angels, leprechauns, and Jesus Christ. Plus, I hated the feel of the chalk in my hands—it felt like a dead man's finger to me.

I decided I could not live up to Mama's new expectations, nor could I stand going to school every day. So I played sick. My suffering had no end: colds, stomachaches, sore throats, flus, rashes, fevers. I was sick so much that Mrs. Ritly said my hygiene must be lacking.

Allowing the illnesses was an important kindness my mama showed me in the months following Daddy's death. She didn't have it in her to stop hollering for most any little thing, but she let me stay home whenever I wanted and she never called me on my maladies, even though I'm sure she knew I was faking.

So I spent a lot of time being a pint-sized vagrant, wandering the acorn-strewn grounds of The Travelers Motel, searching for the dark-skinned old woman who smelled like the sea, steering clear of Mr. Ippolito, who scared me just because he was a man, sailing through the many shadows of morning and noon, a band of squirrels and a limp dog trailing in my meandering wake.

THIS IS THE mystery of love: forgiveness. It was a mystery that flitted all about my mama's heart, sometimes resting there but mostly not. I believe she purely hated and loved my daddy, and while she would cry in the middle of a dark night and say into the still air, "I love you, Billy Jackson. Yes, I forgive you," hers was a forgiveness undermined by wrath.

It is true that in the first couple of weeks following Daddy's death, Mama mourned with such purity that it was difficult to believe he'd ever been mean to her. She mourned with dignity: her righteous wearing of black, her wailing tears that would crest in mid-sentence or just as she was lifting a coffee cup to her lips, and then there was that rice-eating. One morning when we were still in the grove, Phoebe, Mama, and I sat at the kitchen table, trying to down breakfast. I was nibbling a piece of toast. Phoebe was drinking orange juice. And Mama was glumly eating a bowl of cold rice. I asked, "Mama, why ain't you having anything besides rice?"

She set down her fork, took my hand, and kissed it. Her lips were slobbery wet. Her face was so pale it looked as if she was suffering from blood loss. "It's a custom in our family, Bird. You've seen people on TV get married, how all the well-wishers throw rice on the couple?"

"Yes, ma'am."

"Why do you think they throw that rice?" She picked up a grain and rolled it between her thumb and middle finger.

I shrugged my shoulders. "Beats me."

"The rice," she said as she squashed the grain, "is supposed to bring the couple luck and prosperity. But if the husband dies, the widow should eat only rice for as long as she can stand it in order to make sure the luck and prosperity remain with the survivors." Then Mama's sad face crinkled up, and she proceeded to laugh so hard she cried.

When she got control of herself, she offered the bowl to Phoebe and me and ordered, "Here, eat some."

Her mourning subsided once we got to The Travelers. Or at least, the way she mourned changed. She gave up the black clothes, ate what she wanted, and seemed less able to ignore Daddy's evil side. Day by day, the bad things Daddy had done tattooed themselves on her soul. The result was an endless inventory of Daddy's sins, a list she recited whenever the mood struck: "Your daddy cheated on me so many times that after a while I didn't even care"; "Your daddy stole the best years of my life"; "Your daddy hated his own mother"; "Your daddy was a glutton for food, booze, and women"; "Your daddy didn't know how to truly love us, and that's a crying shame." One afternoon I heard her tell Mr. Ippolito, "It's easy to forgive good people. But if you're called on to forgive somebody who had a monster inside them, that's a whole other ball game."

But maybe, just maybe, forgiveness exists not to excuse the sinner but to heal those who suffered. This idea seems true and honest to me for this reason: As Mama became less able to forgive my daddy, her anger grew like wildfire and began to burn us all.

Her temper would flare with the slightest wind. One morning after deciding not to go to school—claimed I had a sick stomach—I was in the kitchen fixing a glass of iced tea, and Mama was standing at the sink, melting wax under hot running water so she'd have a fitting smile when motel guests walked into the office. I heard her cuss Daddy under her breath. She said, "Goddamn bastard, this is your fault."

I reached for a canister on the counter, took off its lid,

spooned what I thought was sugar into my tea, took a deep swallow, and then spewed it out. "Salt!" I said. "Yuck!"

"What's wrong with you?" Mama asked.

"I, I, I thought that was sugar," I said, and I wiped my tongue on my sleeve.

Mama started laughing, and then I laughed, too. What a funny mistake to make! I held my sides and closed my eyes; I was tickled to death, and so was Mama. But then she cleared her throat and said, "You're so stupid it makes me sick. You and your father, two of a kind."

My laughter flew away, just as if it had been snatched by the Devil, and I became statue still, cast my eyes on the worn linoleum floor and its curled edges. I bit back tears and hateful thoughts. And a voice spoke to me—it wasn't mine; maybe it belonged to my guardian angel, or maybe it was the voice of the adult I might become, I don't know. But it said, "Avocet Abigail Jackson, you are not to blame. The past stalks your mama, won't let her go, is like a stone in her shoe that keeps her conscience and memory forever rubbed raw."

Mama turned her back to me, and I slowly eased into my bedroom. *Just forget it,* I told myself, *she didn't mean it.* I took my chest of spring out of the closet and laid the contents on the bed. The faded blossoms and stiff wings looked beautiful against the white sheet. I picked up a yellow butterfly, held it in my open palm, closed my eyes, and blew on it. I pretended that my breath was full of magical, invisible seeds. They rushed through the butterfly, filling it with life. The wings stirred into motion. The butterfly flew out of the trailer, down the road, and lit upon a patch of wildflowers, where it lived happily ever after.

"Bird, I'm going to work. I'll be home at lunchtime to

check on you. If you get any sicker, come down to the office and get me," Mama called.

"Okay," I yelled. Mama slammed the trailer door. I opened my eyes. The butterfly had not moved. So much for magical breath. I put everything back in my treasure chest. *That was something nice Daddy had done,* I thought, *making me this chest.*

I got dressed and decided I didn't want to stay indoors. It was a nice day for exploring—blue and cloudless and not too hot. I put on my flip-flops and headed outside. There wasn't anybody out, not even Old Sam, the gimp dog. I wandered by a vacant cottage with its door wide open. "Hello! Anybody here?" I called. There was no response, so I ventured in. The place smelled like liquor, tobacco, stale sweets. The odors needled my curiosity. The sitting area looked untouched, so I walked into the bedroom. It was full of clues. The *Tampa Tribune* was turned to the engagements page. The ashtray overflowed with stubbed-out butts. A Sweet Sixteen donut bag was open on the bed. Three powdered sugar donuts were left, so I took two. A drinking glass was on the side table in the middle of a sticky trail of rings. I sniffed the glass, coughed at the strong odor, and then saw a bottle of tequila, almost empty, lying on the floor beside the bed. You didn't need to be Perry Mason to know somebody had been jilted, and jilted bad. Then I spied the Gideon Bible half hidden in the covers.

I set down the glass, picked up the Bible, decided it was mine. Then I remembered that stealing was a sin, but how could God get mad at me for snatching His Word? I had tried to read Phoebe's fancy gold-trimmed Bible once, but she caught me, slapped my hands, and said it was not a play-toy. She was afraid I'd break the spine—something she'd never do since she behaved as if the Good Book were Pandora's box, a scary treasure never to be opened.

Maybe it was God's plan, my finding this Gideon Bible, His way of helping me to become pure and holy. Like maybe any moment I'd be transformed into a teenager. And not just any teenager, but a young Mary Magdalene. Boys would think I was lovelier than air. But, of course, because of my saintliness, none of those fellas could so much as lay a little finger on me. I hugged the Bible to my chest and prayed, "Dear God, I'm going to read this fiery testament cover to cover, just you see."

That very day I started. I sat at the edge of the pool and dangled my feet in the refreshing water and began at page one, Genesis. And I'm sorry to admit that I skipped the boring parts like who begat whom, but all the stuff with the serpent I enjoyed. Paradise lost for no good reason fit my bones.

Nobody could accuse me of being a half-assed Bible student, of not at least trying to keep my promise to God. Slowly, just as if I were a fisherman with lead balls in my boots, I waded through the Old Testament, tried my best to stay afloat in those holy waters. I read about how in Eden, God got so pissed off at Adam and Eve that He wrecked His own creation, ruling not only that men and women would never get along, but that women would forever birth children in sorrow and nobody would be kind. He even said the Tree of Life would bear nothing but thorns and thistles. Now, that's some heavy-duty curse-making. It scared the bejesus out of me, and so did this: Whether I was staring into my mama's black eyes or the tissue-thin pages of my Bible, forgiveness was not in abundance. But the wrath of God surely was.

THREE WEEKS AFTER we moved into the trailer, on a blazing hot Saturday afternoon, Mama—who'd been drinking all day, claimed the liquor refreshed her nerves—called Phoebe and me into the living room in order to lay down the law. We were in our bedroom instead of at the pool because that morning when I asked, "Can we go swimming today?" Mama had snapped, "I want you two to keep your fat asses at home." So I was reading a Pippi Longstocking book, which I'd checked out of the school library on one of my rare attendance days, and Phoebe was studying something that looked too difficult for words. That's when Mama called, "Get in here. I'm going to lay down the law." And I thought, *Again?*

Phoebe and I shot each other worried glances—Mama had been drinking an awful lot since we moved to Tampa, and even though she explained that, for her, booze was medicine, I had my doubts. We two girls closed our books and trudged down the hall. The kitchen and living room in our trailer were really one room, with the kitchen being an afterthought thrown in the corner. Mama was at the refrigerator, retrieving a coffee mug filled with beer, a newly acquired manner of drinking. I guess she thought if she was sipping out of a mug with blue daisies on it we wouldn't know she was hitting the bottle.

Mama was dressed in red shorts and a white top, her wax teeth were chipped and pitted, and she was sweating because she'd just come in from trying to plant zinnias in our pitiful yard. She stood by the kitchen sink, guzzled the beer in one long swallow, went back to the fridge and set her mug inside next to the milk, got herself another cold one but tried to keep us from seeing what she was pouring. I could tell by the way she stood—feet wide apart to stop any give-away sway—that she was at least two sheets to the wind.

Phoebe and I sat at the kitchen table, made of plastic wood, and Mama, mug in hand, leaned against the stove, took a deep breath as if what she was about to reveal was grave indeed, and then, staring over our heads, said, "I've had about all I can take out of the two of you. You're going to listen to me and listen to me good. You got that, Bird?"

"Yes, ma'am."

"Phoebe, look at me when I'm talking to you and wipe that holier-than-thou expression off your face. I'm trying to do the best I can for you girls, but I don't know if I can keep going. I don't deserve this. How in God's name did I manage to raise such lousy children?"

She smoothed her shirt over her belly—she'd gained weight since Daddy died—and touched the tip of her tongue to her upper lip. She seemed to be fighting back tears. "I try to make a decent home for us," she continued, "work my fingers to the bone, and you two lie on that bed in there *reading*!"

"I was doing homework," Phoebe said.

Mama slammed down the mug, her eyes flashing like wild lightning, and said, "Don't you interrupt me. Don't you dare lie, you good-for-nothing whore. When was the last time either of you helped out around here? With God as my witness, Mr. Ippolito is going to kick us out of here if the two of you don't stop behaving like bitches in heat. We'll be out on the street. Do you want that?"

Phoebe's face folded in on itself. "No, ma'am."

"Bird?"

I could not speak. All of me—my fists, my scalp, my voice—lay in a heap on the floor like some dead dog.

"Answer me, Bird. Don't start in with that not-talking crap. It's your hellish behavior—pulling shit like you're pulling now—that killed your daddy. He couldn't take any more of you, and I'm just about ready to walk out myself."

In my head, I screamed. I wanted the voice that calmed me the day I put salt in my tea to speak again, to tell me I was not worthless. But if the voice was trying to comfort me, I could not hear it.

Mama pursed her lips, gazed at Phoebe and me. I think she was sizing us up, trying to decide if we were sufficiently cowed. She gulped her beer, then smiled and said, "Ladies, here are the rules. I want this trailer spotless morning, noon, and night. If you have to scrub until your knuckles bleed, fine! But this place better be clean. Got it? Secondly, there is a crazy old black woman who lives in one of the cottages in the back. I am trying to get Mr. Ippolito to evict her. There's garbage all over her yard. It's an embarrassment. Bad for business. He's so superstitious he lets her get by with that and only God knows what. But I can call a spade a spade. She's dangerous. So stay away from her until I get her kicked out. Bird, you hear me?"

"Yes, m-m-m-ma'am," I stuttered, but my words meant nothing because my fingers were crossed behind my back.

Mama pushed aside the mug, lit a cigarette, and an "aha!" expression rumbled across her face. She said, "We have to keep up appearances. Don't you dare dress like common trash. Iron your clothes before going out of this trailer. And be polite to Mr. Ippolito. Bird, don't pester his sons. And you, young lady," Mama aimed her gaze and her cigarette at Phoebe, "if I catch you chasing after one of those Ippolito boys, I'll beat you black-and-blue and senseless."

Phoebe regained her bearings. She rolled her eyes.

"Don't you roll those eyes at me! You think you're so smart. Let me tell you a thing or two. Men are out for only one thing: to get in your pants. I don't want you to go through the pain that I did. So don't encourage boys. If I ever see you behaving like a bitch, you'll never step foot out of this trailer again. Men, they're no damn good."

Then Mama got off our backs for a while as she carried on about how bad men were. This, of course, made no sense. I'd seen Mama point out cute boys to Phoebe, Louis Ippolito included. I thought, *Mama wants us to hold our shoulders back and suck in our stomachs so that we'll be as pretty as possible, but then she calls men monsters, useless sex hounds.* What were we to do with such frayed-end information?

I closed my eyes and tried to remember what Mama looked like before the last beating, before Daddy paid that man to make her less attractive and more scared. But I couldn't do it. My slim, trim, smart-talking mama was gone, and in her place was someone whose beat-up features reflected a bruised and swollen heart.

Mama ranted, "I'd better not catch either of you going out that door with hot pants on," and suddenly the sweet voice of my angel broke through, blocking out Mama's hateful spin: "You did not kill your daddy, you did not kill your daddy, you did not, you did not, you did not."

DESPITE THE FACT that Mama wasn't coping too well with that bed of nails called widowhood, she was trying to make a life for us. And I appreciated it. She planted those zinnias of various blazing colors in front of the trailer. She sewed curtains out of yellow dotted swiss for our bedroom windows. Best of all, she painted a picture of a vase of flowers, which we hung above the kitchen table. It was beautiful, rich in shades of blue. Mama, she was a creative person sometimes.

But snaking through both the meanness and the nest-making was a sadness Mama could not shake. She cried herself to sleep nearly every night. I heard her in there, on that nasty olive-drab couch, muttering and sobbing. It made me feel that I ought to run away, that she'd be so much better off if she didn't have a bad daughter to worry about. Sometimes, though, right in my bedroom, even as Phoebe slept, that mysterious, wise voice would fill the room. It would say, "Go to her, Bird. She needs you."

So I would gather my courage as if bravery and goodness were pebbles scattered all over the floor and I had to pick up those rocks of decency, one by one, and place them in the sack of my soul. And when the sack was full, I would get out of bed and stumble in the darkness until I reached Mama. She would hug me as if she was hugging a part of herself that she'd been missing, and her tears would wash my face. She'd say stuff like, "Thank you, Bird. My baby girl, I'm so sorry. Goddamn, life is so rotten. I don't know how I'm going to go on."

And I'd say what that voice told me to: "Everything is going to be okay, Mama. I promise. Life is going to get better."

THE FIRST HOLIDAY season without Daddy was staring us in the face—Thanksgiving was but a few weeks away, and the weather was behaving as though it were June—when Mr. Ippolito invited us to join him and his sons for Sunday brunch. I didn't want to go, but the invitation perked Mama and Phoebe right up. Mama said Mr. Ippolito loved to cook, wasn't that an interesting hobby for a man to have, and we'd better eat every bite off our plates so as not to insult him. She said, "Your father liked to make hot sauce to go on our oysters, but other than that he never lifted a finger in the kitchen."

I was tempted to remind her of the times he threw our dishes against the kitchen wall, but I guessed she wasn't counting temper tantrums as finger-lifting.

Mama told Phoebe to wear the shorts set she'd made her last year at Easter, the set she'd sewn out of the pink rose fabric. She didn't instruct me as to what I should wear—I don't think she remembered the long lecture about our wardrobe and bad behavior—so I put on a pair of yellow shorts and a blue top. The colors looked good together, I thought, and Mama didn't say otherwise. Mama wore one of her nice cotton shifts—she never dressed in shorts if she was going visiting, said she had too many broken veins in her legs that had been put there from bearing us children.

We walked from our trailer down to Mr. Ippolito's apartment. When we passed cottage eight, out stumbled a couple wearing crumpled clothes and carrying not even a single suitcase. The woman had a Twiggy haircut and long false lashes. She didn't look at us. But the man—dressed in wrinkled, button-up bell-bottoms—shot us a sidewinder grin. My mama said in her pleasant motel-office voice, "Good morning."

They said "good morning" and then got in a red Pontiac with Hillsborough County plates, which was the county we lived in. Mama said the man and woman claimed to be Mr. and Mrs. William Smith, but she was positive they were lying. "They're shacking up," she said.

"What's that mean?" I asked.

She and Phoebe laughed, and Mama said, "You don't need to know."

As soon as we reached the office door, we heard Mr. Ippolito, from somewhere in his apartment, singing Italian opera. That man sang when he worked, sang when he walked, sang at the top of his lungs. If he was singing and you walked past, he might raise a hand in greeting, but he would not trip over one note of his song.

Mama said he was a tenor. I liked his voice, but I wished I understood the words. One day when I was kneeling in the bushes by cottage fourteen, trying to find a chameleon that had rushed into the azaleas, Mr. Ippolito sauntered by singing a particularly beautiful melody. It sounded so sad I knew it had to be about love. Right there and then I made a private vow to myself to learn Italian. Maybe when I was grown up I'd live in Italy and a handsome man who owned a gondola would marry me.

The Ippolitos lived in back of the office, behind a red curtain hung in a doorway. Mama pushed back the curtain and called "hello," and I sniffed deeply because I loved the scent of garlic. That's what everything in Mr. Ippolito's apartment smelled like. He told us to come in, come in. He offered Phoebe and me Dr Pepper. He got Mama a cup of coffee and asked if she'd like some brandy in hers, he was having it in his, and she said, "Well, in that case, of course."

He said Manny and Joe wouldn't be eating with us, they had gone over to a friend's house to watch football, and then Louis Junior—whose nickname, Mr. Ippolito said, was L.J.—walked out of his bedroom wearing a gray T-shirt and blue jeans so tight they brought to mind things girls are not supposed to think about.

"Hi," he said, and he flashed an Elvis grin. His hair was a jumble of brown curls. I'd seen pictures of Roman gods. Well, pictures of statues of Roman gods. They all had leaves covering their privates. My brain played a trick on me and I saw Louis Ippolito, Jr., naked except for a bouquet of leaves sticking out of his crotch. I had to press my tongue to the roof of my mouth so that I would not start giggling. I know Phoebe's heart must have been cartwheeling.

Mama asked if we could help cook, and Mr. Ippolito

said no, not at all, that we were to relax. L.J. poured himself a glass of milk. The kitchen overlooked the living room, so I could see everything that went on. Mr. Ippolito handed us our drinks. Mama sat on the barstool at the counter, facing into the kitchen. I caught her looking at L.J. She told me to sit on the couch and not spill anything. I did as I was told, except I had a difficult time relaxing.

"She is such a clumsy child," Mama announced. "Sometimes I just don't know what to do with her."

Photographs of the Ippolito boys were everywhere. Baby pictures, class photos, football and basketball team shots. A portrait of President Kennedy hung above the TV, and stuck behind the frame were two miniature flags—the American and the Italian. A Virgin Mother figurine held a place of honor on top of the TV. She was gorgeous—slim nose, Ivory soap skin, and rosebud lips. White rosary beads wound around the hem of her blue, gold-trimmed robes. I wanted to touch her face and trace my finger along that twenty-four-karat trim, but I did not because I didn't want Mama to slap my hands and call me a wicked name.

Mr. Ippolito fixed what he called Italian eggs. They were full of garlic, onion, and green pepper. He winked at Mama and called the three ingredients the holy trinity of Italian cooking and Mama laughed and said celery, onion, and green pepper were the holy trinity of southern cooking and L.J. spoke up and said all his friends thought that the holy trinity was beer, bait, and ice. That caused a big laugh out of everybody but me because I didn't really know what they were talking about.

But at least everyone seemed to be having a good time. And even though I did not care for the combination of eggs and green peppers, I choked them down because I didn't want to get in trouble. Mama and Mr. Ippolito did most of the talking. They didn't know what was becoming of America's youth. Mr. Ippolito seemed particularly concerned that boys were wearing their hair long. Mama said even though she enjoyed some of the new music, lots of it simply wasn't to her liking. They agreed that President Johnson was doing a good job and people ought to quit protesting the war so we could hurry up and get it over with. That way, fine young men like L.J. wouldn't have to go to war even though Manny probably would because he would be eligible for the draft in just seven months and there was no way that "the conflict," as Mr. Ippolito liked to call it, would be over that soon. I wanted to ask, "What about Joe?" but I suspected we were deep into children-are-to-be-seen-and-not-heard territory. Mr. Ippolito said something in Italian and he made the sign of the cross and Mama said, "Amen."

When everybody was done eating, Mama told Phoebe and me to clear the table and wash the dishes. "No, no! There be none of that. Today you are my guests, and guests, they no do dishes!" Mr. Ippolito said. Even though he scared me, I sure liked getting out of cleaning.

Then L.J. stood up from the table, tossed back his head so that all those curls fell in new and interesting angles, and said to my sister, "You want to go sit out on the porch?"

Phoebe blushed and she looked at Mama, whose eyes turned to stone even as she forced a tight, thin-lipped smile. I knew that look. It meant, "Don't you dare." But I got the shock of my life because Phoebe's feminine blush gave way to womanly defiance. She coiled a strand of black hair around her finger and said, "Sure. I'd like that."

Mama downed the last of her brandy coffee and then called to Phoebe, who was already out of sight, "Don't stay out there too long." Then to Mr. Ippolito, "I think I'll have another cup, if you don't mind."

Mr. Ippolito gave me a second Dr Pepper without my even asking for it. "What do you say?" Mama demanded.

"Thank you," I said, but I kept my face turned away. I had to pee but didn't want to ask to use the bathroom. Too embarrassing. So I just sat there, slowly sipping on a drink I sure didn't need, feeling my bladder get fuller and fuller, and listening to Mama and Mr. Ippolito chatter about their lives.

Mama wanted to know why his ex-wife didn't have the boys with her. Mr. Ippolito explained that his ex-wife was a good woman but she'd gotten mixed up with some people who told her she ought to be independent and live her own life. She had decided she wanted to go to college and get a degree in psychology.

"She needs a psychology!" he said, and then he revealed that the boys spent most every summer with their mother although Joe was out of school and not really a boy anymore and Manny was almost grown, too. So then I knew L.J. was the baby, like me. Mr. Ippolito told Mama that a situation such as his—the wife not raising the children—was unnatural. "A woman needs her children. She needs a husband." Then he shot Mama an important stare.

"Well, I'll never get remarried," Mama said. "My husband was not a perfect man, but I loved him. I just couldn't bring another man into the lives of my girls. It wouldn't be right. Not in their eyes, nor in the eyes of the Church."

I turned my gaze on the Holy Mother, but I heard Mr. Ippolito loud and clear: "Who knows? Maybe you change your mind."

MAMA SEEMED TO be having fun, drinking brandy and shooting the breeze with Mr. Ippolito, but I knew her mood was changing when in mid-sentence she said that it was time to leave.

Mr. Ippolito had been talking about Miss Zora—that's what he called the old black woman I'd been hoping to meet. Mr. Ippolito said she had lived at The Travelers for as long as anyone could remember, she was there when he bought the place six years prior, never gave him a minute's trouble, paid her rent on time, stuck to herself unless you poked in her business. Which was fine with him.

"Why's it fine?" Mama asked. "Don't you want to know what she does day in and day out in that cottage?"

"No, I no want to know. She different, like powerful. Can give you the evil eye if you're not careful. She stay, she pay her rent, she keep the place safe, she don't bother nobody, I don't bother her. As long as I own this motel, Miss Zora is free to live here. I no want to get into how, but she helped this place once when we really needed it. Your talk of eviction, Glory Marie, I don't listen to it. Miss Zora, she good for my business. And a good woman."

Mama puffed on her cigarette and then chided, "You're not superstitious, are you, Louis?"

"Superstitious? No. But I don't kick luck in the teeth."

Wow—a spooky colored woman with special powers. She sounded right up my alley! Maybe she burned black-cat bones, drank lizard blood, talked to toads. Maybe I could get her to put a spell on my teacher, or better yet, one on my mama, to make her nicer. Wouldn't that be the best!

"Bird," Mama snapped, breaking my daydream to bits, "I know you have to go to the bathroom. Go on, now. And give me that Dr Pepper. Don't set it on Mr. Ippolito's coffee table. Goodness, child, you're stupid. Move! Do as I say. Now!"

In my mind's eye Mama was a drill sergeant—I'd seen one in a movie Phoebe and I had watched on TV when we lived in the grove. The drill sergeant yelled orders at absolutely everything and everybody he laid eyes on. The image of my mama in an army uniform spouting off to the point that she appeared to be nothing but one gigantic mouth took some of the sting out of my having to parade past them and into the bathroom. *Hex on you!* I thought.

"Down the hall, first door on the left, little girl," Mr. Ippolito said, and I felt myself blush.

The bathroom floor and walls were tiled a baby's-breath-pink color, and I thought it was funny that four burly men peed in a room of pink tile. The toilet seat was up, which made me sort of sick. So I rolled off a wad of toilet paper, put the seat down using the paper as a barrier between my fingers and the seat, and then I squatted, not letting my butt touch anything except air. I do not know why I was so squeamish about other people's bathrooms, but I was.

When I came back into the living room, Mama was laughing, which I was relieved about. She didn't seem at all angry that Mr. Ippolito had told her what-for about Miss Zora. Mama clutched her cup and said, "I once went to a palm reader to get my fortune told, and that damn woman had the nerve to say . . ." Mama quit talking and a flash of reckoning tiptoed across her face. That's when she snapped, "Bird, come on, let's go home."

She thanked Mr. Ippolito, and he ignored the suddenness of our departure and said the pleasure was all his. We walked through the office and out to the front porch, and there on the bench sat L.J. and Phoebe. L.J. was telling some sort of braggart story, and Phoebe was soaking it in, staring at him as if she was a movie star and the part called for her to look starry-eyed.

Mama said, "Phoebe."

My big sister understood the warning tone and this time decided to heed it. She stood, fear wiping away those stars.

Mama once more thanked Mr. Ippolito and told him and his son that we'd had a wonderful time. Then we started walking toward home, and Mama's polite going-visiting smile slid off her face. I saw it fall in the dirt like a Halloween mask. She stared into the merciless distance, her jaw set hard, that vein in her temple a sickening purple. She didn't say a word. I knew the signs. Mama was summoning a fury.

As we walked by the overgrown path that I'd seen Miss Zora hurry down the day we moved into The Travelers, I looked for her, but she was nowhere in sight. A bird's shadow crossed in front of us, and I looked to the sky but didn't see anything besides a few clouds that looked as if they were sitting in a basket of branches.

Mama's hands were shaking when she unlocked the trailer door. Once inside, first thing she did was get the bottle of bourbon she kept stashed in the cupboard. She poured herself a tall one. Phoebe headed to the bedroom, and Mama said, "Where do you think you're going?"

"To my room. I have homework," Phoebe answered.

Mama looked at her as if she were staring at a liar. "Homework, is it? You certainly didn't seem to have homework on your mind when you traipsed out to the front porch with your precious L.J."

"We just talked, Mama, I swear," Phoebe said.

"Talk, my ass." Mama stepped into the hall, blocking Phoebe's way. "Little hussy, how dare you behave that way in front of Mr. Ippolito."

"But, Mama, I didn't . . ."

"Don't contradict me. The nerve of you!" She slapped Phoebe hard across the face. "Get in the bathroom. I'll teach you to defy me, useless piece of shit."

Mama grabbed Phoebe by her hair and yanked her down the hall. Phoebe yelled, and Mama said, "Don't ever, ever embarrass me again. Understand, ugly bitch?"

Mama shoved Phoebe into the bathroom. "Please, Mama, stop! You're hurting me!"

I ran and looked in. Mama's hair was flying, and her face was tangled. Through clenched teeth she shouted the words "slut" and "whore." She hit Phoebe all about her head with a long-bristled hairbrush. Phoebe tried to shield herself from the blows, but Mama was strong—she raised her arm high into the air and then pounded Phoebe so hard that my sister fell to the floor and hit her head on the toilet. Blood gushed as her brow split open. Mama hammered the hair-brush and her fists into Phoebe's mouth, arms, chest, legs.

Out of the corner of a crazed eye, Mama saw me standing there, and she yelled over her shoulder, "Get out of here, Bird, or you'll be next."

It felt as if my feet were tied together with bundles of rocks. I tried to walk fast but kept stumbling. In the kitchen, I tripped over a chair, banged my knee. I limped toward the door, my hands moved in slow motion. Finally I gripped the knob. "Goddamn you," Mama yelled. I pushed the door open. The afternoon light was too bright, too hot. I had to hide. Mama could not find me. No. And I didn't want to see Mr. Ippolito, couldn't run into L.J., didn't trust myself to keep quiet. After all, I had a big mouth. Whippings were nobody's business but ours. *We can't tell on Mama because nobody else could love us.* Bad, bad children. Phoebe screaming. Mama cussing. So bad we nearly killed her. Rough on us for our own good. What a burden we were! Stupid children are always a burden. No wonder our daddy was dead, couldn't stand having rotten daughters. Mama sacrificed so much. So much. She was our only hope. *Run to the pool. Jump in. Swim. No. You'll bump into somebody you'll have to watch your big mouth hide hide hide. The field, of course, the field.*

And I ran. Blue-eyed grass, ragweed, goldenrod, dandelion, beauty berry. All around me, pretty, sweet-smelling. Cicadas humming. Farther and farther until Mama's voice floated away. Only the sounds of insects and birds. I tripped and fell, disappearing in a thicket of wildflowers. Fear poured off my bones, drip, drip, drip. My breathing slowed, as did my pounding heart.

Like a little ground dove safely out of sight, I listened to the cicada song and watched the trailer, which looked like a blood blister rising out of a green sea. Now and again, a bird's shadow rippled over me. Those bolts of darkness were a relief from the sun, and I did not search the sky because I wasn't afraid of this bird. It wasn't like those vultures who killed my cats, or the blackbird who stole my voice. I felt good here; this field was a different sort of place than the grove.

Hidden in the tall reeds of grass, I thought how nice it would be if I were a big stalk bending this way and that. If only I could take root in this sandy soil. If only my legs would turn into thin, golden blades, rustling in the breeze. If only I would break into a million seeds that the wind would scatter across the earth. If only the hard shells would crack open, sending tender shoots up, up, up. I would no longer be a little girl who caused her mama great sorrow. I would be faceless, forever reaching toward heaven.

I stayed in the field until dark, buried my hands in the dirt, imagined they were roots growing strong and healthy. When the bedroom light flashed on, I shook off all the loose earth that I could, then stood tall and straight and let the wind carry me home.

I OPENED THE trailer door and peeked in. Mama was passed out on the couch, snoring to beat the band. Guessing I was safe, I came inside, tiptoed to the refrigerator, and looked for something to eat. There wasn't much in there except for an open package of hot dogs. I took two and ate them raw. I drank cold water straight from the jar and then wandered down the hall to the bedroom. Phoebe was lying on the bed, a washrag filled with ice pressed to one eye and her algebra book opened. Notebook paper filled with scrawled formulas was scattered like giant snowflakes all across the bed.

"Hey," I said, "what are you doing?"

"Algebra."

"You hurt bad?" I went over to the bed, moved some papers, and sat down.

She shook her head no, but took the ice pack off her eye. She had a nasty cut, and the bruise was already showing. Both eyes were swollen, her bottom lip was bloody, and her skin was scratched—head to toe—from those bristles.

I patted her leg. Except for the scratches, her skin felt like velvet. Two weeks before, she had argued with Mama, trying to get permission to shave her legs, and finally she just went ahead and did it. The girls at school had been making fun of her about being Hairy Mary, so really she didn't have any choice but to defy Mama.

"Phoebe," I said, "I'm sorry."

"Wasn't your fault. You don't have anything to be sorry about."

I felt a little hurt because she wouldn't accept my sympathy. Her face looked so hard I understood how easily it could be shattered.

She said, "As soon as I can, I'm getting out of here. I hate that bitch."

"Phoebe, don't say those kinds of words! If Mama ever catches you talking like that you'll be in bad trouble."

"I don't care, Bird. I can't take this anymore." Her eyes

filled with tears, but none fell. She stared down at her algebra book. "Go get ready for bed. I've got a lot of studying to do."

"Wh-wh-what," I stuttered, "are you gonna say happened to you?"

"I don't know. I fell down some stairs or something. Quit asking stupid questions."

When I got under the covers, Phoebe stacked all her papers on her side and continued to scribble and fret deep into the night. I put my arm over my shut lids to black out the glare of the overhead light. I prayed to Jesus that He would not take my Phoebe away from me. This was not a purely kind prayer. I knew if Phoebe left, I'd suffer the full brunt of Mama's fury. At least with two of us at home, the bad times were spread around.

DADDY SNEAKED INTO my dreams that night. I felt so happy being with him again that I wanted to never, ever wake. I could just stay in Sandman Land with Daddy. He and I were sitting on our front porch swing in the grove. He wore a T-shirt and boxer shorts. He strummed that six-string guitar and sang "You Are My Sunshine." *Please don't take my sunshine away.* He sang these words so plaintively it was as if God had stuck a stake in his heart. As I watched and listened, I thought, *My sweet daddy ain't someone who could commit evil deeds.* In my dream, I had special powers. I could see his thoughts. It was as if we switched places. He wanted to live forever. Me, I was the one who loved the notion of falling off the edge of the earth and tumbling into the gaping hole of death. And if I did, Daddy would catch me, he'd bring me back home, he wouldn't let me kill myself. "Leave us alone, death," I whispered. Then I patted Daddy's freckled knee and said, "I won't go away, Daddy, I promise, I won't."

But come morning, as Mama yelled down the hall, "You two wake up. You're going to be late for school," I knew that promises were nothing but good intentions destined to be broken. There wasn't any way for me to hang out with the dead.

I couldn't stand the idea of going to school, so I feigned my tried-and-true excuse, a stomachache. Phoebe put on a lot of makeup to try to hide her bruises. Mama came into the bedroom and watched her. I was lying under the covers, looking as sick as possible, and Mama stopped at the foot of the bed. Under her breath, she whispered, "Dear God." She bit her lower lip and covered her mouth with a shaking hand. She said, "Phoebe, I'm so sorr—" but she stopped short of finishing the word. She tossed back her head as if she were trying to recover her pride, trying to be a good mama again, and she said, "Here, Phoebe, let me do that for you."

Mama walked over to my sister, took the bottle of foundation from her, and began to gently dab the liquid on Phoebe's bruised cheek. She tilted Phoebe's face to the light, rubbing here and there, smoothing and blending, as if she were an artist. Phoebe did not speak and kept her expression as blank as a fresh piece of paper. Mama said, "Wait a second. You need some loose powder."

Then Mama went into the bathroom and I heard her open the medicine cabinet—that's where she kept her cosmetics.

"I think she feels real sorry," I whispered to Phoebe, but she just shrugged her shoulders.

Mama came back with a jar of face powder and a makeup brush. "This will smooth out your skin tone, sweetie," Mama said lightly, as if she and Phoebe were two friends sharing beauty tips. "Close your eyes for me."

Phoebe did, and then Mama dusted my sister's face. Mama stepped back, admired her handiwork, and said, "I think that will do it."

Sister opened her eyes and studied her reflection. Mama had done a good job—I couldn't see any bruises at all, but I bet if Phoebe was in full sun, they would show.

"What do you think?" Mama asked. From the tone of her voice, I knew she was fishing for forgiveness.

But Phoebe wasn't in a forgiving mood. She picked up her books from the bureau and tried to walk past Mama.

"Phoebe," Mama started, "I, I—" Her eyes welled with tears, and she never finished her sentence. Instead, she kissed Phoebe on the forehead, walked out of the bedroom, and the next thing I knew, the trailer door was banging shut.

My sister headed down the hallway. I got out of bed and followed her. "Phoebe, she's trying to make up with you," I said.

"It's too late." Then Phoebe, her arms laden with books, said, "I'll see you later," and she left, too.

I stood all alone in the shadow-filled trailer, and I

stomped as hard as I could. The jalousie windows rattled, and I pretended that the tin walls and leaky ceiling fell down all around me and Channel Thirteen showed up and put us on TV and a rich family took pity on Mama, Phoebe, and me so they bought us a nice house and Mama got a good job and she didn't feel moved to beat her children and the words "I'm sorry" never again got stuck at the back of her throat.

I took a shower, dressed, went in search of something to eat. I grabbed some saltines and two raw hot dogs and washed them down with half a bottle of Yoo-Hoo. Then I took the remaining hot dogs outside, pinched them into chunks, and set them along the shed's rail for the squirrels. Bruno, the largest, was so tame he would eat out of my hand. I studied the oak tree that canopied the garage. No squirrels in sight. But Old Sam was wandering down the road, and when he saw me and caught a whiff of the hot dogs, he limped over. I fed him a few bites, and then he licked my hands clean.

There was a light breeze, which caused all the grasses of the field to rustle. I liked the sound. It was music. I patted Old Sam's head and said, "How about you and me go for a walk today?"

Old Sam was a good-natured dog who had gray around his mouth and eyes. He'd been hit by a car right in front of the motel the very week the Ippolitos bought the place. Mr. Ippolito said, "Best lesson the dog could have learned," which made very little sense to me. I hugged the dog's neck and then said, "Come on."

We waded due west into the field. I wondered if there was any water out here, a lake or a pond. Maybe there would never be any houses, maybe it would always be a meadow full of lizards and birds.

After we'd walked maybe ten or fifteen minutes, we came upon a patch of knee-high grass topped with clouds of tiny red blossoms. I ran my hand over the wispy petals and said, "I name you red-haired grass."

I looked around and realized I was surrounded by at least a jillion different plants and didn't have a clue about hardly any of them. I remembered my brother saying to me a long time ago, "Bird, if you're going to stay in one place for any time, you've got to learn the lay of the land."

Well, ain't that the truth, I thought to myself. So I began naming things. I dubbed the thick-stalked plants with pointed purple blossoms star grass. There was a wild lily of deep red—almost burgundy—its edges outlined in yellow, so I named it rich girl's lily. There were tall brown reeds sturdy enough to be woven. *I name you basket grass.* Butterflies swarmed over a plant of orange-and-yellow clustered flowers. *You're a butterfly bush.*

The names rushed at me like a full-moon tide. Sun daisy, glory vine, starburst, fire flower, white crown, wise cotton, lizard weed. And as I named the bounty of the field, I began to feel responsible. Not as if I owned the place, but that these wildflowers, red birds, skinks were my brothers and sisters—as if my peace of mind depended on theirs. For a little while the sadness of my family life unwound itself from my throat, and there I was, walking with dragonflies and bumblebees. The cicadas hummed. I think they sang, *I will not harm you.*

Yes—*I will not harm you*—that's what I was hearing in my head when the air suddenly turned salty and something big moved behind me. I spun around and caught my breath because rising up from the earth, a bundle of oats in her hand, was that black lady I'd been desiring to meet. With one hand on Old Sam, I said, "Hi. You must be Miss Zora."

She softly chuckled, came closer, and bent down on one knee. Her eyes were golden brown. She wore a big hat and a man's blue denim work shirt with a feather stuck in its breast pocket. "Indeed, I am," she said. "You know my name. Now tell me yours." She pushed a wisp of hair out of my eyes.

"Bird," I responded, and I remembered how that boy in the grove had made fun of me when I'd told him my name.

Miss Zora put one hand to her face as if she was floored and said, "Bird! What a beautiful name! Such a fortunate child!"

She was a kind lady, I just knew it. Why, she almost glowed! I liked her all at once and was moved to tell her my whole life. I thought she might listen. How nice for somebody to listen. I said, "My given name is Avocet. But people call me Bird for short."

"No! Avocet? Really?" Her eyes grew round, and she cocked her head as if she absolutely could not imagine it. I nodded yes, it was so, and she said, "I think you may be the luckiest little girl I ever met. Child, how did you ever get so lucky as to be named after one of God's prettiest birds?"

I giggled. I had never known an avocet was a favored bird in God's eyes. Then I said, "I don't know what one looks like."

She touched my cheek. "Are you pulling my leg?"

"No, ma'am. I'm serious. I ain't never seen one."

"Hmm. Maybe we'll fix that," she said, sounding as if she was talking more to herself than to me.

I gazed at her face with its road map of wrinkles and wondered how old she was. "Mr. Ippolito says you have lived here forever and to stay away from you. And my mama, she says you're dangerous."

Miss Zora threw back her head and laughed. Her teeth gleamed against her blackberry lips. "My, my, my. What folks will say about one another!" Then her good humor settled like powder into the crevices and lines of her leathery skin. She held her head high, as if balancing a tray full of tender pride, and asked, "Do you think you should stay away from me?"

I listened to the autumn breeze unfurl across the field. The smell of earth and salt rolled with it. I glanced past her shoulder and saw grasses move under the weight of the wind. The field shimmered, rising and falling, just the way the sea does. I looked again at Miss Zora. What would happen, I wondered, if I traveled down the many wrinkles of her face? Where would those rutted roads lead? Why did that voice in my head whisper, "Take the journey"?

"No, Miss Zora," I said, "I do not think I should stay away from you."

BONES. THEY WERE strewn like stardust all about Miss Zora's house. She told me they were the bones of birds and that she was their keeper. "When winged creatures cross over to the other side, their bones need to be cared for, prayed over, so that as they journey through God's many skies, their wings will be sheathed in gold."

I gazed at a pile of bleached bones stacked willy-nilly beside her front door—I guessed that was the trash Mama kept bitching about—and asked, "But why?"

"Because, Miss Avocet, the birds need that gold on their wings so they don't burn up like little puffs of paper as they fly past the sun. Just what do you think gives us our sunsets, hmm? All those colors painted across the horizon don't show up out of nowhere. What you're witnessing are the moods of God reflected off the golden wings of my birds as they leave this earth and soar toward the seas of heaven."

When she told me this, the very day I met her, she was wearing a wide-brimmed straw hat with feathers of various sorts stuck at odd angles all over it so she looked as if she had a chicken on her head. And that made me want to laugh. But the beauty of her words and the serious glint lighting her eyes made me want to curl up in her lap and hear more.

Miss Zora's cottage was off to itself, at the end of a long dirt road that ran east to west on The Travelers's grounds. There was one cottage next to hers, but Mr. Ippolito never rented it. He probably thought all those bones would strike the fear of God into whatever wayward traveler he might put there. The field surrounded the rest of the cottage, so Miss Zora had a dandy setup out at the far reaches of the motel, away from the office and pool and nameless guests.

I spied a shiny fender sticking out on the other side of

her cottage. "What's that?" I asked, pointing, thinking maybe I'd found more of the trash Mama was angry about.

Miss Zora took off her hat, patted her forehead dry with a gingham kerchief she had pulled out of her back pocket, then put her hat back on. "The heap of metal that brought me here. A 1949 Dodge pickup."

"Does it run?"

"Of course it runs. I wouldn't have it junking up my yard unless it worked." Miss Zora patted Old Sam's fanny. "Would you two like to come in and have something to eat?"

I knew if Mama caught me, she'd beat me till I couldn't walk. *Don't do it, don't do it, don't do it,* said my fear. But my heart spoke louder. I tried my most winning smile. It felt like I was slipping free of a ball and chain as I said, "Yes, Miss Zora, we would love to."

Old Sam and I followed her in. Her door was not locked. I said, "Why don't you lock your door when you're not home? Mama says there are burglars everywhere in Tampa."

"Well, child," Miss Zora said as she set down a basket full of grasses and flowers and weeds she'd picked in the field, "if anybody needs what I have, they are welcome to it."

That was certainly a new way of thinking to me. And so was the way she had decorated her cottage. My eyes could not move quickly enough. Herbs and grasses tied with twine hung from a piece of knotty wood that stretched the length of the room. Flowers in mason jars perfumed the air. From the ceiling at the room's center hung a prism that cast rainbow colors all across us. There were piles of baskets filled with seashells and bones. On the wall next to the door was a framed picture of some sort of large bird, and next to it was a map of south Florida. A stack of books cluttered her kitchen table, and bookshelves lined the wall above her couch. This place was a library and a nature museum wrapped into one. I said, "You sure do have a lot of books."

"Mind food," she said as she fixed us two tall glasses of sweet tea made pretty with lime wheels. "Do you read, Miss Avocet?"

"Yes, ma'am. I love to. Books help me to forget."

She pulled two plates down from her cupboard. "Forget what?"

"Not really forget," I answered, and I picked up a seashell and put it to my ear so that I could hear the ocean. "The words just take me someplace else."

Miss Zora nodded as if she understood, and I remembered what she had said about helping birds get to heaven. She must be really smart, I decided. So I set down the shell and asked, "Do you know what happens to people when they go to heaven? Do any of them make it, or do they get burnt up in the sun?" And then I had a most terrible idea: Maybe Daddy had not visited me in my dreams or back in the grove. Maybe all that had been wishful thinking and he was nothing more than a shower of ashes.

Miss Zora motioned for me to sit down on her couch, which was identical to the couches in most of the other cottages except hers smelled like mint, not mothballs, and hers looked nice because she'd covered it with a flowered spread. She handed me my tea and a slice of homemade spice cake. She gave Old Sam a little piece all his own. Then she sat in a wooden rocker across from me and said, "Don't you be worrying about dead people, little girl.

They take care of themselves. And that's what you've got to do."

"But what if when they were living they were sinful people?" I asked, and I kept my cake close to my chest so Old Sam wouldn't get it.

Over the rim of her glass, Miss Zora shot me a stare so potent I felt my skeleton shake. She said, "I'm not sure. But I don't think anybody burns in hell, if that's what you're asking. No, I do not believe in hell."

I had never heard of somebody not believing in hell. Why, that changed everything. It meant a person's good deeds had equal weight with their bad. I thought, *If there's no hell, that means the Devil is nothing but a story grown-ups tell to frighten me.* "No hell?" I asked. "But the Bible says—"

" 'But the Bible' blahblahblah. That's what Jesus was for. To get rid of all that fire and brimstone and damnation stuff that takes up half the book and wastes our time."

"Oh. Well, I haven't gotten that far yet," I confessed.

Miss Zora reached over, patted my arm, and laughed. She said, "Child, you are funny. What a fine brain you have. Now eat that cake. It's full of good stuff, herbs that will make you healthy."

"Like what?"

"Plants and flowers that grow in the field. This here cake I call my Calm Cake. It soothes fears."

When she said that, I realized how very hungry I was. I ate the cake in about three bites and washed it down with the tea. "Mmmm, it's really delicious," I said.

"Thank you, Miss Avocet." She took away my empty plate, refilled my tea glass, and sat back down.

"How old are you?" I asked.

"Why do you want to know?" She tapped her long, slender fingers against the worn arms of her rocker.

"Mr. Ippolito says you have been here forever and that you're really old."

"Well, Miss Avocet, thankfully the man is wrong. I've been walking this earth for just over half a century, which is no time at all. Although I've been through a lot, that's for sure." She scratched her knee and said, "I'd like to live long enough to see a hundred. And you know what, even if I do live that long, when my time comes I'll be protesting, saying, 'But, wait, I've got more to do!' So don't let these lines in my face fool you. They come from the sun and a few other things we won't talk about."

"Why not?"

"Because sadness has a way of giving birth to more sadness, and we don't want that. Do we?"

"No, ma'am."

Miss Zora leaned forward, looked me in the eye. For some reason, her directness did not disturb me. I stared right back. But I wasn't sure what to say next so I took a gulp of tea.

She sat back in her rocker, clasped her hands in her lap, and said, "So, your daddy, I see he's not around."

"He's dead. Had a heart attack," I lied. "Last summer."

"I'm sorry to hear that. And your mama, what about her? How's she doing?"

My lips sealed themselves shut, and in my mind I locked my mouth at the corners and flung the key out the door. *Stick to chit-chat. Do not spill the beans. Do not say, "My mama is a good woman full of bad deeds."* Damn, I wanted to tell on her, wanted to holler, "I think Mama's gonna kill one of us one of these days."

I opened my mouth, ready to speak the truth, and then I thought, *If I say anything bad, like how much she drinks or how she beats us or how she accuses us of being filthy evil and of killing our daddy, I will feel so guilty I'll have to run home and wash myself off in scalding water and a whole bar of soap.* So I erased my true thoughts, stared at my dirty feet, and mumbled, "She's fine."

"And how are you doing, Avocet Jackson? Tell me about yourself."

I looked up at Miss Zora, surprised that anyone would want to know anything about me, and I felt that tearful lump rise in my throat.

"Come here, baby, come here." She held out her arms, and even though I wasn't a little bitty child anymore, I found myself compelled to sit in her lap and rest my head on her shoulder. Miss Zora was a bag-of-bones woman, but when I lay against her, she grew soft and fat, as if she sported the wide lap of the grandmama I'd dreamed of having. She rocked me softly to and fro, but I did not talk.

She did. She told me all about myself. It was as though I was a tiny person wearing a thousand layers of clothes that she took off me, one piece at a time, so that I could finally get a good, long look at myself and all the layers in between. I was a sweet girl, with pure and honest intentions. I had a good head on my shoulders.

She brushed aside my bangs and whispered, "Trust yourself, little girl."

Miss Zora told me I was pretty and that when kids said mean things, they were really talking about themselves. My mama and daddy were not bad people, their mistakes were opportunities for me to practice forgiveness.

"You have a merciful heart, and that's a very precious gift."

Then, as the sun filtered through her window and struck the prism that hung from her ceiling, spinning a rainbow of color across the room, she told me my future.

Lulled by her words, which sounded like the sea, I fell deeply asleep. And when I woke up, I was in her bed, under a cotton throw with bluebirds embroidered all across it. "Miss Zora," I called, but she did not answer. I sat up. On the table beside the bed was a bowl of strawberries with a note propped against it.

Dear Miss Avocet,

I had to run across town to check on a friend who has not been feeling well. Could not bear to wake you. Please eat these fresh strawberries. I grew them myself. What a lovely visit we had! I trust it won't be our last!

Your new friend,
Miss Zora

I reread the note three times and then leaned back into the pillow. I needed to get home. But no, not yet. I wanted to stay just a little longer. Miss Zora's cottage seemed so clean and safe. What had she told me? I had to remember. I pulled the bluebird cover up close to my chin, riffled through her voice, sifted through her sentences and pauses. But her words that had laid bare my destiny were lost, as if she'd revealed all the sorrows and joys of my days only to strew them across the earth. I looked out the window and stared at the sky. I imagined that I was flying, flying, flying. I felt my eyes turn dusky gray, then hawk yellow. High in the sky, the wind was pure and cold. My feathers, sun-soaked, glistened. I flew over open water, searching for pieces of my life. And like an osprey hunting mullet, I noticed each shadow that darkened the aqua sea.

I CONTINUED TO VISIT Miss Zora whenever I thought I could get away with it. And let me tell you, there was a whole lot more to her than simple magic. For instance, she taught me to bake biscuits using whole wheat flour. We ate those fluffy morsels right out of the oven, drizzled them with tupelo honey made by a cousin of hers in north Florida. She taught me all the verses to "We Shall Overcome," told me I had "a nice, clear, fruitful voice." Three mornings a week she volunteered at a soup kitchen near downtown. A lot of her time was spent writing letters to Washington, even to the president himself. She read me a few, and her concerns were many: didn't want "our sons" dying in Vietnam; wanted stricter laws banning pesticides so that "beasts, birds, and babies would be protected from such awful poisons"; wanted President Johnson to "do more than run your mouth. Make sure the civil rights laws are enforced." Because Miss Zora's heart was always in the right place, I suspected she could give most anybody what-for and get away with it.

One afternoon when Mama had gone grocery shopping, I slipped off to Miss Zora's and found her in her rocker, knitting an afghan. Said she was making it for a homeless man who was new to the soup kitchen and that he wasn't cut out for life on the street. She feared he might freeze to death in the coming winter because "he's not like some of the others—he doesn't have any will." She inspected her work and said, "I hope this afghan keeps him warm."

I ran my hand over the pretty colors—grass green and crown gold. "He's lucky to have you," I said.

"No, baby, it's not luck. We all ought to take care of one another."

She looked up from her knitting and told me there were lemon balm cookies and raspberry tea in the refrigerator. "Would you do the honors?"

"Yes, ma'am," I said, and I felt so important, fixing us a snack right there in her spotless kitchenette. As I got two small plates out of her cupboard, my whole body ached with the wish that Mama and she would become friends. But I had to admit, the chances were slim. Just the other night, Mama had said that Mr. Ippolito was being a damn fool about "that crazy colored woman" and that when she asked him "How in the hell is she paying her rent?" he had told Mama it was none of her business. Maybe if I could find out where Miss Zora's money came from, Mama would back off and act nice. I poured the tea, taking care not to break anything, and when I handed Miss Zora her glass and then the plate with three cookies—she said three was her limit—I asked, "Miss Zora, how do you live? You ain't working or nothing."

She set her knitting in a basket by her feet, took a sip of tea, smacked her lips, and said, "That's a long story, Miss Avocet, one I really don't want to go into now. But I will say my family, we owned some acreage—in fact, still do. But part of it I sold. And there's some pension money on top of that. Since I don't live high on the hog—never have, never will—I manage to get by. Why? Who's been asking?"

"Nobody. Just wondering." I kept my eyes on my toes because I hated lying to Miss Zora. I was positive she knew I was telling a tale, but she let it slide.

As Thanksgiving neared, I daydreamed about inviting her to the trailer and us spending the holiday together. I saw it so perfectly: Hank—we still hadn't heard hide nor hair from him since we left the grove—would blast into town in that ragtop MG. Mama would adore Miss Zora, they'd become best friends. Hank would tell us that he was leaving Kentucky so he could go to college in Tampa. Over a delicious turkey and giblet dinner, we'd decide to get a big house together—one that didn't have any roaches or spiders. Friends would visit after school. I'd have a room of my own—its windows would be draped in breathtaking lace curtains. And under Miss Zora's influence, Mama would blossom.

I took my daydream so far as to actually ask Miss Zora how she was going to spend Thanksgiving. I stopped by her place the Sunday prior, early in the morning while Mama slept. Miss Zora was standing in her backyard, studying some bones that were laid on the ground on a piece of blue silk. She explained that she was saying her Sunday-morning prayers.

"Oh," I said. "Well, I was just wondering, what are you doing for Thanksgiving?"

She said, "Working in the soup kitchen until two or three."

"What about after that?"

"Nothing, honey, I'll just be home." She shooed a fly off a bone.

"By yourself?"

"Yes, sweetie, but I like being by myself."

I told her that maybe I'd pay her a visit and maybe my big brother would be in town and he'd visit her, too.

She stared down at the bones; her face grew long with some horrible kind of sad. "No, Miss Avocet. Thanksgiving is a day for families. You stay with yours."

"What about your family?"

"They're busy, bumblebee. Now run along home. I've got to take care of these bones."

As I left her yard, I thought, *Maybe we should quit having holidays.*

I walked back to the trailer, playacting that I owned the place—queen of The Travelers. I tried to step regally, as if my tennis shoes were silver slippers. The acorns that were scattered all over the ground were gold coins I'd left there so that the poor villagers would find them and not go hungry. The sandy soil was diamond dust. When it rained, the dust turned into jewels. I walked up the stairs to my front door, being ever so careful not to let my invisible crown fall off my head. Then I flung open the door—that's how I imagined an empress would enter her palace—and there stood Mama in the middle of the living room, compact in hand, sliding on some raging red lipstick. "Where the hell have you been so early in the morning?" she asked.

I veered past her and to the fridge. "For a walk in the field. With Old Sam."

"Jesus Christ, Bird, you're going to get snakebit. Why don't you ever think? I can't afford a hospital bill."

I slammed shut the fridge door, slumped into a kitchen chair, and asked, "Do you think Hank will be home for Thanksgiving?"

"I doubt if we'll ever see the no-good son-of-a-bitch again. That boy, he isn't much of a brother and even less of a son. Don't get your hopes up, young lady. I don't want to deal with your tears." Mama dropped the compact and the tube of lipstick into her pocketbook, patted her hair, which looked funny because the day before she'd pin-curled it wet and the result was that her ringlets were wound way too tight—maybe she was trying to have hair like L.J.'s, I thought—and then she walked out, saying, "Don't let your sister sleep all day."

DADDY ALWAYS SEEMED to enjoy Thanksgiving. He behaved as if the day was one long party, and Mama stayed too busy to push his buttons. On the last Thanksgiving of his life, he paraded around the house with nothing on but his undershorts and the paper Indian headdress I'd made at school, asking if any of us had seen some Pilgrims, that he'd heard they "knew how to do up a turkey" and he hoped so because he was starving.

Well, so much for memories. Thanksgiving morning Mama woke up in a foul humor, said she hated holidays, and for Phoebe and me to straighten up and fly right—all before we'd been awake long enough to cause her trouble. She wouldn't even let us turn on the radio.

We did not have a TV or a hi-fi, two things that might have distracted us from being a lousy excuse for a family. Grumbling something about memories, trash, and wasted time, Mama had left both means of entertainment in the grove. We'd lived at The Travelers for about two weeks when Manny Ippolito—the wiry middle son whose eyes shifted when he talked so you didn't know if he was a liar or simply high strung—had shown up on our doorstep with a radio, said his daddy wanted us to have it. Mama seemed to enjoy the music. And on Thursday nights we listened to "Mystery Theater," which I loved. But when Phoebe flipped on the radio Thanksgiving morning, Mama snapped, "Turn that goddamn racket off. I can't take any noise today."

I glared at Mama, but she wasn't paying me any attention so I marched into our windowless, airless bathroom, locked the door, and muttered to the darkness, "Dear Jesus, please bring Hank home. Please fill our trailer with company who'll stomp out hurtful Daddy memories." Then I heard something crawling. I screamed, flipped on the light. A giant cockroach scurried along our toothpaste tube.

I got out of there fast, and as I tumbled into the living room, Mama snapped, "Now what's wrong with you, you little jackass?"

"Nothing is wrong with me," I said. I sat on the floor next to the coffee table and picked up my playing cards. Printed on the back were palm trees that swayed against a blazing sunset. I thought about what Miss Zora had said—that sunsets are the moods of God reflected off the wings of birds. *I hope so, I really do.* Then I dealt myself a game of solitaire. But the cards conspired against me and I lost without claiming even one full suit. I was about to try again, thinking I might possibly cheat, when there was a knock at the door. *Hank! Hank! Hank!* My hope spilled all over the place.

Mama, she stood in the kitchen, shaping ground beef into patties—we were having hamburgers for Thanksgiving because we couldn't afford a fancy meal. She slapped a ball of meat on the counter, glared at the door, and said, "Bird, see who in the hell that is."

I scrambled up, threw open the door, positive I would see Hank's smiling face, but instead I stared into the round mug of a postman. "Special Delivery for the Jacksons," he said.

Mama wiped her hands on a dishrag, came over to the door, and took the letter. She said, "Thank you."

The postman said, "Happy Thanksgiving."

"Yeah."

Phoebe came in from the bedroom. The two of them had been getting along, but that's only because Phoebe steered clear of her and Mama still nursed a guilty conscience. "What's going on?"

"A letter from your brother," Mama said as she tore open the envelope. She read us parts of it. The priest at Immaculate Conception had given him our address. He wasn't coming home for Thanksgiving because he had a job and they wouldn't give him the time off. He was sorry he couldn't call, but since the trailer didn't have a phone, that was impossible. He suggested we call him collect from a pay phone after nine P.M., he would sure love to hear from us. He claimed that in January he would start his second-to-last semester of school.

Mama said, "That's a damn lie."

Her disbelief made me mad. I thought he deserved the benefit of the doubt.

Hank covered the bases about his trip to cowboy country, writing that the West was truly awe-inspiring yet not all that it was cracked up to be. He promised that he'd be home for Christmas.

Mama said, "I hope so. It would be good to see him," but her voice was weighted down as if her words were little balls of buckshot that fitfully rolled up through her windpipe without any firm sense of direction.

Hank wrote Phoebe and me each a special line. Mine was, "Dear Bird, you are not alone. You are in my thoughts always. Take care of Mother. I love you. Your big brother, Hank."

I memorized that part. I liked him writing me.

We sat down to eat about three o'clock—Mama said she wanted to get the meal over with. She barely ate, and the liquor she drank did not cheer her or propel her into a hissing spell. She was, all in all, quiet and moved slowly. Maybe there was something wrong with her blood, I thought. Maybe she needed some iron pills. She apologized for not cooking a turkey but said we needed to save money and that our tiny kitchen was "no place to cook real meals." Then she looked at Phoebe and said, "But at least we've got each other."

I asked if we were going to call Hank.

"Bird, not today. Don't bother me about it."

After supper, Mama got herself three beers and sat outside on the steps to have a smoke. I was scared that Mama might be fixing to tie one on. Since that bad beating she gave Phoebe, Mama seemed to be trying not to drink so much. But maybe the holiday was too much for her. Phoebe and I cleared the table, and we let the dishes soak in the sink for a couple of minutes before we set to cleaning them. Phoebe tossed me a dish towel, told me that she'd wash and I could dry but to do so carefully, she didn't want me breaking anything, Mama couldn't take it. We'd had the dishes only a month. Mama had bought a matching set at Goodwill and had ordered us not to damage them, they were the only nice things we owned.

I scooped up a handful of suds and blew. The bubbles whirled through the air, light as feathers. Phoebe started washing the dishes. She handed me one, and I dried it. I said, "I wish we'd invited people over. I bet if she'd invited the Ippolitos, they would have visited."

My sister said, "Don't cry over spilled milk."

"I ain't crying. I just think that if we'd filled the trailer with people maybe we'd be having fun right now, maybe we wouldn't be walking around here on tiptoes for fear of stepping on a Daddy memory."

A dish slipped out of my sister's hands, into the soapy water, and landed against another plate with a dull thunk.

"Shit," Phoebe said. She brought up the dish. It was in two pieces, split down the middle, even Steven.

"Uh-oh," I said.

Phoebe looked over her shoulder to see if Mama was turning the doorknob. Then she tucked the broken plate under her shirt and headed down the hall.

"What are you doing?"

"I'm hiding the plate so she won't know." Phoebe opened her underwear drawer and hid the evidence at the very bottom. "I'll throw it in the big Dumpster behind the shed when she's at work. Now, quick, we've got to finish the dishes and get them in the cupboard before she finds out."

We hurried back into the kitchen, and I worked hard because I knew we needed to. But I still was wishing somebody would stop by. I said, "If you go down to the office and ask, I bet Mr. Ippolito and a son or two would come down here. Maybe even L.J."

"Forget it, Bird," Phoebe said as she stacked the plates in the cabinet. "Mama's mad at Mr. Ippolito."

"But maybe she's over it."

Phoebe shook her head no, and I knew why. Earlier in the week Mama had said that Mr. Ippolito had made a pass at her, so "from here on out it's strictly business."

I watched Phoebe wipe the kitchen counter. A roach crawled along the backsplash. Phoebe whacked it with the towel. She didn't even make a face, as she was getting used to killing them. I thought about how Mama was still trying to discourage Phoebe's lust for L.J. She hadn't again tried beating the lust out of her but she was continually dropping little reminders such as, "I will not encourage any hanky-panky between you and that young man."

But that was a silly thing for Mama to say because they didn't need any encouragement. I caught Phoebe and L.J. smooching behind the garbage shed one day when Mama was working in the office. I'd sneaked around the corner on tiptoe and watched them grope and breathe heavy and kiss each other as if they were searching for something at the back of each other's throats. I was having a helluva good time until a rat raced along the edge of the shed straight at me. One look at the rat and I screamed. Phoebe—her face trapped in a snarl—said, "Pest, leave us alone before I tear your hair out!" L.J. started blowing me kisses and laughing. I sang long and clear, "I'm gonna tell on yoooooouuuu," and Phoebe sassed, "If you do, I'll tell Mama about your visits to Miss Zora."

"Don't you dare! You promised not to say a word." Shortly after I'd met Miss Zora, I'd told Phoebe about her. When good things happen to you, it's just too difficult to keep the news all to yourself.

Holding L.J.'s hand, Phoebe said, "I mean it."

And I said, "Okay." So that was that. We kept each other's secrets.

After Phoebe and I finished cleaning the kitchen, I asked, "Well, now what are we going to do? We're stuck in here. She's out there guarding the door like some old grumpy bear."

"Maybe she'll let us listen to the radio since she's done cooking," Phoebe said.

"I'm not going to ask. She's been drinking all day."

Phoebe was staring out the window, figuring her chances, when Mama read our minds. She jerked open the door. "Why don't you two get your lazy asses out of the trailer and out of my sight for a while."

We did not hesitate. We shot past her.

Phoebe and I walked to the pool, and she said, "I've got some change. Do you want to go to the office and get a cold drink out of the machine?"

I said sure, and I knew it wasn't really a cold drink we were after. She was hoping to run into L.J.

Then I had a brilliant idea. "Let's stop by Miss Zora's on the way to the office."

Phoebe looked annoyed, so I whined, "Please, Sister. She's all alone. We'll only stay a minute. Cross my heart and hope to die."

"Well, okay," Phoebe said, "but only a minute."

I walked fast and Phoebe said it looked like I had ants in my pants and I said I was hurrying so we could see L.J. sooner.

When we got to the cottage, Phoebe looked at the bones and said, "This is weird."

"No it ain't. She can explain everything."

Her door was closed, but the truck was there. I said, "She must have gone for a walk."

"Let's go, then."

"No, I want to show you inside. It's okay. She don't ever lock the place."

I started to open the door, and Phoebe said, "Bird, don't do this."

Too late. The door swung open. But I stopped stock-still. Miss Zora was sitting in the rocker, her back to us, and she was crying. Her shoulders shook under the force of her tears.

"Oh, Miss Zora," I said, "please, please don't cry."

Without turning around, she said, "Go away, baby, go on. I'm not taking any visitors today."

"But, Miss Zora . . ." I was going to explain I'd brought my sister to meet her, but Phoebe grabbed my shirt and whispered, "Let's go. Now!" She pulled me toward the door.

"I'll see you later. Happy Thanksgiving!" I said, and slapped Phoebe's arm away. I closed the door as quietly as I possibly could.

In the yard, Phoebe tripped over a bone. As we headed

down the drive she said, "I don't think you ought to be going over there, Bird."

I didn't argue with her. I was too upset. Seeing my Miss Zora that way was too terrible.

Phoebe slipped her arm around my waist. "Don't worry about it. Lots of people get depressed at Thanksgiving and Christmas."

I said, "I know, damn it all to hell, I do."

Then my sister started chattering about a girl at her school who stuffed her bra and everybody knew it. This was interesting, helped me ease Miss Zora to the back of my mind.

"Between first period and seventh, she grows at least two bra sizes," Phoebe said, and this got me to giggling. We walked to the office and stood in front of the drink machine, running through our choices—I wanted a root beer, Phoebe wanted a calorie-free Fresca—and we both straightened our posture, tried to look sophisticated and bored because maybe, just maybe, L.J. could see us from the office window.

"Oh, shoot," Phoebe said, "I thought I had some change. All I've got is two ones."

"Where'd you get that?"

"I save my lunch money. Don't tell Mama."

"What are we going to do? The machine don't take paper dollars."

"You could go in the office and ask for four quarters."

"Why don't you do it?"

"Because I can't look obvious."

She dangled the dollar bill in front of my nose. I grabbed it, and she said, "Do *not* tell him I'm out here."

"Don't worry. But, Big Sister, you can start figuring out now how to pay me back for this favor."

I walked into the office and rang the buzzer. I heard some low conversation I couldn't make out, but then somebody said, "L.J., it's your turn, you get it," and a chair scraped against the tile floor. Boy, this was Phoebe's lucky day.

L.J. came out from behind the red curtain, took one look at me, and asked, "What are you doing, squirt?" He sauntered behind the counter and leaned against it. He wore cutoffs and a blue T-shirt. Blue was a good color on him.

"I need change for this here folding money."

"Why? You going shopping or something?" he teased.

"My sister and I are desiring a cold drink."

"Oh yeah? Where is she?" he asked, and he showed off by vaulting over the counter and out the door.

Next thing I knew, we were being invited inside, cold drinks in tall green glass tumblers were being shoved in our hands, all three Ippolito boys were looking pleased at having our company, and we were being told not to talk real loud because "Pops is taking a nap."

The boys were in the middle of a poker game. L.J. asked, "What about it—should we deal you in?"

Manny, the shifty-eyed one, said, "Yeah, come on. The stakes are high. We're playing for Sweet'n Low tablets." He pointed to a pile of small white pills on the table in front of him.

Joe—he lifted weights, worked construction, had a bad limp from childhood polio, was the oldest of the three, and could give them all a run for their money in the looks department despite his limp—said, "Girls! I don't want to play poker with girls!" Then he graced us with that Ippolito smile so we knew he was kidding.

But I was in trouble because I didn't know how to play poker. It turned out neither did Phoebe, so Joe and L.J. took us on as partners.

Joe stretched his arms over his head—his muscles were very well developed—and he said, "Sit in this chair next to me, little girl. I'm not going to bite. It's about time you learned to play poker. What's your name again?"

"Bird."

"Well, Bird, watch close. We're going to burn this table up." Joe smelled like aftershave, and that made me think of Hank.

I asked, "Can I shuffle?"

"Only if you do it right."

"I'm a good shuffler. You'll see," I said.

Daddy had taught me how to handle cards back in the grove. And I did real good—even cut the deck—except I didn't know how to deal a game of poker. All in all, though, I think they were impressed.

L.J. and Phoebe won the first hand. L.J. called her his good-luck charm. Phoebe's eyes shone bright. L.J. took good care of her—kept her glass full of Tab, repeatedly moved her hair off her shoulder and back again, sometimes stopped everything he was doing to stare at her exactly as if she were balm for his eyes.

I tried to learn the game, but I was having more fun just being there than paying attention to the details of full houses, royal flushes, two-of-a-kinds. On the third hand, I dealt Joe and me two aces and two kings. Even a beginner knew that combo was good. I beamed, and Joe said, "Honey, you've got to develop a poker face. Like this." He made a face as boring as oatmeal. "Otherwise you give us away to these card sharks."

"Sorry." I wiped the grin off and tried to look blank. I said, "Two days ago Mama killed a tree spider the size of my fist. It was crawling across the living room ceiling."

L.J. looked at me over his cards. "How big did you say it was?"

I held up my hand.

"Shit, that's nothing. They get way bigger than that. Last summer I had to kill one with a baseball bat."

"Really?" My eyes were popping.

"Yeah. I went in to take a shower and there it was, in the tub. Think it wanted a drink of water."

Joe said, "No lie. You should have seen it. Giant body, long hairy legs, 'bout a foot across. Looked like an octopus."

"Must of weighed ten, twenty pounds," added L.J.

Joe said, "L.J. called me in there, screaming, 'Bring the bat, Brother, this is a big one.' "

"It was the most hellacious creature I've ever seen," Manny agreed. "I heard my brothers yelling, so I ran in there, and old L.J., he was whaling on that spider. Had to hit it five, maybe six times before it died. Guts all over the place." Phoebe squealed. "Had to pay a professional to clean up the mess."

"God!" I said. "That's awful. What happened with what was left of the spider?"

"Buried him out back," L.J. said.

"Had to dig a—" Joe started and the other two chimed in—"big, big hole."

Then the three brothers whooped and hollered and

Manny said between the laughter, "Keep it down. We're gonna wake Pops."

We played poker and told stories until way after dark. I had to swallow my pride and pee in their pink tile bathroom. I looked in the tub to make sure there wasn't another spider lurking. Mr. Ippolito eventually woke up. He came out of his bedroom with just his pants on, scratching his gray chest hairs. He wanted to know where our mama was, and we lied, said she was home sewing. He fixed us each a turkey sandwich but he didn't join the game, just sat on the couch and watched TV. And that Manny, he won the night, had a huge pile of Sweet'n Low in front of him.

He said, "I guess this means I'm the sweetest."

"I think Phoebe would disagree," Joe said.

L.J. leaned over and kissed her cheek, Phoebe blushed, and Mr. Ippolito said, "None of that!"

Phoebe and I were sort of scared to go home, but we didn't have a choice. L.J. offered to walk with us. Joe told me I was a good player, and Manny said, "Yeah, she'll probably beat us next time."

When we got to the trailer, Phoebe told me to go inside and see if Mama was still awake. If she was, I was supposed to come right back outside and say, "Phoebe, did you find your earring yet?" That was code language for "Get your butt in here before Mama finds you outside with your boyfriend."

But I didn't get to say the code words because Mama was snoring and mumbling in her sleep, so Phoebe and L.J. were safe. I went to my room and got ready for bed. I checked the sheets for spiders, figuring I'd have a heart attack if I ever found one the size that L.J. beat with the bat.

I couldn't kill something that big and I didn't think Mama could either. It would probably eat us alive.

When I was sure there wasn't anything crawling in the bed, I lay down. I thought about how much fun Thanksgiving turned out to be after all, despite Mama's foul mood and Miss Zora's blues. As soon as I could, I would visit Miss Zora and stare into her autumn-colored eyes and tell her she was the nicest person I knew. I tried to stay awake until Phoebe came in. I wanted her to tell me all the loving words L.J. must have been whispering in her ear. Such knowledge could prove helpful to me someday. Maybe they'd get married and I could live with them. Mama and Phoebe and I, we weren't much of a family, no we weren't. I reimagined us. Glory Marie, Billy, Hank, Phoebe, Bird—there we were, gathered around a Thanksgiving honey-baked ham, swapping stories, passing biscuits, our mouths running over with decency. We ate until we couldn't breathe. Then we sat on our couch and watched TV, drank 7-Up–spiked Kool-Aid. Hank and Daddy got along perfectly well. Mama was pretty.

As I drifted asleep, my perfect family began disappearing. But then Daddy sat on the bed, smoothed my hair off my forehead, and kissed me. "Good night, sunshine."

"Good night, Daddy."

Then Mama and he, talking softly, walked down the hall to their room. There weren't any arguments the whole night through.

THE FIRST DAY back to school after Thanksgiving break, our teacher handed out a magazine for children. It was full of puzzles, word games, articles about science and history, stories written by other kids. She told us to turn to page three and read the article entitled "Africa and Its Animals" and then answer the questions at the end.

But my attention was snagged by a photograph on the facing page. A skinny, long-haired blond girl stood—looking so smart—next to a cherry-red bike with a banana seat. I was seized with a sudden, unshakable longing for that bike. I'd read in the Gideon Bible, "Do not covet." But I couldn't help it. I saw myself racing past the cottages of The Travelers Motel, guests pausing to watch me, throwing compliments my way: "What a great bike!" "I wish they had made bikes like that in my day." "Look at her fly!"

I ripped the picture out of the magazine and slipped it into my notebook.

That afternoon I walked home, but in my heart I was riding my brand-new Christmas-gift bike. As soon as I got back to the trailer, I changed my clothes. That morning had been cool enough to stir Mama to say, "Bird, you'd better wear your sweater to school." And I did, but I took it off and had to batten down both tears and anger because Suzy Smith—the girl who sat behind me—laughed and told everyone that I was so poor I had holes in my stinky sweater. But come afternoon, the weather had warmed up pretty good right along the edges. So I put on a pair of Bermuda shorts and tucked the picture of the red bike in my rear pocket.

Then I checked in with Mama at the office. Mr. Ippolito and she were leaning against the counter and agreeing that LSD was going to be the ruination of all people under thirty, especially unsuspecting girls. Mama seemed to be enjoying the conversation, so I guessed she wasn't mad at him anymore. She asked me how school was.

I said, "Fine. Look at this here picture of this bike." I held the ripped page in front of her face. She took it from me. *Please, please, please, God, make her understand.*

"That's nice," she said, and then turned to Mr. Ippolito. "My children believe that money grows on trees."

So, convincing her wasn't going to be easy. I would have to tape the picture to the refrigerator when I got home. Maybe what she needed was a constant reminder. But I knew not to push. "Can I go play with Old Sam?"

"You have to ask Mr. Ippolito."

"Can, can, can I please play with Old Sam?"

"Yes, little girl, if he'll move, be my guest. Old Sam, he is a lazy."

As I walked out of the office, I heard Mama say, "That child sure does love her animals."

Old Sam was lying in the middle of the driveway, napping. "Come on, let's you and me go for a walk."

He batted his feathery tail and then stood and slowly stretched. His right rear leg was the one taken in that accident, but he didn't seem to care that he was a tripod dog. We headed off first in the direction of the trailer so that if

Mama was watching she wouldn't see us making a beeline to Miss Zora's. A couple of times I had to hurry to keep pace with that gimp dog.

When we arrived, Miss Zora was sweeping out her cottage.

"Well, good afternoon, Miss Avocet. What brings you by on such a lovely day?"

"We just come visiting," I said. She seemed fully recovered from her sad spell. I wanted to say, "Miss Zora, I love you," but when feelings get so strong they're woven into my bones, I can't talk about them without crying. So instead I said, "Miss Zora, you're my best friend." Which was true, too.

Miss Zora rested the broom against the cottage wall and said, "Thank you, Miss Avocet. Hearing you say that means everything." She hugged me and whispered, "You're such a good girl."

Then she invited Old Sam and me inside, and we had a luscious snack of oatmeal-raisin cookies with apple slices. I washed mine down with a cold glass of milk. And I showed her the picture of the bike.

"What kind of seat is that?"

"A banana seat—see how it's shaped?"

"What will they think of next! You ought to have a bike like that." Then she said, "It's so nice out, why don't we go for a walk?"

"Where to?"

"Maybe the water."

"Water?"

"Yes, Miss Avocet. Far out in the field. It's beautiful."

"I didn't know there was water out there."

"Most people don't."

Miss Zora put an apple in each of her pockets, and then we headed into the field. We walked for a long time. If I hadn't been with Miss Zora, I would have said we were lost. But the walk was definitely worth it, because the pond was deep green, full of lilies and small darting fish, surrounded by a thick stand of bald cypress. On the far side, an egret stood so still in the water that it looked like a statue. Miss Zora said the bird was fishing. "If we're real quiet, the bird just might stay," she said. She took the apples out of her pockets and handed me one.

I bit into it and tried to chew without making any noise. I reminded myself not to laugh too loudly if Miss Zora said something that tickled my funny bone. Old Sam, he lay down by my feet and took up again with his nap. I spit out a seed and whispered, "Are there ever any avocets around here?"

Miss Zora squinted down at the water. Her reflection lapped against the shore. "I haven't ever seen any," she said. "But, you know, I don't come here every day. So they might visit every now and again. Where I come from, I sometimes saw them during winter. I'm not sure, but I don't think they are regular visitors to this part of the state, not anymore. Golf courses, farmers and their pesticides, you know, take a toll on birds. But creatures that have wings can end up almost anywhere."

"The place you come from, Miss Zora, where is that?"

Miss Zora took off her hat and repositioned it so that it sat firmly on the crown of her head. The hair framing her face was silver-veined. "You probably never heard of it. I was born, raised, married, and reared a daughter in a little village on the edge of the 'Glades. They call it Ochopee."

"The 'Glades! I always wanted to visit there. I mean,

my mama said we went once but that was right after I was born, so I don't remember. I asked if we could take a trip to see it right after we moved here, but she said no, that it was just a bunch of mosquitoes and still water."

Miss Zora laughed and shook her head. "Sounds like your mama wasn't too impressed. I admit, you got to have a certain kind of eyesight to appreciate that land."

"What kind of eyesight would that be?"

Miss Zora put her finger to her lips and then pointed at the egret, who darted its head into the water as if its neck were a spring-loaded coil, but it came up empty-billed.

"Oh well, better luck next time," Miss Zora whispered to the bird. Then she said, "The 'Glades," and she shut her eyes as if remembering, "is a magical place. It's like . . ." She paused, then gazed at her hands, which she held in front of her as if she were cupping water. "It's a place of new beginnings, a place where life starts over again every day. Yes. That's exactly right. It's the beginning of creation. Forever."

I tossed the apple core on the ground and picked up a stick, jabbed it into the mud. "How come you left? What about your husband and that daughter?"

"Look at you. So full of questions today." She shot me an annoyed glance, but I caught her. I stared deep into those yellow eyes and I would not let go.

"I guess I'll tell you. But you keep all this to yourself. Promise?"

"Yes, ma'am."

Miss Zora tapped her long, brown fingers on the side of her face. My teacher had said long fingers were required if a person was going to be a great piano player. I would have to ask Miss Zora about that later.

"Ages ago, miles and miles of the 'Glades were drained off for farmland," she said as she grabbed a dandelion dancing by on the wind, "and that's how my husband's family and mine made a living. We grew crops—tomatoes, lettuce, melons. Through the years—and it wasn't easy—both families managed to own and hang on to quite a bit of acreage."

She handed me the dandelion and squeezed my hand shut. "When my husband got out of the service after fighting in World War II, he came home just full of good ideas about how to make the most of our farm. We didn't know how bad pesticides were for us, so we dusted our crops, you know, from a plane. Now, I regret that decision, but I will say that we had a very productive farm."

Miss Zora tossed a nibble of her apple into the water, and a silver fish came along and ate it. "But five years after the war, on July 22, 1950, everything changed." She rubbed her eyes the way an Egyptian lady might rub a magical lamp, and then she said, "It was a clear, blue-sky morning. So clear you could hear angels fly. And my husband was up there among them in our little gnat of a crop duster. I was sitting in my backyard mending one of our fishing nets. The occasional click of my needle against the net's wooden floats and the drone of our plane were the only sounds. Every time he took to the skies, I played a game with myself, and this day was no different. I imagined he was a blue jay and I was so smitten with his beautiful colors and the way he cut across the heavens with seemingly no effort at all. In my head, I created this little scene—I flung the net so high that I caught my blue-jay husband, and he showered me with kisses. That's just how I was thinking when everything went wrong."

Miss Zora stopped talking. Her eyes glazed with what I thought to be both memory and tears. I touched her arm, and she patted my hand. "That old engine failed, Miss Avocet, and my dear husband—he was an excellent pilot—he tried to land on the road that ran alongside our lettuce field, but he didn't make it. Got snagged in the electric wires. Died in the air. Golden flames shooting everywhere—looked like the plane had gotten swallowed up by the sun. But you know what shakes me up the most—the thing that never stops haunting me?"

"No, ma'am."

"How pretty the sky was. I just can't seem to get over that beautiful sky."

"I'm sorry, Miss Zora," I said. "I really am."

"Thank you, sweetheart," and she planted a kiss on the top of my head. "But don't worry. In a way, it's ancient history, almost twenty years ago. His name is Moses. Moses Aloysius Williams. And what's not ancient history is that I love him now as much as I did when he was alive."

"Was he a good man? Did you fight?"

She looked out over the water. "No, Miss Avocet, we did not fight. We had our disagreements about silly things, but we always made up and we followed my mama's advice, which was never to go to bed angry and never to go to sleep without kissing each other good night. To this day, as soon as I lay my head on my pillow, I say, 'Good night, Moses, I love you.' And I kiss the air." Miss Zora closed her eyes and kissed the autumn wind. Then she turned and looked at me. "Yes, he was a very good man."

I rubbed Old Sam's fanny with my foot. He wagged his tail but kept napping. "What about your daughter? Where's she?"

Miss Zora picked up two pine needles, braided one, and stuck it in her hat. "Actually, I raised two children, but my son, Moses Junior, I lost him. Pneumonia. Couldn't get a doctor to come visit as we were black, and there was a white doctor down there, but he wouldn't have a thing to do with us colored people. I tried all the cures I knew, but nothing worked. I sat there night and day by my baby's side—he was just about your age, not even in his teens—and I watched him die. It was hard on us. A parent never gets over a baby dying.

"And as for my daughter," she said, and she shook her head, ran those fine fingers over her eyes. She picked up another pine needle, dipped it into the water, and shook it. "Well, I've lost her, too. Says I embarrass her. Says I need to change out of my dirty clothes and wear some respectable city threads. Says I ought to forget about hoodoo and healing and all my little animals, both beast and fowl, that I care for. Says she won't recognize me as her mother until I behave civilized." Miss Zora flicked her wrist as if she was tossing away something bad-nasty. Then she reached over and touched my cheek. "I'm sorry, Miss Avocet, I should not have told you that. Just forget it. Goodness, child," and she widened her eyes in disbelief, "I think you're the only person I've ever told all that to."

I took Miss Zora's hand again and squeezed tight. How could anybody not want Miss Zora to be her mama? What was good and just about someone as kind as my Miss Zora suffering so many troubles?

"Miss Zora," I said, "I'm sorry bad things happened to you. But you'll make up with your daughter. I bet you will. She's back in that town you come from?"

"No. She's too grand for Ochopee. She lives in Miami.

Just a stone's throw across the swamp. But you see, Miss Avocet, when she told me I was an embarrassment and to stay out of her life, well, because I love her and because I couldn't become what she wanted me to be, I did as she asked. I left. Went far enough away that she doesn't have to worry about me anymore."

"But, Miss Zora," I said, "don't you talk? Or write? You never see each other?"

"No, little girl." Miss Zora's face went slack, and I knew—at least in part—who had drawn those wrinkles on her coffee-colored skin. "Ten years this Christmas."

I skimmed a stone into the pond. It fell into the dark water with a hollow thump. The egret stretched its neck forward and then rose like a spirit into the sky, squawking as it flew. Miss Zora and I watched until the bird disappeared beyond the naked gray branches of the cypress.

But we did not leave. We sat there, side by side, Old Sam at our feet. And we did not mutter a single word. But I'd swear on a stack of Bibles that as the cool wind swept over us and as the sun dipped down below the tree line and as a heron and its mate flew unseen but known through their strange cries, we were both thinking, *If only* . . .

AS SOON AS I got home, I taped the picture of my bike to the refrigerator. Just like with the savings bonds, sometimes objects could seal themselves to my soul, and

I'd think I was going to die if I didn't get them. I watched Mama closely as she fixed supper. She seemed not to notice that I'd taped my Christmas wish onto the refrigerator. She went about her business, ignoring me and my blazing red hint.

But the bike had made an impression, it sure had. That night, over Mrs. Paul's fish sticks and fresh coleslaw, Mama told Phoebe and me that when she was a girl her family never exchanged store-bought presents. They were too poor. But it didn't matter because spending money was not what Christmas was supposed to be about.

I jabbed my fork into my fish stick and thought I heard failure rumbling down the tracks. What would I say the first day back to school after Christmas vacation when we had to write that yearly paragraph, "What I Got for Christmas"? If failure came, I would lie. I'd say I sure did get my super-slick bike. Or better yet, I'd be absent.

Mama didn't have her wax teeth in and she was drinking fast out of that coffee mug with the blue daisies. "I'm not going to be able to meet the rent if I have to buy you presents," she said, and by her tone of voice, a person could have decided she resented us kids.

"Fine," Phoebe said. "We don't get presents. So what?" Seemed to me that of late, Phoebe was either overly cautious or else she threw it to the wind and spouted off without regard to her health. Sister's hair was pulled back into one long snake-black braid that followed the bony ridge of her spine. I wanted to yank on that roped hair to see if that would get her to shush.

"Well, I was thinking . . ." Mama's voice rose, and her dark eyes looked watery. She gazed at the ceiling as if there were answers scrawled in its water stains. "Maybe we could have an old-fashioned Christmas and we could make presents for each other. Nothing fancy, but like I said, they'll mean more than store-bought because we made them ourselves."

"Fine with me," Phoebe said saucily. Then she did one of her famous eye rolls and mouthed "drunk" to me. Quickly, I looked at Mama. Her eyes were closed as she gulped her beer. I guess it was because the full intent of Mama's words hadn't sunk in, or maybe it was because I saw an open window when Phoebe got by with the "drunk" jab, or maybe my hopes had been so high that it was taking a while for them to crash to earth. All I know for sure is that the words spilled out before my better sense could cork them in. "So I'm not going to get my bike this Christmas?"

In an instant Mama's eyes blazed open and her face contorted into something truly fearful to look upon. Before I could duck, she slammed that coffee mug into the side of my face.

ON MY NEXT visit to Miss Zora's, she wanted to know how I got that "bruise the size of Jupiter" on my temple, and I told her I'd been hit while playing tetherball. She pursed her lips and arched her eyebrows and asked if I was sure.

"Yes, ma'am."

Thinking that she would sympathize with me and maybe even talk bad about my mama, I told her we weren't going to buy Christmas presents.

"No Christmas presents?" she asked.

"Well—we're going to make each other presents. We're not allowed to buy any."

Miss Zora said, "Child, that's a grand idea!"

"It is?"

"Yes! Don't you think so?"

"But I wanted—" Then I stopped and looked around.

Miss Zora's cottage was virtually store-bought-free. From her baskets to her picture frames to her pine chest—she'd made them all. It dawned on me that that was why her cottage felt warm and inviting instead of like a motel room. Then I thought about how much I wanted that bike. But maybe it wasn't time for me to own anything so fancy. Maybe I needed to—as Mama often ordered—grow up.

"Yes," I mumbled, even though my heart was hurting, "it's a real good idea."

I looked at that prism hanging from Miss Zora's ceiling and decided that at least one of the presents I would make would catch sunlight. "You have any glitter?"

Miss Zora bit her bottom lip. Her eyes darkened as she concentrated. "Glitter," she said. "When Mary was your age she loved glitter, too."

"Who's Mary?"

"My daughter, the one you were so curious about the other day." She walked over to the pine chest that she used as a side table. She moved some books and a lamp onto the floor and then opened the lid. The chest was full of papers, photos, boxes, and who knows what. She knelt down, and I looked over her shoulder as she sifted through memories.

Mary's first report card. School pictures of Mary. She had been a pretty little girl. Had her mama's light eyes and a smooth complexion. Miss Zora paused over a photograph of five black men with shotguns, two dead hogs, one 'gator.

"Wow! They killed that 'gator?"

"Yes, ma'am, they did. This fellow with a hat on is my uncle Jake. And the tall good-looking man with his foot on the hog—that's my pappy. The two in the middle were our nearest neighbors: the Morgans—Jerome and Charles. And this one over here, leaning on his rifle, I don't have a clue about. But just look at my pappy. Wasn't he the most handsome thing!"

"Sure is," I said. Miss Zora had his eyes but not his nose. "You got any pictures of your mama?"

"Yes, somewhere in here," she said as she set aside the photo and grabbed another stack.

I picked up a dog-eared picture that was half hidden under a stained lace doily. "Who are these people?"

A young couple, the woman holding a baby, stood on the front porch of a picture-book clapboard farmhouse. A wild rose, heavy with blooms, climbed the porch rail, and two tall, bone-skinny coconut palms towered like shimmy dancers on either side of the oyster-shell walkway.

"Goodness, I haven't seen this photograph in ages," Miss Zora said, and her eyes glowed with a wistful, faraway light. It was the same look folks get when they're in a picture show viewing places they've longed to go and people they've always wanted to be.

"That's my men, Big Moses and Little Moses. Lord God, they made my life a happy place. And that's me. What a long time ago! Fine house, though, isn't it?"

"You were beautiful, Miss Zora."

"Why, thank you. I did have my admirers."

"Your house was pretty, too. Who lives there now?"

Miss Zora set the picture aside. "Nobody. It's still mine. I hung on to it, thinking maybe one day I'd return. You know, maybe Mary and I would finally see eye-to-eye and I could go home. I've got family down there who look after it."

"I can't believe you own that nice house and you're living here."

"Well, Miss Avocet, life does tend to throw at us problems and sores that we don't always know how to contend with. But we do our best. Don't we?"

"Yes, ma'am. I guess so."

Miss Zora stacked the photos into one pile and set them gently back into the chest. "I'm not sure where the picture of my mama is." Then she lifted out a cigar box. She opened the lid and muttered, "No, no, not this one."

"What's that stuff?" I asked, pointing to the cigar box.

"Important things. Shells, stones, dried herbs, scraps of old clothes—all charms I use for divining."

"Divining? What's that mean?"

"You know, divine the future, cast spells. That sort of thing."

I put my hand on her shoulder. "Miss Zora, are you a witch?"

She placed the box on the floor and rooted some more. "Witch? No, baby. But I do believe in the old ways. Mother Earth, she has powers. To heal, you see."

"Mr. Ippolito, he thinks you keep this motel safe."

"Is that what he said?" Miss Zora opened a small

wooden box that contained a pair of gloves and then snapped it shut.

"And my mama told him he was foolish and should kick you out."

Miss Zora paused from her rooting and turned to me. "Miss Avocet, does your mama know you come over here?"

I shook my head no.

"And I bet you'd be in some hot water if she found out?"

I didn't answer, just gazed back at her, terrified that she was going to say I couldn't visit anymore. I could not lose my Miss Zora. Not that. A scream started to form way deep in my belly, a bring-down-the-rafters yowl.

But Miss Zora plucked it right out. She said, "Fine. We'll be careful, then, like a couple of little mice who come in from the cold at night and who don't disturb anything so much that the people find them out. And when the time comes, I'll talk to your mama and we'll make everything right. A lot has happened to her. She's still adjusting. Deal?"

"Deal."

"Good," she said, and then she turned back to the pine chest. I sneezed because she was stirring up dust. "God bless you."

"Thank you."

"Ahhh! Here's what I'm looking for." She picked up something covered in layers of faded violet tissue paper.

"I like that color," I said.

Miss Zora slowly unfolded the wrapping and then stared down at a card made of red poster board shaped like a heart. Her eyes teared over again, and I sent up a silent prayer that I was witnessing tears of joy, but in my bones I knew regret was souring the mix.

She said, “Look here. See what a fine job Mary did with that glitter?” The front of the card was spangled in sparkling snowflakes. Miss Zora opened it and read the message, written also in glitter, “ ‘Merry Christmas to my mama. Love, Mary.’ ”

“It’s beautiful,” I said, and immediately I knew that I would make glitter cards for Phoebe and Mama.

“Yes. Yes, it is.”

Miss Zora started to rewrap it, and I said, “The card is so pretty, why don’t we leave it out? We can set it on the table. It’ll be your Christmas decoration.”

She traced her finger along the edges of a snowflake as she mulled my suggestion. “That’s a good idea, Miss Avocet. But I can’t. Not yet.”

She bundled the poster-board heart in the sheets of violet paper and set it back in the chest. Her eyes swept across her treasures one final time, and then she shut the lid.

“Sweetheart,” she said, “life sure is a mysterious journey.”

IT SEEMED AS if we’d just gotten over Thanksgiving when Christmas sprouted all around us. Mr. Ippolito and Joe strung candy-colored lights throughout the office.

Manny bought a can of snow and sprayed the words "Noel, Noel!" on the windows of every cottage that faced Nebraska Avenue. Then he went a little crazy and sprayed the palm trees. My teacher took to wearing a Santa Claus hat. Mama found the bells that had hung from our front door in the grove and tied them with a red ribbon to the trailer's door.

These holiday touches were cheerful, but they weren't enough to take the sting out of the fact that we didn't have the money to buy a Christmas tree. And that broke my heart. Not having a tree only made the obvious harder to swallow: my family was not like others. We did not fit into the scheme of things. There wasn't a comfortable place for a widow with two children. We were square pegs in a round world.

To Mama's credit, she was trying to get past Christmas by behaving better. Maybe all the talk about goodwill and peace on earth soaked in. And also, the three of us stayed so busy making presents for one another that we didn't have much time to stew.

I made Phoebe a twig basket—Miss Zora taught me how—and then I visited a stand of maples that grew along the eastern edge of the field and collected its scattered gold and red leaves. A basketful of fall—I thought Phoebe would love it, and the earthy and splendid colors ignited to ward off death reminded me of my sister's beauty.

Mama's gift was more troublesome. I was afraid that nothing I could make would be grand enough, and I sure didn't want to displease her. Miss Zora told me not to worry so much, that I'd discover what to do when I wasn't even thinking about it. And she was right.

I had gone to the office to get a cold drink out of the

machine, and on my way back to the trailer I stumbled on a bird's nest under a mess of Spanish moss. We'd had a thunderstorm that morning, and the wind must have blown the nest out of the tree. It was larger than the one in my pine chest where I kept my hurt pieces of spring. A shattered blue eggshell was embedded in the webbing of feathers, leaves, pine needles. I pressed against the side of the nest to see how sturdy it was, and felt a sharp sting. The jagged edge of a shell had stuck me. Drops of my blood trickled down the tip of my finger and into the nest. I didn't want to give Mama a present stained with my blood, so I tried wiping away the drops but succeeded only in bleeding more. But as my blood dried, it disappeared. So I felt okay. Mama would never know that the nest held anything other than air. I hid it under my shirt, and as I started toward the trailer, I decided to make a twig basket to set the nest in, like a cradle.

During art in school—I was attending more regularly because math class played second fiddle to fun Christmas activities—I made Miss Zora's present. I visited the school library and studied a book filled with beautiful paintings of birds. My heart's desire was to make her a poster-board avocet. But avocets were complicated creatures. Their bills were all wrong—long, skinny, black, and curved up toward heaven instead of down at their food. I wondered how they got enough to eat with beaks aimed the wrong way. The book said that avocets changed colors. In winter their heads and necks were a soft gray, but come breeding time the gray blossomed into burnt pink. Even if I could have managed to cut a skinny enough beak and stilt legs that looked like sticks instead of stumps, I could not have chosen between their winter or breeding plumage.

So I abandoned my idea of an avocet. I considered trying a blue jay, but didn't want to risk making Miss Zora sad. From living with my mama, I knew widows didn't like being reminded of their husbands. Mama had told me that because I looked like Daddy, she sometimes couldn't stand to see me.

After a lot of hard thinking and studying every bird in that book, I decided to make a dove. It was a gentle bird and simple to draw. I have to say, I did a good job—coated the feathers in gold glitter, and on top of the gold, in silver glitter, I spelled out "Miss Zora." Even some of the kids who made the worst fun of me said the dove was pretty. I punched a small hole in the bird's back and threaded a string through it so that the bird could be hung from the ceiling.

I knew that the dove, to some people, brought to mind Jesus, the Prince of Peace. Miss Zora didn't seem religious in an ordinary Christian way, so she might not think about Jesus as the dove spun in the bright light of her cottage, moved in the breeze the way the pictures of ice cream floats twirled in the cool air at Beckett's Pharmacy. And that was fine with me, because I was dead certain that Jesus had jilted me back in the grove. Troubles didn't grow like weeds in the souls of girls who are loved by Him. In the longest time, I hadn't had daydreams of the two of us walking into the sunset, hand in hand. No, my crush was finished. Now, I wasn't ready to say I didn't believe in God, and I still read that Gideon Bible, trying for the life of me to understand the mysteries of faith, but I didn't feel special in His eyes anymore. And when you've been jilted by the Son of God, there's no easy way to get over that sorrow. So it didn't matter to me if Miss Zora thought about God or not when she watched her paper dove spin. But I was hoping she would murmur to herself, "That Avocet Abigail Jackson is a wonderful child."

Mama had instructed Phoebe and me not to make anything for Hank, that she doubted he would be home for Christmas. But my hopes told me otherwise. I made him a snowflake mobile. I thought he could hang it in his window up there in Kentucky. And Mama, I must have inspired her because she gave in and started knitting him a muffler. "If he doesn't show up, I guess we can mail our gifts to him."

Two days before Christmas, a cold front blasted us with some bone-chilling weather. I told everybody I saw, "You know, I think it might snow." Mama turned on the oven and opened the door to try to heat the trailer. She borrowed a space heater from Mr. Ippolito, but it was useless unless you stood right in front of it. The bathroom was freezing, so the three of us took sponge baths in the kitchen. But we couldn't do anything about our bladders. We sorely hated setting our butts down on that icy toilet seat. But it got to be funny because every time one of us went to the bathroom the first sound was the closing of the door and the next was a scream or a curse as our bare fannies touched that frigid seat.

About noon on Christmas Eve, Mama came home from the office, her nose red from the cold, and put on a pot of chicken and dumplings. Since hitting me upside the head with her coffee mug, Mama hadn't laid a hand on me. And she hadn't beaten Phoebe since the whipping she gave her the day we ate brunch with Mr. Ippolito and L.J. I wasn't sure if it was out of guilt or if she was truly mending her ways, but after Thanksgiving, Mama began trying to make up with Phoebe, buying her cheap jewelry and offering beauty tips. That was the biggest change, her deciding that Phoebe had a right to look nice.

I watched Mama cook, tried to make small talk. I said, "My teacher burped right in the middle of calling roll the other day. A boy who sits in the front row started laughing, and the teacher said if he didn't behave she would send him to the office. I don't think that was fair. She was the one who burped. Did you know no two snowflakes are alike?"

Mama glanced up from the dough, which stuck to her hands like glue, and said, "Bird, you're driving me crazy. Go find something to do."

Phoebe was in the bedroom, reading a beauty magazine, her hair rolled in orange juice concentrate cans. This means of hairstyling, she had told Mama and me a few weeks earlier, was taking her classmates by storm. Belinda Clark, a girl Phoebe had made friends with, gave her a sack of cans that she didn't need. It seemed she came from a large family that drank lots of juice. Mama had looked into the bag of cans and said, "Hell's bells. Whatever works, I guess."

The first time Phoebe rolled her hair in such a fashion, Mama and I sat on the bed and offered advice.

"I think you should wind less hair per can," I said.

"Well, I'm trying to do my best, but I don't have enough rollers," Phoebe answered in a tone usually reserved for desperate situations. "I'll just have to get some more from *somewhere*."

"I think if you use Dippity-Do, that will help," Mama said. "Your hair is fine, like mine. The Dippity-Do will give you some control. I don't think it's very expensive.

Remind me and I'll try to get some next time I go grocery shopping. But Bird's right. You're rolling too much hair on those cans."

Phoebe slammed down her comb. "If all you two can do is criticize, I would appreciate it if you left me alone."

Mama said, "With God as my witness, I don't know where you came from. You with your high-and-mighty attitude."

So I didn't think Phoebe had a snowball's chance in hell of getting that Dippity-Do. But I was proven wrong. Mama bought her a jar of that neon pink goo the very next visit to the grocery store. Phoebe used it for the first time on Christmas Eve. I was shocked that the gel's color disappeared once it was out of the jar and on the head. But what interested me even more was that as Phoebe sprawled on the bed, reading her magazine, in those oversized rollers—Belinda Clark had given her a whole other sackful—my sister looked like a science fiction creature: part robot, part girl, part gigantic mouse.

I said, "Your head looks huge."

She ignored me, just kept on with that glamour magazine, so in my singsong voice I chortled, "I know who you love. I know who you love."

"Bird, don't you have anything better to do than act stupid and bother people?"

"I'm not bothering anybody. And my teacher says I'm not stupid. I just need to apply myself."

"Then go apply yourself somewhere else."

I stuck out my tongue at her and then retrieved from under my bed a box full of the presents I'd made. They were all wrapped except for Miss Zora's because we'd run out of paper. I didn't know what to do about that. I was afraid I might have to give Miss Zora a naked, unwrapped present. "Look." I held up the golden dove. "I made this for Miss Zora. Ain't it beautiful!"

Phoebe looked and then turned a page. "Yeah. It is pretty. But you better stop waving the thing around. If Mama sees it, you're in trouble."

"There's nothing wrong with Miss Zora," I said. "Mama doesn't know what she's talking about. Why, Miss Zora, she knows about all kinds of things." But before I could detail Miss Zora's knowledge, I was interrupted by a conversation in the living room. Mama distinctly said, "What a nice surprise!"

When I heard the voice of our visitor, my eyes got big and I said, "Oooooo!"

"Shut up!" Phoebe snapped. She leaped from the bed like a track star and began ripping those cans out of her hair.

"Phoebe! Bird! Get in here. We have company," Mama called.

"Shit!" Phoebe said as she tried to flatten her hair. Those curlers and that Dippity-Do had done their job a little too well. Her black hair ballooned around her face and shoulders, making her look like the star in a movie named *Teenage Hussy from Outer Space.*

Phoebe pressed her hands to her hair and groaned. "What am I going to do? I can't go out there looking like this."

"You got two choices, Sister. You can go out there as you are and L.J. will mistake you for a Martian, or else put your hair in a ponytail. That's what I'd do."

"Girls, get in here!" Mama yelled.

"But I don't have a rubber band!"

"Check the top drawer. There's probably one in there. And tie a ribbon in your hair. That'll look neat," and then I left her alone.

As I walked down the hallway, I heard Mama say, "L.J., this is really nice of you and your family. Please, thank everyone for us."

"Hey, squirt," L.J. said. "Santa brought you something."

"What?" I asked, and it hit me that L.J. was so cute that if I were older, Phoebe and I would be fighting over him. And what would Jesus have to say about that!

"Over there. By the couch, Bird," Mama said.

I looked, and what I saw filled me with unspeakable joy. I couldn't believe anyone had been so kind as to fulfill one of my most immediate wishes. "Oh! Oh! Oh!"

In the corner by the couch was a small and perfect Christmas tree. "Is it ours?" I asked, my voice shaking.

"Of course it's ours," Mama said. "L.J. didn't bring it over here just to tease you. Now what do you say?"

I was so happy I could barely stand it. I threw my arms around him. "Thank you, thank you," I said into his black turtleneck sweater. He smelled like cedar and soap.

"No problem, Bird." Then I heard him say, "Hey, Phoebe. You look real nice tonight."

I let go of him and ran into the bathroom. I didn't even get a look at Phoebe's hair, because I couldn't bear to have L.J. see me cry. Even though he wasn't my boyfriend, I was beginning to have the kind of pride that responds to the opposite sex.

In the cold, tiny room, I buried my face in a towel to muffle the sound of my sobs. I was scared Mama might barge in and demand to know why I was behaving like a goddamned fool. If she did, what would I tell her? Would I say I was crying because I'd gotten my Christmas wish, that I was caught up in the moment of a dream coming true, that religion and life were two pinballs forever colliding in my head?

I turned on the faucet, washed my face, then stared at my reflection. I looked pale. Mama liked to say that my skin was the color of peaches and cream. I guess that was good, but I wished I had Phoebe's complexion—she didn't ever get sunburned. My freckles looked like cinnamon stars scattered across my nose and cheeks. But boys hated freckles. I blinked and then opened wide. Even though I had my daddy's eyes, we didn't see the world the same way. No we didn't. That would be awful if I saw just like him. It would have meant I was destined to be a failure.

Mama's voice rumbled through my memory: "You will make something of yourself, goddamn it."

Somebody walked down the hall and went into my room. I figured Phoebe was in there doing some touch-up preening, maybe making sure her hair was still under control. I opened the medicine cabinet and grabbed Mama's jar of face powder. I patted it on and immediately turned two shades darker. Boy, I didn't look good at all. I guess I wasn't made for cosmetics.

"Bird, what's going on in there?" Mama yelled. She was right outside the door. She knocked on it.

"Nothing. I'll be right out."

"Well, hurry up."

As quick as I could, I wiped that powder shit off my face, flushed the toilet so they wouldn't know I had gone in there to spill baby tears, and before walking out said to my reflection, "I'm fine just the way I am."

Everybody was in the living room. L.J. and Phoebe were untangling two strings of lights. Mama stood on the other side of the couch, watching.

Phoebe's hair looked luxurious. She'd taken my advice and tied it with a blue ribbon. And even though the ribbon had been my idea, I had a sneaky urge to pull on it. L.J. would be shocked—Phoebe's hair suddenly so big. I thought, *My sister has the nicest boyfriend.* Not only did he bring us a tree, but he brought lights and a box of red Christmas balls.

L.J. looked at me. "Want to help?" he asked.

I eased over to the two of them, and as I ran my hands over the blue, green, and yellow bulbs, a magical feeling shot through my fingers and up my arms. If I concentrated hard enough, maybe through sheer brainpower I could make the lights flash on. Somebody had told me Russians could bend spoons just by thinking. I grabbed hold of a green bulb and shut my eyes. *Light up, light up, light up.*

"Bird, what are you doing? Quit fooling around," Phoebe ordered.

"I'm not fooling around."

"Then what do you call it?"

"Give it a rest," Mama said, and then she looked at L.J. and asked, "Did you spend a lot of money on these decorations?"

"No, ma'am," L.J. answered. "This is extra stuff we weren't using."

"Well, it sure is sweet of you and your family," Mama said. She seemed not to mind that L.J. was visiting and helping us decorate the tree. I thought, *That's the thing about Mama—she's like a volcano: you never know when she's going to blow.* And though we all walked lightly for fear we might set her off, I think she enjoyed having company. She turned on the radio and tuned in a station that was playing Christmas music. When "The Little Drummer Boy" came on, we all sang the pa-rum-pum-pum-pum part. Mama set out Co'-Colas and put bourbon in hers. When we plugged in the tree we cheered, and Mama said, "This isn't going to be so bad after all."

Phoebe suggested we stack our presents under the tree, and when I went to get mine from beneath the bed, I remembered that I'd left Miss Zora's golden dove on the dresser, but it wasn't anywhere in sight. I thought that Phoebe must have hidden it for me.

Mama was so good-humored that she even invited L.J. to stay and eat supper with us. He said that even though he'd already eaten, he was still hungry and would love to. L.J. was very polite to Mama. He behaved as if his new goal in life was to butter her up. We crowded around the small kitchen table, which didn't look so shabby in the soft glow of the Christmas lights. After one bite of Mama's chicken and dumplings, L.J. said, "This is great! What is it?"

That got us all to laughing, because we realized that L.J. had never before eaten chicken and dumplings. He said Brooklyn wasn't big on southern cooking but ought to be. This pleased my mama. She said, "You just wait and see. It will catch on one of these days."

After supper, L.J. offered to help wash the dishes, but Mama wouldn't hear of it. And when he said he needed to get home because he and his brothers were going to midnight folk mass with guitars and everything, would we like to go, I jumped in and said, "Oh, Mama, that would be so much fun! Can we?"

"I always loved midnight mass," she said. "But no, we can't. Not this time. Thank you for asking, though."

I wanted her to give me one good reason why we couldn't go to church, but I knew if I spoke my mind I'd sour her good mood. So I stayed quiet. And that voice in my head whispered, "You're lucky you got the tree."

When L.J. left, we stood on our concrete steps and wished him "Merry Christmas! Merry Christmas! Merry Christmas!" Young love and heartache flickered across Phoebe's face as she watched him walk away. I thought I understood what she was feeling.

The three of us went back into the trailer, shivering due to the winter air. "Judas Priest, I hate cold weather," Mama complained.

I walked over to our tree, and Mama said, "Do you want to open gifts?" Our custom was to open one present on Christmas Eve and leave the rest for morning, but Daddy always went hog-wild and made sure there were tons of presents under our tree. They weren't expensive or anything. Chocolate bars and hankies, water guns and flip-flops. But volume mattered.

Phoebe and I looked at our budget of gifts and we both said no.

"Maybe if we wait until morning, Hank will be here," I said.

Mama leaned against the kitchen counter, lit a cigarette, reached for her bourbon and Co'-Cola, and said, "Bird, don't get your hopes up."

As I fell asleep that night, I realized I was becoming aware of the goodness in common people. L.J., I'd love him forever because of that tree. And Miss Zora, she was a house of peace. Maybe, I thought as my mind grew drowsy, people such as L.J. and Miss Zora were the world's guardian angels. Maybe they possessed invisible wings.

Right before sleep took me, I saw myself entering Miss Zora's cottage. On my arms were bangles of gold. My toes shimmered with emerald and garnet glitter. I wore a crown spun from diamonds and stars. And I carried a golden dove that cooed so beautifully even the wind paused to listen.

SOMETIME THAT NIGHT, when I was so deeply asleep that I wasn't even dreaming, Phoebe shook me awake. "Bird, do you hear that?" she whispered. "Somebody's outside!"

I groaned and pulled the covers up closer around my chin. "Leave me alone," I mumbled.

"Wake up, damn it. I mean it. Somebody is out there."

Sure enough, as soon as the words were out of her mouth, I heard the sound of footsteps in the fallen leaves Mama had scattered over the yard to keep the dust down.

The first thing that came to mind was the story Phoebe told so well about the crazy man from Chattahoochee. I was positive we were about to come face-to-face with the real thing. Probably Mama had rented a room to a mental patient. "Let's hide under the bed," I whispered, and right then there was a rapid *taptaptaptap* on our bedroom window.

Sister and I screamed, bolted upright, and grabbed hold of each other.

"Phoebe, Bird, let me in. I've been knocking on the front door forever!"

"Hank!" Then we erupted into squeals and giggles. We threw off our covers and beat a path into the living room. Phoebe flipped on the overhead light, and Mama groggily lifted her head from her pillow and said, "What the hell is going on?"

I opened the door and Hank walked in, grinning from ear to ear.

Phoebe and I hugged him, and he said, "Hey, you two. Hey, Mama."

"Well, Jesus Christ," Mama said. "Somebody get me my robe."

I took it off the back of a kitchen chair and handed it to her. Hank said, "How in the blazes is everybody?"

"We're good," I said. "Look at our tree! L.J., Phoebe's boyfriend, gave it to us." I plugged in the lights.

"He's not my boyfriend," Phoebe lied.

"He is too!"

"Boyfriend! What are you doing with a boyfriend?"

"He's not—"

"Don't start fighting, damn it!" Mama stood up and secured her robe and said, "My God, son, it's good to see you."

They hugged, and I clung to Phoebe. Mama said, "Sit down, Hank. Just push my covers to the side. Would you like something to eat?"

Hank flopped on the couch and said, "That would be great, Mama."

"Phoebe, put the chicken and dumplings on the stove while I fix a pot of coffee."

Feeling triumphant, I sat on the floor beside Hank's feet. I had believed all along he'd come home.

My brother rubbed his eyes and said he was dog-tired, that he'd driven straight through from Kentucky because his part-time job at a hunting and sporting supply store required him to work Christmas Eve day. But as soon as his shift was over, he got in the MG and headed south.

Mama murmured, "I just can't believe you're here." She came into the living room with two cups of coffee, handed Hank his, and sat beside him.

"I said I'd be home for Christmas and, by God, I meant it." Then he laughed and pinched my nose. "Ain't that right, tiger?"

I slipped my hand into his and kept it there. We told him about Mr. Ippolito. "He's bald," I said, "and he sings opera."

Hank asked where, and that threw us into a laughing fit and Mama managed to say, "Anywhere he feels like it."

Phoebe fixed him a plate. He took a bite and said, "Man, this is good food. I sure have missed your cooking." Then he stabbed a dumpling and asked, "The trailer is kind of small, isn't it?"

"We manage," Mama said, her expression darkening into a scowl. "Don't you worry about us. There's nothing wrong with this trailer."

"Didn't mean anything by it, Mama." Hank stared at his plate, clenched and unclenched his hands a couple of times, and said to no one in particular, "Everything is okay." Then he cleared his throat and began to tell us all about himself. He said that he'd been "getting his life together," that the trip west had been good for him because he'd done some serious thinking on those "long, lonely stretches of highway."

"Yep," he said, his voice lowering into a timbre of importance, "I'm going to make something of myself. This is one old boy," and he tapped his chest, "who is not going to live a wasted life." Then he set the plate on the coffee table, pushed it away from the edge, and wiped his mouth.

Mama didn't say a word, just puffed on her cigarette. I guess she was used to hearing men talk that way. Daddy had done it all the time. I patted his leg and asked, "You going to have to go fight in that war?"

"Me? No. I'm out of that one. As the only surviving male in the family, I am destined to remain in civvies."

"What's a civvy?"

"It means he's not going to be drafted," Mama said.

"Oh. That's good. Hank, there's a swimming pool here."

My brother said, "Really? Right here at this motel?"

I nodded yes, and Phoebe said I acted like that swimming pool was the be-all and end-all, and Hank said, "Man, I could use a swim!"

Mama said, "You'd freeze your ass off."

"Naw. After the initial shock it will feel great. How about it? You girls game?"

I yelled yes. "Hank, it's really cold," Phoebe said.

"Listen here, there was three feet of snow on the ground in Kentucky. This is like summertime."

"You're not serious," Mama said.

Phoebe tossed back her ponytail. "I'll do it if you will, Hank."

"Me, too!" I chimed, even though the thought of that freezing water terrified me.

Mama couldn't help herself. She flicked her ash and said merrily, "You all are damn fools."

"Girls, go put your suits on. Shit, I almost forgot about Buster. I've got to bring in something from the car," Hank said, and he winked at me.

"Uh-oh, what have you done now? I'll bet my bottom dollar it's something wild," Mama said, but her words did not carry their usual venom.

While Hank was outside getting the surprise, Phoebe and I went into the bedroom and changed into our bathing suits. I was hoping Hank had brought me home a cat. But no, when we came out, Mama and he were standing by the kitchen table, staring at a turkey. Hank had carried the bird all the way from Kentucky in an ice-filled trash bag.

"Yum, turkey!" I said. "We're going to have turkey."

"What?" Hank asked in floored surprise. He did look tired—his hair was standing on end, he smelled like cigarettes and B.O. "You want to roast my traveling companion? We can't eat Buster."

For two seconds I took him seriously, and then I realized I was being played with. "Are we going to go swimming?" I asked.

"Yeah. Hurry up. We need to do it before the sun comes up or it won't be as much fun."

"But you just got here," Mama said. "And you shouldn't swim on a full stomach."

Hank put his arms around her, kissed the top of her head, and said, "Put on your coat and come with us. If the girls want to swim, by God, that's what we're going to do."

Mama started to say something but stopped. She looked confused. Maybe all this was just too much for her. She fiddled with the satin collar of her robe and said, "Well, all right, but help me get the turkey in the refrigerator. We don't want it to spoil."

"No, we don't," said Hank, and he tickled my ribs.

Mama opened the refrigerator and began making room. She muttered and fretted, and Hank said, "That's good enough, Mama." He slid Buster in.

"Can we go now?" I asked.

"Whatever," Mama said, as if she'd come to terms with the idea that her children were nuts.

We bundled up and trooped into the night. Mama was dressed in her coat, robe, and nightgown. Phoebe and I were in our coats and swimsuits. Hank wore a leather jacket, jeans, and T-shirt. He said, "The air feels fantastic!"

As we walked across the driveway and past a row of cottages, Mama warned, "Don't make any noise. You'll get us thrown out." But I didn't think we were at risk of getting in trouble because I remembered that there was only one guest and he was checked into cottage two, by the office. Mama had said he was some poor drunken bastard down on his luck and depressed because it was Christmas. I didn't think such a person would be mad about our swimming in frigid temperatures in the deep dark of night.

"We're just going for a dip. That's not illegal, is it?" Hank chided.

"Actually," said my Miss-Know-It-All sister, "there's

not supposed to be any swimming between ten P.M. and eight A.M. It's a rule."

Hank imitated her, using a hoity-toity voice, and then said, "But the rules don't apply to us because we live here!"

The pool looked gorgeous in the dark, glowing like a giant aqua bean. Hank unzipped his jeans and stripped down to his underwear. "My God, son," Mama said.

But he ignored her, walked over to the diving board, betrayed no chill whatsoever, and climbed the ladder. He stood at the back of the board, tall and straight. Then, one, two, three, jump, into the air, graceful, his body arched like the silver-gray curve of a dolphin. "Wow!" I said between chattering teeth. "I didn't know he could do that!"

Hank entered the pool with barely a splash, and Mama said he'd been on the diving team in high school. Hank came up for air, hollering, "This feels great! What are you two? A couple of chickens?" Then he clucked at us.

I threw off my coat and did a cannonball. Phoebe held her nose and jumped in feetfirst. The shock of the cold water was so intense it caused Phoebe and me both to scream, and I thought my heart stopped beating. But Hank was right, after a few minutes, the only parts of me that were cold were the parts not in the water.

So that's how we brought in Christmas, behaving like we were Yankees, as if the frigid weather didn't bother us. "It's going to snow," I announced.

"God, I hope not," Hank said, and then he played tugboat, dragging Phoebe and me behind him. I bet Phoebe a thousand dollars that I could hold my breath underwater longer than she could. I lost. Hank swam laps. I doggy-paddled into the deep end and pretended I was far out to sea and that I wasn't a little girl. I was something else—a seabird who could fly great distances. The ocean and the heavens were my home, and I was happy because there weren't any predators anywhere near. There was just my crazy, good-hearted brother and my bossy, beautiful sister and my mama, who for once in her life forgot her anger. That was what really made me happy—my mama, standing at the edge of the pool, wrapped in her overcoat, holding out her hand to see if there were snowflakes swirling through that Florida sky, and then laughing at our antics. Yes, Mama, throwing back her head and letting her joy dot the stars.

THAT NIGHT HANK slept on the floor, but Christmas Day Mama went to the office and got him a room. Mr. Ippolito wouldn't accept any payment. Four nights for free. Despite the fact that I feared Mr. Ippolito just because he was a grown man, I also knew he was being more than kind.

When Mama got back from the office, she told me to take a shower. I had to admit, I did smell like chlorine. As I closed the door to the bathroom, I heard her announce that Christmas dinner would be ready at two. That meant that after we ate, I'd have the afternoon to sneak away to Miss Zora's and give her my present. As I turned on the shower faucet, I reminded myself to ask Phoebe where she'd stashed the dove.

Once the turkey was in the oven, we were allowed to open our gifts. We sat around the tree, Mama on the couch and the rest of us on the floor, and we oohed and aahed over our handmade treasures. My desire for the banana-seat bike seemed a dream of some other girl.

Phoebe had strung us each a necklace of love beads. We immediately put them on. Even Mama. Hank said he'd never take his off.

Hank, of course, was exempt from the homemade rule, and he gave my sister and me silver charm bracelets with St. Christopher medals dangling from them. Mine also had a cat charm and a cross. Phoebe's, a cross and a ballerina slipper. I helped Phoebe clasp hers, and then she helped me with mine. Mama said our bracelets went well with the love beads, and Hank pointed out that there was plenty of room for us to collect more charms.

Mama opened her present from Hank and said, "Oh, it's beautiful!" She held up a turquoise sweater that had a row of white seashells sewn around the neck.

"It's a good color on you," Hank said.

Mama blushed and set the sweater aside. "Thank you, son."

From Mama, Sister and I got granny bags—they were all the rage. She had cut up clothes that we'd outgrown and sewn them together in starburst shapes. The long handles were made out of velvet edged in lace. At first I thought Mama had cheated and bought the lace brand-new, but then I recognized the lace as having been taken off of an old, stained tablecloth she'd brought with her from the grove. Mama sure was handy with a needle and thread.

When Hank unwrapped his present from Mama, he tied the muffler around his neck and said, "Boy, this is just what I need. Thank you." He kissed her cheek.

Phoebe gave Mama a needlepoint purse of a sunflower. She'd made it in home ec. Mama said she had no idea that Phoebe was so talented.

When Mama unwrapped her present from me and saw that bird's nest with its broken eggshells, she said, "Oh. Thank you, Bird. How nice." Even though she set it and its basket on the knickknack shelf next to the front jalousie window, she didn't look or sound as though she liked her gift very much. Her face didn't light up the way it did when she caught a glimpse of the sweater. No sweet compliment like she paid Phoebe. My eyes stung, and I blinked fast to beat back the tears, glanced at Phoebe and Hank to see if they noticed. Hank hugged me and said, "That was real nice of you, tiger."

All three of them seemed to like their glitter cards, though. Phoebe set them on the kitchen table—they made a gorgeous display.

Mama wouldn't let me leave the house before we sat down for Christmas supper. She said she might need me. But Phoebe was helping her cook and there wasn't room for a third person in that cramped kitchen, so I chalked it up to her being mean.

Hank asked me to play cards. "Okay," I said. "You play poker?"

"Poker! Yeah, I play poker, but where did you learn to play a gambler's game?"

"Nowhere. Let's play rummy," and I shot a look at

Mama to see if she was listening. Hank and I spread out on the living room floor—he wouldn't let me keep score—while Mama and Phoebe bitched and cooked and hovered over the stove. Mama asked Hank if he wanted a beer, and he said, "No, thank you. I'm trying to cut back."

Despite Mama's doubts about cooking a big meal in a kitchen the size of a footlocker, she turned one out, using stuff we had on hand. She made giblet stuffing, collard greens, mashed potatoes, gravy. We didn't have any cranberry sauce, but I didn't complain. Mama had fixed a feast. We crowded around the kitchen table—my glitter cards a fitting centerpiece. Hank asked, "Where'd you get these beautiful dishes?"

Phoebe and I stole glances. As far as we could tell, Mama had not noticed that a plate was missing.

"At Goodwill. Can you believe it?" Mama said.

Hank picked one up and held it to the overhead light. Mama said she thought the pattern was Virginia Rose, and Hank raised his eyebrows and semicircled his mouth to show he was rightly impressed. He set the plate back on the table and said he thought we should say a prayer before we ate.

"Go ahead," Mama said, as if she couldn't care less.

We shut our eyes and bowed our heads. Hank thanked God for his family and for the supper and then he said, "May you bring peace and comfort to us all, living and dead."

I sneaked a peek at Mama to see if she got that part. She seemed to because her lips folded in on themselves, forming a watertight seal.

The food was wonderful. Except for Phoebe, who was on an everlasting diet, we ate with a vengeance. But best of all, we were actually getting on real well—like a normal family—by talking about nothing important. And then Hank mentioned Daddy. I could not believe it. There he was, in his white T-shirt and sailor-button bell-bottoms and all cleaned up, when he rested his knife on his plate, planted one elbow on the table, leaned forward to draw us in, and said, "You know, I never saw anybody who loved Christmas as much as Billy Jackson."

Mama paused, her fork in midair above the greens. *Oh no, here it comes.* I sank down in my chair, scared at what might happen next. But Mama showed me. She nodded, poked at her greens, and said, "That's for sure." Then she laughed and her face turned dreamy. She began to speak, tamping down her ill-natured tendencies, and I could see that talking about Daddy was painful but maybe good for her.

"He was just like a little kid," she said. "He couldn't wait to open his packages. And he decorated the yard like it was an amusement park. Reindeer, snowmen, lights everywhere, even on the azaleas."

She paused and toyed with the rum and eggnog Hank had fixed them. She looked at my brother, and a sad smile floated up from the past and warmed her face. "Remember the Christmas he dressed up like Santa? He borrowed the suit from that fellow in Lily who always played Santa Claus in the parade. Billy had to be at least two feet taller than that man. But he stuffed himself into the outfit anyhow. His face turned red, those clothes were so tight!" Mama covered her mouth with her hand and chuckled.

"He looked like he'd put on one of the elf outfits by mistake!" Hank sputtered. "He looked like a sausage!"

Mama, Phoebe, and Hank hollered with laughter. I

laughed, too, because good times really are contagious, but no matter how hard I tried, I could not remember Daddy dressed like Santa. As I giggled, I wondered if eventually I wouldn't remember anything about my daddy—not his voice, not his smell, not the funny, kind, or evil deeds he committed.

"It's a damn shame," Hank said, "that he couldn't stay sober. He had a great voice. He could have been a star."

"Yes, indeed," Mama said. "He completely fouled up that audition in Nashville. That recording contract came down to two people. Billy Jackson and Tex Williams."

I never knew Daddy had gotten that close to amounting to something. I wiped my mouth with the back of my hand. My mind reeled at what life would have been like had Daddy not failed. "Wh-wh-what happened?" I asked.

"The usual," Mama said. "He got scared. And when he was scared, he drank. The morning of the audition I was feeding him soda crackers and seltzer, trying to stop the vomiting brought on by spending the night with Jim Beam. But it was useless. He didn't even make it to the studio."

Mama looked at Hank as if she was about to accuse him of something. "He could sing circles around Tex Williams."

"Damn straight," Hank said.

And then Mama and he went on telling stories about Daddy, one after another. They couldn't stop; words rolled off their lips like broken rosary beads careening on a hard church floor. Daddy talked himself out of every speeding ticket he almost got. Daddy bet Amos Barwick that he could eat more blue crabs in thirty minutes than anyone else in the Creekside Bar. Daddy won, drove away on Amos's brand-new 1958 panhead Harley. But then he wrecked it beyond repair on Devil's Curb, trying to get home in a rainstorm the night I was born. Daddy hosted high-stakes poker in the back of the general store, and when the police visited during one game, suddenly there weren't any weapons, poker chips, or money to be seen—Daddy quickly shuffled the cards, dealt a hand of rummy, invited the officers to stay awhile. Daddy and his band, the Ramblers, played in a stripper bar in Daytona Beach for three weeks straight, and Daddy didn't get lucky once.

"That joint was no low-class affair," Mama said. "It was a respectable bar. The girls were talented. Ribbon dancing was their specialty. One strip at a time until they were naked as newborn babies. But they performed artfully. A lot of the women were single mothers trying to make a living and, let me tell you, they were strictly business. No hanky-panky. They showed up for work on time, danced, then went home. And not a one of them would have anything to do with your father. Which drove him nuts. By night's end he'd look like a puppy deprived of mother's milk."

Hank and Mama laughed so hard they cried. Even though I knew my mama was the sort of woman who would always keep her clothes on in public, I couldn't stop myself from imagining her as one of those ribbon dancers. Maybe if life and Daddy's fists hadn't taken their toll on her, she'd be pretty enough to make a good living. But neither strip joints nor offices wanted a woman with missing teeth and a busted nose. Besides, I wouldn't want my mama to dance in front of a bunch of leering drunks. That'd be awful. I gazed at my family and decided I loved hearing these stories. They fed an ache in me, fattening my longing for a nice life.

When Hank finished wiping the giggle-tears out of his eyes, he fiddled with his plate and said, "Look. I've got something serious to discuss. This seems like a good time."

Mama turned to face him, the laughter not yet gone from her eyes. Hank went on, "I'm not going to lie. Everybody sitting at this table knows that Billy Jackson and I had our troubles. He could be a mean son-of-a-bitch when the mood struck him, and I felt a God-given duty to protect my family. But—now this is my point and it's something I've got to say—I didn't have anything to do with his death. I know I talked big after everything came down. But listen here. Mama, I know this isn't easy, but you need to hear me out. I found him earlier that evening at Joe's Elbow Room. He was engaged in some serious drinking, but despite that we did have a conversation. And, yes, I told him if he did not go voluntarily to the police and turn himself in, I'd do it for him. But I never thought the crazy bastard would shoot himself. How was I to know that? How could anybody know that?" Hank looked at Mama imploringly, waited for an answer.

Phoebe kept her head down. Mama threw her napkin on the table, got her drink and cigarettes, and said, "You all need to leave me alone for a few minutes." Then she stormed outside.

Hank asked, "What did I do?"

"Nothing. That's just her way," Phoebe said flatly.

I put my arms around him.

"You know, I love you two girls."

"We love you back," said Phoebe.

I kept quiet—didn't trust my voice—but I was full of amazement, because for the first time I knew I wasn't the only one in the family who felt responsible for Daddy's death. Maybe that's why Mama accused me of killing him, to take the sting out of her own guilty feelings.

Phoebe sighed. Her sighs were so rich, they practically told stories.

"Bird," she said, "help me clear the table."

While Phoebe and I straightened the kitchen, Hank busied himself by picking and eating white meat off the turkey. I wanted to say to Hank that I had believed in him all along, but I was scared to start anything. So I let it rest.

Hank was telling us about a buddy of his who could stuff three tennis balls in his mouth, when Mama opened the door and said, "Son, I want you to go down to the office with me. Meet Louis Ippolito and get the key to your room." Then she shut the door before he could say anything.

Hank shot us a grin and whispered, "I guess she's over it." Then he went off with Mama.

Phoebe and I continued with our cleaning. I washed our Virginia Rose dishes so fast I was nearly out of breath. I wanted to be done and down to Miss Zora's before Mama got back to the trailer. I set the last plate in our new rubber rack—Mama had decided air-drying was better, that we might not be so prone to break one. This made me suspicious that she knew about the plate Phoebe broke at Thanksgiving, but she never came right out and said anything. I wiped my hands dry on my shirt and asked Phoebe where she hid Miss Zora's present.

"I didn't hide it," she said. "It was on the dresser last night when I came out to see L.J."

"You didn't hide it? You must have."

"Well, I didn't. I told you to put it away."

A sinking feeling filled my soul. I ran past Phoebe and to the room. I must have hidden the dove, must have forgotten where. I searched under the bed and through all the drawers, opened the closet and pushed aside boxes and shoes. How could I have left it out? Why couldn't I remember? Why was I so stupid? Maybe Phoebe was lying.

The dust caused me to sneeze. I searched quickly, even though I was scared of those roaches and spiders. I started to back out of the closet but then saw something small, golden, and familiar in the corner, next to my treasure chest of spring. I picked up a torn piece of paper. Glitter stuck to my hands. *God, no.* I pulled out the pine box and opened the lid. There, among my dead lizards, dragonflies, and fallen nests, was Miss Zora's dove, snipped to hell and back with Mama's pinking shears. *God, no. God, no. God, no.* Mama must have found the dove Christmas Eve when I ran into the bathroom to cry in private, or maybe this morning before we opened our presents. That's right, I took a shower so that I wouldn't stink of chlorine all day.

"Thought you were going to put something over on me, didn't you?"

Slowly I turned around. Mama stood in the doorway, cigarette in hand, smirking.

"I, I, I—"

"Shut up. I don't want to hear your excuses." She reached down and grabbed a fistful of my hair. I closed my eyes and tensed, ready to take the hit.

Mama pulled me up by my hair. The more I squirmed to get away, the harder she yanked. She brought her face close to mine. Coffee, cigarettes, bourbon, spit. "You've got a few days to think about what you've done," she said.

"I'm not going to punish you while your brother is here. So for the next four days I want you to stew, you useless lying bitch. Think about your lies, about all the heartache you bring me. Four days. Now get out of my sight. Go to your precious Miss Zora. She's not going to be able to help you out of this, Bird."

Mama let go with a shove. My scalp stung as if it had been pricked with hot needles. I rushed past her. Strands of my hair were tangled in her fingers.

I felt boneless. But I did as I was told. I ran to Miss Zora. And through blinding tears, I told her I didn't have a present for her because one of my sister's mean friends had visited and torn up her beautiful golden dove for pure spite.

THE DAY BEFORE Hank left, I took him to meet Miss Zora. What else could Mama do to me now that she knew I was regular friends with the woman? I didn't make a big deal out of walking with my brother down to the cottage at the end of the road, but I didn't much hide the fact either.

We sat on Miss Zora's front stoop—the cold weather had taken its leave—and ate boiled peanuts. Hank and she hit it off. Hank complimented her on that old rattletrap truck, saying it was a classic. Miss Zora said it was a piece of junk but got her where she needed to go. Hank was keenly interested in the place she'd come from and said he was thinking about moving to south Florida after he graduated. "I hear there are jobs down there."

"I suspect that's true," Miss Zora said.

"And I'll be closer to my family. I think the girls need me."

"They need a steady hand."

"Yeah," Hank agreed. Then he stared down at the space between his feet.

A mockingbird in the loquat ran through her entire songbook. Miss Zora shelled and ate a handful of boiled peanuts. Hank continued to stare at the dust between his feet, evidently knocked off kilter by her "steady hand" comment, but finally he said, "That picture on your wall. That's not a bald eagle, is it?"

"No. Osprey. Some folks call them fish hawks. I put the picture up there because it reminds me of home. And to write my congressman."

"Oh, yeah," Hank said, as if it was all coming together for him. "DDT, right? It does something to the shells—the eggs—of birds of prey. Osprey, eagle, what have you. Thins the walls of the eggs so that the baby birds can't hatch right. Is that what we're talking about?"

"You got it. Makes me sick, all these chemicals we're putting in the air and water and soil. Folks need to be more upset about it. I bet some of us are walking, talking toxic dumps."

That got a laugh out of Hank. He said, "Yes, ma'am, it is a crying shame." Then my big brother and Miss Zora chatted about the world's problems and solved most of them. They even came up with a few million-dollar ideas—business schemes for Hank the dreamer.

We visited for about an hour, and when we left, Miss Zora hugged Hank and whispered in his ear. He looked in her eyes and said, "I know. I'm working on it."

She kissed my cheek. I said, "I'll see you later."

"Yes, you will."

Then Hank and I walked home. The oak-shaded drive was speckled with winter light. Songbirds chirped carelessly, as if troubles weren't part of this world. Hank slipped his arm around my shoulders. "She's a good woman," he said.

"Mama don't want me seeing her."

"Your mother is just scared."

"Please don't go back up north. Please stay."

"I can't, Bird. You know that. I've got to finish school. One thing about your old brother: I have lived some wild times, but that doesn't mean I'm not going to contribute to this world. I'm going to. I swear. Your daddy's fate won't be mine."

I stopped walking and turned to him. "But Mama's mean to us, Hank. Sometimes real mean."

Hank hugged me and ran his hand over my hair, which hurt because my scalp was still tender from Mama pulling on me. "Listen, tiger," Hank said, "I will be back. I'm not leaving forever. I'll talk to Mama. I know she's rough on you. She's got a temper that could scare a viper. Hell, she broke a broom across my back once. Didn't want me dating the girl I was seeing. But she doesn't want to hurt us. I guess she just can't help herself. And you know, Bird, she's having a real tough time."

A guest—an old man in plaid pants, carrying his ice bucket—walked by and said hello.

"How are you?" Hank asked.

"Very good, sir, very good."

I took a deep breath, waited until the old man was out of earshot, then told my most honest thought: "I think she hates me."

"Wait a minute." Hank's tone and his face turned iron stern. He looked like Mama except for that dimpled chin—must be his daddy's chin. "Your mother does not hate you. She loves you, us. Maybe too much. Believe me, I know. I've been through hell with that woman. One day when you're older I'll explain. But I want you to understand one thing. I'm getting my life together. I've sworn off excessive drinking. Those days are over. I'm not going to be Billy Jackson. I'm going to be a man who can hold his head high and look a powerful son-of-a-bitch in the eye and say, 'It's a pleasure to meet you. Let's get down to business.' You'll see, Bird. Things are going to be all right."

I hugged him because I felt that was the proper thing to do, even though his speech did not comfort me. It seemed all the answers in the world were for the benefit of other people. Hank was the one person in this universe I even dared talk to about Mama's harsh ways, but his well-meaning words about his future left me feeling more alone than ever. I jabbed my toe into the dirt, and a fear raked me. Maybe the three of us—Hank, Phoebe, and I—were like those baby birds born in a web of DDT: doomed from the start, some other creature's lunch before we even had our wings.

WHEN MAMA GOT home from the office on Hank's last night, she informed us that twenty dollars had been stolen from the office cashbox and that Mr. Ippolito was fit to be tied. She said she'd stake her life that Miss Zora was the culprit, and Hank said, "I don't think she'd do that," and Mama snapped, "What the hell do you know? Just stay out of it."

Phoebe was standing in the kitchen, putting leftovers in one big pan. Hank and I were sitting at the kitchen table—I was trying to clip his fingernails because he'd said a friend of his gets manicures and I offered to try to give him one. I thought I was doing a good enough job to be a candidate for beauty technician school. Hank studied his snipped nails and said, "Miss Zora's not so bad, Mama. What don't you like about her?"

"The damn woman puts all sorts of crazy notions in Bird's head. That's what's wrong with her. As if it's any of your business." Mama opened the fridge and got herself a beer.

Hank's speaking up that way made me bold. I said, "Mama, she's a widow, like you. Y'all would be best friends if you'd just give her a chance."

"Young lady, you're in enough trouble already. You'd best keep your filthy mouth shut before I shut it for you—permanently."

Hank shoved his chair away from the table and stared at the wall. Phoebe stood motionless, a spoon heaped with mashed potatoes in her hand. Me, I felt my insides shiver, realized my mama could hurt me in ways I wasn't able to imagine.

The rest of the evening, I stayed quiet. Hank blabbered about nothing important, and Mama blabbered back. But after Phoebe and I went to bed, Mama and Hank started fighting. It reminded me of those endless nights back in the grove.

Mama said, "Lower your voice. You're going to wake the girls."

Hank said, "Maybe we should wake them. Maybe they ought to come out here and talk this through with us."

I fiddled with my sister's hair. "What are they fighting about, Phoebe?"

"Us, I think."

"Phoebe?" I wrapped my arm around hers.

"What?"

"Do you believe in God?"

"Of course I believe in God. Everybody believes in God."

Mama yelled, "You worthless jackass. How dare you try to tell me how to raise my two girls!"

I put my hands to my ears and said, "No they don't, Phoebe. No they don't."

I TRIED TO act grown up about Hank leaving, but I did not succeed. I embarrassed myself by falling victim to heaving tears, the kind that steal your breath. Hank whispered that he loved me and handed me a piece of paper with his work and apartment numbers scrawled on it and said if I ever needed to I could call him collect.

Mama said, "Hank, don't interfere." Then she kissed him on the cheek and said, "Good-bye, son."

As Hank's car rounded the corner and sped out of sight, Mama reached toward me. I ducked. She wasn't the kind not to keep her word about a beating, and I expected her to fulfill her threat right away. But instead she snatched Hank's phone number out of my hand and said, "Bird, make yourself useful and clean the trailer. Phoebe, watch your sister for me." Then she walked down to the office.

Out of habit, I sent up a prayer. *Dear Jesus, wipe Mama's memory clean. Don't let her come home and beat me all because of Miss Zora's golden dove.*

Phoebe helped me clean, and when we were done I asked her if she would roll my hair in orange juice cans. I wanted to see if I, too, would look like a space queen. But Phoebe said, "Why don't I try to do your hair in a French twist instead?"

"What's a French twist?" I suddenly imagined myself

in front of the Eiffel Tower, a beret smartly angled on my head.

"It's a real sophisticated bun. Sit down at the kitchen table, and we'll give it a try."

Phoebe twisted and pulled and pinned and Dippity-Do'ed and even though it hurt because my scalp was sore, I let her create for me a wonderful hairstyle. She gave me a hand mirror and asked, "What do you think?"

I could barely believe my eyes. With my hair swept up and off my face, I could get a good look at my bones. I had good structure. "You know, Phoebe, I think I've got potential."

"You do. I know it. Why don't we try a little lipstick?"

"No, I don't think so. Mama would kill me."

"I bet not. We'll put it on real light so there's just a hint of color."

I held up the mirror again and looked at the side view of my French twist. "Well, okay."

Phoebe went into the bedroom. I heard her rummaging through her top drawer, and then she came out with a tube of Burnt Coral. "It will go good with your skin tone," she said.

With her left hand she held my chin steady, and with her right she dabbed my lips with color. I felt a little bit important.

Phoebe stopped and examined her handiwork. "Just a smidgen more in the corners. Open your mouth. No, not that wide. I need to smooth the color, not inspect your tonsils."

She dabbed twice more, stepped back, and said, "Not bad, if I say so myself."

I looked in the mirror. I didn't want to hurt her feelings

but I thought she'd put too much on me. However, I could see that as I grew older, lipstick would become one of life's necessities. I said, "I put on some of Mama's powder but it looked awful. I don't think I can wear makeup."

"Everybody can wear makeup," Phoebe said, as if I'd said the dumbest thing yet. "But Mama's powder is far too dark. You need a lighter shade. Hold on, we've got to blot your lips." She disappeared into the bathroom and came out with a sheet of toilet paper. "Here. Press your lips on this."

I did, and I knew how because I'd watched Mama put her makeup on a thousand times. She always tossed aside the lipstick-smeared toilet paper, and I often went behind her and picked it up because, if you thought about it right, the crushed, red-tinted tissue made a perfect paper rose.

Phoebe cocked her head. "That's better," she said.

She held the mirror for me. "Wow! I look sort of grown up. The toilet paper really helped."

After that, I didn't move too quickly. At least not my head. The French twist caused me to feel top-heavy. Any sudden moves might cause my hair to tumble down. So when I walked through the trailer, it was with my shoulders back, my head high, as if I were some sort of society girl.

I was sitting on the couch, getting a stiff neck from holding my head so still, reading a library book, *Nellie Bly—Girl Reporter,* and fantasizing that I was brilliant and talented and in New York City taking that town's newspaper by storm, when Mama came home. She looked at me, half snorted, half laughed, and said, "Judas Priest."

Knowing I needed to get out of there, I closed my book

and asked if I could go outside. "Sure," she said, "but put on your sweater."

She handed me my green button-down with the deep pockets and moth holes.

Phoebe came out of the bedroom. "How do you like Bird's hair?"

"It's quite a 'do" is all she said. Then she knelt down and I backed away. Her hands scared me. "Come here, silly," she said. "I want to button you."

I stood stiff as a tin soldier. She ran her hands down my sides and said, "Huh, what's this?"

She put her hand in my pocket and withdrew a twenty-dollar bill. "Well, what do you know! Now where do you think this came from?"

I eyed the twenty. It was more money than I'd ever dreamed of owning. "I, I, I don't know!"

"You goddamn bitch! What are you doing? Stealing for her?"

"I swear to G-G-G-God, Mama. I d-d-didn't steal no money!"

"Twenty-dollar bills simply don't grow on the insides of pockets. You're going to march your fat ass down to the office right this second and return the money to Mr. Ippolito. You're going to apologize."

The tears flowed and so did my wailing pleas of innocence, but Mama had me trapped. She shoved the folding money back in my sweater pocket, spun me around, and pushed me out the door.

"You lying bitch. You think you're so smart. You look like a goddamn fool in that hair and makeup. Everybody who sees you is going to laugh." She clamped her hand on the back of my bare neck and pushed. Scared she might decide to choke me, I walked stiff and fast. The world was a blur.

We barged into the office. Mr. Ippolito was sitting behind the counter, reading the *Tampa Tribune*. He looked up over the paper.

Mama said, "Louis, this lousy excuse for a child has something to give you. She has done a terrible thing. Hand it over, Bird."

I took the money out of my pocket. I could barely breathe. I set the twenty on the counter.

"Tell him what you did."

"But I didn't—"

"Tell him!"

"I st-st-stole the money."

"I see," Mr. Ippolito said. He let the paper fall on the floor. His face lost all hint of good humor. He looked grim—that wrinkled brow, those mad eyes.

Please, God, don't let his sons see me like this.

"This is bad, little girl. Very, very bad."

He stood and shook his finger in my face. "You no allowed in this office no more! I see you here, I call the police. What a bad girl to put your mother through this. I no want to see you here again. Ever! You understand?"

I think I said, "Yes, sir," but there were so many sounds rushing through my brain that I couldn't clearly hear myself.

"Thank you, Glory Marie," he said. "This no could be easy for you."

"I'm real sorry, Louis. I don't know what got into her."

I began to back out the door. Mr. Ippolito was saying that if I was his daughter he'd give me a spanking.

"I'll give her worse than that."

By the time I was just outside the doorway, I realized my pants were wet. I was peeing in my pants.

"It's the influence of that colored woman."

Mr. Ippolito raised his palm in the air as a signal he didn't want to hear any more. I looked down at myself. Wet, stinking, foolish in that fancy hairdo and lipstick. Mama was right, I was worthless. I turned around and ran.

When I got back to the trailer I washed myself, scrubbed my face, took my hair out of the French twist, and put on clean pants. The entire time I heard a voice in my head. "I hate you, Mama. I hate you. I hate you."

I closed the bedroom door—didn't know where Phoebe was, maybe at the pool with L.J., maybe just hiding out—and got under the covers with one of my favorite Mrs. Piggle-Wiggle books. I loved Mrs. Piggle-Wiggle because she was kind and she was magic. She could help children see their way past their parents. And she could teach kids lessons about cruelty. Like one time she gave a mean child extra-sharp hearing so that he heard the insects scream when he stomped them.

Before long I heard the front door swing open, then those heavy footsteps down the hall. Mama busted into the bedroom, looking triumphant, as though she'd had a good time.

"Don't ever lie to me again, Bird. I always get even. And don't come out for supper tonight. You can starve, for all I care. If you know what's good for you, you'll stay in here and read your stupid book and cry your crocodile tears. But I'm warning you, I don't want to see your ugly face."

Then she walked out, slammed the door. Her words hung in the air like blades of broken glass.

I TRIED TO walk the straight and narrow after that. I quit Miss Zora—didn't have a choice, Mama had grown too crafty for me to stand up to her. It's as if her evil trick with that twenty-dollar bill had sucked away my spunk and courage. I cried to Phoebe about it, but she said I'd be doing Miss Zora a favor if I stopped seeing her.

"Bird," she said, "if you keep going over there, you'll just give Mama more fuel to light a fire under Mr. Ippolito about Miss Zora. And you don't want that, do you?"

"No, Phoebe," I said, "I don't want to cause her no trouble." I didn't even have the backbone to tell Miss Zora I couldn't see her anymore.

I became a shadow that trailed and trembled behind Mama. Mainly I felt only one emotion, and that was fear. Sometimes the fear was so great I couldn't breathe. Nothing bad had to be happening. I could be sitting still on the couch, drawing a picture or reading a book, and suddenly my throat would close up on me.

Mama decided it was asthma, said some kids just weren't born right. She bought me an inhaler. Instructed me to use it only when I really needed to because it was expensive medicine. But the Devil bent my ear. He convinced me to walk into the field and spray the inhaler until it was empty. Finding a way to defy her felt so good—it was as if somebody came along and unscrewed the lid of the firefly jar for a few minutes, gave me some fresh air.

When Christmas vacation was over with, I began going to school like clockwork. And in the afternoons, instead of visiting Miss Zora, I stayed in the trailer by myself and waited for Mama to come home. One cold afternoon in early January, I was sitting on the couch playing cat's cradle, when Mama walked in from work, poured herself a bourbon, and said Mr. Ippolito wanted to know if she'd punished me enough for stealing the money. As soon as the words were out of her mouth, my fingers got tangled up and my breathing shut down.

"Get your inhaler," Mama ordered.

As I gasped for breath, I managed to tell her that I'd been suffering terrible spells at recess and had used up all the spray.

"Well, that's just great, Bird," she said, "because we're down to our bottom dollar. I was trying not to tell you, but I guess I have to. Our government check is late. I guess it's because of these goddamn holidays. But if we don't get it soon we're going to be in dire straits. Now go outside and see if that helps."

Four days later Mama told me to put on my shoes, we were going over to May Ellen's Cafe and Truck Stop. I brightened. Maybe she was going to be kind and buy me a piece of pie. But no. Instead, we walked across the street and used the pay phone. Mama said she didn't want Mr. Ippolito knowing our business. She called the Social Security and Welfare office. After waiting in a cramped, dirty phone booth for what seemed like forever, Mama shouted over the traffic noise, "We never got our check!"

Some government secretary told her that if our money

didn't appear within the next two weeks, she needed to come in and fill out a form.

Day after day went by, and the postman brought nothing but junk mail and bills. Every afternoon, upon returning from the office, Mama started in on the Early Times, fretting over nickels, dimes, and our shrinking bank account. She visited the Nebraska Avenue Gun and Pawn, took me with her, and a burly man with a pistol on his hip gave her thirty dollars for her wedding band. Mama spent it all on booze and groceries. She bought me another inhaler. I felt so guilty that this time I did not waste it. There wasn't enough money left over to pay the electric bill. We went back to that pay phone, called Tampa Electric. Mama pleaded our case. They gave her three weeks to pay.

February arrived, cold winds and all, and still no check. We'd eaten the same pot of beans for well over a week, and what started as a thick bean soup made rich with ham hocks eventually thinned into onion tea.

It was during this time that Mama caught L.J. and Phoebe holding hands as they walked from the office to the trailer. Mama knew they were going steady—after he gave us a tree for Christmas, Mama told Phoebe he was a decent boy and that she approved of them seeing each other so long as it "didn't get too serious." But our money woes had eaten a hole in Mama's heart. She forgot everything sweet she'd ever said. She ordered Phoebe home. Standing right in the living room, she called her a slut, balled up her fist, and hit my sister square in the face. Busted the inside of her lip, must have banged against her teeth.

Phoebe stayed away from the trailer as much as she possibly could after that. Yes, she slept at home a few times a week, but that was about all. Her excuse was that she was studying in the library or staying over at a friend's. About three days after Mama had belted Phoebe over L.J., my sister—before she left for school—told Mama she would be home late, that she wouldn't be eating supper with us, she was doing research for a term paper. Mama called her a liar and slapped her. That was the last straw. Phoebe slapped her back. Mama cried all night long. Between shots of Early Times, she expressed utter disbelief that one of her children had hit her.

The third week of February, I came home from school and opened the refrigerator to see if there was anything to eat. The fridge wasn't running. I went into the bathroom to pee. I flipped on the light switch, but it was broken, too.

Mama came home, and I said, "Nothing's working."

"What the hell are you talking about, Bird? I don't need you causing me more trouble. Your sister called the office to say she was spending the night at Lori Flagg's. I don't have any idea what kind of family this Lori Flagg comes from. God, I curse the days you two were born."

Mama walked into the bathroom, and when the light didn't come on, she said, "Goddamn, son-of-a-bitch! Bird, do you know if we have any candles?"

Then she searched a kitchen drawer, cursed everything her fingers touched—a rusted bottle opener, a ball of twine, a can of WD-40, and, finally, a fat white long-burning candle.

The temperature dropped into the lower forties that night. Mama and I wrapped ourselves in blankets and, by candlelight, ate mayonnaise sandwiches. Mama opened a new bottle of Early Times and said for me not to read or do any homework, that I'd put my eyes out straining in the dim light.

I sat at the kitchen table and shuffled cards. Mama sat on the couch, drinking. We didn't speak. She was too busy brooding. I dealt myself five cards and came up with two jacks. I tried again, but this time nothing. I separated the entire deck into suits and ordered them by number, aces being the numeral one. Finally, when I couldn't think of anything else to do, I gathered my nerve and said, "Mama, I'm tired. I'm going to bed."

She set her whiskey glass on the coffee table, glared at me from across the room, and big tears suddenly rolled down her face. "Come here, Bird, I need to hang on to you."

There she sat—drunk and cold and, quite frankly, pitiful. She held out her arms. I looked at those violent hands. I did not move.

"Please, Bird, I need you."

The candle flickered wild shadows over us and the walls. I weighed my chances of getting slugged.

"Please, don't make me beg. You're all I've got."

I didn't want to be all she had. I didn't even want to be her daughter. My blood, poisoned with our family sins, turned hot, scorched my veins. Breathing was getting difficult. *I must be the worst daughter in the world not to want to comfort my mama.* Then I heard that voice inside my head. It said, "Go to her, Bird. You have to."

Slowly, I walked to the couch. Mama looked so weak. If I'd been of such a mind, I could have hit her. She reached for me. I took a deep gulp of air and sat. She threw off her blanket, wrapped her arms around me, and wailed so loud I was embarrassed.

She put her lips to my ear. "Your daddy lies," she whispered. "Don't ever believe a word he says. That's all he knows how to do is lie, lie, lie."

"Mama, go to sleep. You'll feel better if you get some rest."

She jerked away. Her skin smelled sour, as if she was rotting from the inside out. "You're just another snake," she said. "Billy Jackson made over."

I stood up, couldn't do this, but she grabbed my arm and pulled me back down. "No. No. Don't leave me. I'm scared. So scared. Nothing is right. My head is killing me."

Each of my bones—one by one—began to turn bitter. I thought, *This is not fair. I won't take care of her. No, I won't.* But then I paused and listened to myself. Jesus, I sounded like a spoiled brat. *Mama needs me. Be a good daughter. Do what's right. Overcome your spoiled ways.* "I won't go away, Mama," I said. "I promise. Let's lie down. That's good. Shut your eyes. Come on now." I lifted her feet and put them on the couch. I fluffed her pillow and ran my hand along her cheek. She quietly sobbed as I pulled the blanket up over her.

"Get me a drink," she said.

"No, Mama. No more drinks."

"Useless, you're goddamn useless." She gripped my face, grumbled something that didn't make sense, and then fell deeply asleep.

I waited until her snores became steady. Careful not to make a sound, I tried to ease off the couch. But the second I shifted my weight, her eyes flashed open, her fingers dug into my arm, and she said, "No. You stay."

SOMETIME DURING THE night, I managed to lie on the floor between the coffee table and the couch without waking Mama. I watched the candle flicker and listened as she jabbered in her sleep—on and off, over and over. Her words and sentences were jumbled—a grab bag of her various sufferings.

Despite her long night, Mama was up at dawn, drinking coffee, smoking cigarettes, making lists of numbers, adding them up, crossing them out. She asked me why I had slept on the floor.

I stammered, "I, I don't know." Explaining was out of the question.

Then she told me to hurry and get dressed, we were going downtown.

I asked, "What for?"

"We've got to get our money."

The drive into downtown Tampa took us about thirty minutes, and it was thirty minutes I savored because the Plymouth had a heater that could blow a person into the backseat when set to full blast. We drove through an area of Tampa I'd never seen. Signs were written in Spanish. Restaurants advertised their specials in their front windows—*boliche,* deviled crab, *fríjoles negras, café con leche, flan.* Too bad I wasn't Cuban—I could make some good food, and my hair would be jet black, like Mama's. We passed the

Catholic Services soup kitchen—a few homeless men stood huddled beside the door—and my heart busted with sadness because Miss Zora's truck was parked out front.

Mama said, "God, what an element. Bird, lock your door."

As we entered downtown, the buildings became taller, but still, bums, winos, and prostitutes outnumbered the businessmen in their shiny shoes who worked in the handful of gleaming new high-rises that shared the sky with dilapidated hotels and offices.

Mama said, "They keep talking about urban renewal, but they'd better put some money where their mouths are."

We sat at a red light on Ashley Boulevard, and I felt as if I were waltzing through a ghost world. No trees or flowers, but plenty of empty-eyed buildings that were so close to crumbling I imagined they were towers of dust. We crossed over the Hillsborough River, and to the right was a magnificent brick structure topped with silver domes that were shaped like Hershey's Kisses.

"Is that a palace? Is that where the mayor lives?" I asked.

Mama said it used to be a hotel for the very rich and that they'd since turned it into a university.

"I'd like to go there."

"Well, then, you'd better shape up and study."

I wanted to mouth off and say that she was the one who was keeping me out of school so that she didn't have to go by herself to the government office, but my good sense told me to can it.

Mama slowed the Plymouth and inspected a group of single-story concrete-block offices. "I think that's it," she said.

The heater was working so well that I was sweating. Mama turned on the blinker, and I sank down in my seat. I didn't want to visit any government office.

About five people stood outside, drinking coffee and smoking. But none of them was talking. And even though they obviously were not related, their faces were all veiled with the same mask of hopelessness—the white woman with a baby on her hip; the old Cuban man whose chest was caved in and whose skin hung on his bones like ancient paper; the worried black lady who felt her little boy's forehead for fever.

"Do we have to go in there?"

"Shut up, Bird. I'm doing my best."

We slammed our car doors, and I kept my eyes on the pavement as we walked past the people on the sidewalk. Once inside, Mama announced herself to the receptionist, who cut her off when she tried to explain our dilemma. The receptionist, a pale, fat white woman with eyes bluer than mine, handed Mama a plastic card with the number thirty-seven on it. Without ever looking at us, she snapped, "Take a seat. A caseworker will call you."

Mama and I turned around and tried to decide where to sit. "Come over here, Bird," Mama said, and she headed for two chairs in the corner.

The waiting room was filled with all sorts of people—men, women, white, Latino, black, old, young, newborn. There were fussing babies and fussing children, but other than to ask their kids to behave, the adults stayed quiet, mainly stared into space.

I punched my thigh. The pain felt good, familiar, not at all like Mama's punches.

We sat and sat, my butt grew numb. I nodded off a

couple of times, but when my chin fell onto my chest, I was jerked awake. A woman whose baby was coughing something awful—Mama said it was the croup—asked the receptionist how much longer before she got to see someone, she needed to get her baby back into bed.

The receptionist smartly flipped a page of the magazine she was reading and said, "Look, I've told you twice, they'll get to you when they can. If you didn't have time to wait, you shouldn't have come today."

The woman, sounding as if she'd just been slapped so hard she could barely speak, murmured, "I'm sorry. Thank you, ma'am." Then she sat down, clutched the baby to her chest, and rocked.

I squirmed in my seat and began to think things over. Maybe the rules for how to treat poor people were written in a government manual. It probably went something like: *Poor people stink. They ain't worth nothing. So treat them like they're shit on the bottom of your shoes. Stare at them coldly. Huff. Act as if their questions are stupid, even insane. When you hand them their official numbers, make sure your skin don't come in contact with theirs because God only knows where they've been and what they do behind the walls of their tar-paper shacks and tin-can trailers.*

I closed my eyes, and in my mind a caseworker, a skinny man with a white shirt and black tie, walked into the waiting room and said, "Everybody against the wall," and we dutifully shuffled over to the plastic partition, and then he gunned us down. He was following orders, a soldier in the War on Poverty. I opened my eyes. We all were still living, but I wondered what for. Hours passed, and not a single person was called by name. "Eighteen." "Twenty-four." "Thirty." At about eleven-thirty, the pace slowed even more. Mama said the caseworkers had probably started going to lunch. And I said, "Well, I'm hungry, too." So Mama got me some cheese and peanut-butter crackers out of the vending machine, and we shared a Co'-Cola.

A few minutes past noon, our number was finally up. Mama and I walked behind the partition, where we were greeted by a man who looked very similar to the gunman in my daydream. He did not say hello but, "Have a seat at the third desk from the water fountain."

We followed him. The room was lined with desks, case-workers, poor people mopping their brows and pleading their cases. The whole place seemed weighed down by file folders and stacks of official forms. Mr. Satler—that's what was printed on the nameplate on the third desk from the water fountain—settled into a swivel office chair and said, as he watched the papers in front of him, "Sit. What's your problem?"

Mama briefly explained that our problem was simple: we hadn't gotten our government check in almost three months, and he said, "Well, you must have moved. You must have done something wrong."

Mama's knuckles went white on that needlepoint pocketbook of hers. "No, sir. We're at the same address as when we first started receiving benefits. And we need that money. I'm a widow, raising two children. Our electricity has been turned off. We have no heat and very little food. I'm here to get this straightened out. My girls are hungry. Sir, I'm here for help because I really need it."

"You and the rest of the multitude," he said, patting a stack of file folders. He opened a drawer and removed a series of forms. Then he filled them in with answers Mama gave to his questions. Names, Social Security numbers, birth dates, Daddy's numbers and date of death, our address. It went on and on, the same questions and answers supplied for various government forms that, like us, were referred to by number only.

After about a half hour of questions and scribbles, Mr. Satler looked up from the paperwork and scowled. We might as well have been flies ruining his Sunday dinner. "I don't know what the problem is here," he said. "The government is not in the business of making mistakes. But whatever, you'll have your checks soon." He wiped his hands as if cleaning off our stench.

Then he stood, walked over to the plastic partition, and called, "Forty-one."

TWO WEEKS PASSED and, at long last, the postman brought good news. Our checks arrived, without explanation for the delay. Mama said it must have been a computer error. We got our electricity turned back on, and Mama filled our cupboards with food, but her mood did not brighten a whole lot. She hit the bottle with a regularity never before seen. And that liquor, it fed her anger. Behind Mr. Ippolito's back, she railed against him for being a fool and a bad businessman. She railed against

Phoebe for being a whore and an ungrateful daughter. She railed against me for being a lazy-assed liar.

If Phoebe wasn't at school, she was with L.J., at the library, or spending the night with her new friend, Lori Flagg. Yes, one or two nights a week I got the bed all to myself, but it didn't matter. I missed my big sister. And just as I'd predicted, with Phoebe out of the house as often as she could manage it, much of Mama's unwanted attention was heaped on me.

I tried to take her trash in stride. I was used to being called names and slapped for reasons only Mama knew. But the drunken ramblings that lasted all night forced *me* to act like the mama—comforting her, making her drinks, urging her to eat.

She would beg me not to leave her side, to pour her another drink, to tell her I loved her, to fix her bread soaked in milk to calm her sick stomach, to sit and hold her while she stumbled through her past in words that I could not cope with. She spoke of rapes, beatings—her daddy whipped her all the time—even a shooting. One night she opened her robe and unbuttoned her pajama top and exposed a startling white breast.

"Look here." She pointed to an ugly Frankenstein scar that ran from her collarbone, next to her armpit, down past her breast. "Somebody I knew before your father. I tried to leave him and the son-of-a-bitch shot me."

Then she cried and complained that her life was wasted. She should have left men alone, finished college, learned how to take care of herself. "But then I wouldn't have you." And she cried some more.

Even though I wasn't skipping school anymore, I was so tired after Mama's all-night crying jags that I took to falling asleep in class. Sometimes I would come home and take a nap. If Phoebe was around, I'd pester her into playing cards or running me through my vocabulary lists—anything to stay away from Mama. When Phoebe was spending the night at her friend's house, I'd fix supper and then wait in the cold, dark trailer for Mama to come home. I tried to act grown up. On those nights when Mama drank until she vomited, I'd offer broth and milk and soothing words. Sometimes she'd accept, but mostly she'd shove me and accuse me of trying to poison her. Then she'd say something like, "Child, just sit here with me. Just let me get my bearings."

One night when Phoebe was home, the two of us stayed in our bedroom. I was reading *Strawberry Girl*, by Lois Lenski. Phoebe was chewing her nails and boning up for a social studies test. Our door was closed and latched on our side—a few weeks before, Phoebe had installed a hook latch to keep Mama out, and, luckily, she hadn't noticed yet.

Mama was in the living room. We didn't know what she was doing—thought maybe she had passed out early because it was so quiet you could hear spiders crawling the walls. The silence was sweet. But it was not to last. Phoebe and I were just minding our own business, reading our books, when suddenly there was a rapid-fire series of crashes in the kitchen. I looked in the direction of the noise. Phoebe said, "Shit, what now?"

It sounded as if Mama was breaking everything we owned. But as fast as the commotion started, it stopped. Then Mama barreled down the hall. She tried to push open the door. "Unlock this goddamn door this second. How dare you lock me out! Open it! Open it!" She pounded and shook that door so hard I thought she was going to rip it off its hinges.

"Go away," Phoebe said, "and we'll unlock it."

"Oh you will, will you? Fine, I'm leaving."

We listened and counted. She always took seven footsteps between the kitchen and our room. But we counted ten, which meant she paused by the stove. Then we didn't hear anything else. Phoebe got off the bed.

"What are you doing?"

"I'm going out there," she said.

"No! She might beat you."

"Let her try."

Phoebe unhooked the latch and walked out. I didn't move.

"What's the big idea of locking me out?" Mama asked, slurring her words.

"I'm not locking anybody out. I simply want some privacy."

Mama snickered and said, "Listen, queen, get you and your sister's fat royal asses busy and clean this mess. Jesus, you make me sick!"

"Bird, get in here. Wear your shoes," Phoebe called. I slipped into my loafers. Then I started praying. *Don't let her beat me. Don't let her beat me.* I inched down the hall and stopped at the edge of the kitchen. The floor was littered with our Virginia Rose plates—all of them broken to smithereens. Phoebe handed me the dustpan. "I'll sweep, you scoop."

"I loved those dishes," Mama said, suddenly sounding as if she were a little girl. "But they weren't perfect anymore." She picked up a jagged piece, showed it to us as if she were presenting a ruby, then said accusingly, "It was supposed to be a service for eight."

She threw the shard at Phoebe, spun around, went and sat on the couch, lit a cigarette, poured a drink, and glowered at us silently the whole time Phoebe and I swept the floor.

When we finished, we went back to our room and re-latched the door. I put on my pajamas and whispered, "Mama's crazy."

"She certainly is," Phoebe said. She picked up a tube of Clearasil and studied her face in the dresser mirror.

"Phoebe, I don't think you should stay away from home so much. She scares me. Makes me stay up with her all night while she drinks. Tells me horrible stories. I can't stand it."

My sister turned away from the mirror, palmed the Clearasil, sat on the bed beside me. She gathered my hair in one long tail and then let it fall around my shoulders. "I'm sorry, Bird," she said, "but I can't. When you're older, you'll understand. I'm through with trying to make up to Mama. Now listen, if you get in trouble and I'm not around, go to L.J. He'll help you. And he always knows how to reach me."

I stared into her eyes—deep and dark and sad. I shook my head. "It ain't enough, Phoebe. And it ain't fair. I don't have anybody. I'm all alone."

I DON'T KNOW why, but my dreams that night were delightful—filled with visions of spring. Bees disappeared into the throats of ruby-colored flowers. The field was blanketed in a rainbow fog created by blossoming grasses—pastel shades of yellow, purple, pink. Baby birds cracked open their shells and drank sunlight. Newborn lizards circled my wrists—bright green bracelets, wiggling, tail to tail. Butterflies adorned my hair and sang songs in angelic, tiny voices. Watching over it all, as though she were a conductor of some fancy symphony, was my dear Miss Zora. She placed golden doves on my shoulders, turned storm clouds into snow-white petals. It was a dream I never wanted to wake from. *Let me stay here. Please, don't send me away.*

But of course, morning came, hurling me back to real life—my scary mama and my hard-faced Phoebe, avoiding each other, getting out of that trailer as fast as they could. Me, I stumbled out of bed, sat at the kitchen table, poured a bowl of Frosted Flakes, closed my eyes, replayed the dream. Yes, yes, what a wonderful world my sleep had created. I felt strong and able. Fear and rattlesnake-tail anger slipped my skin. I gazed into my cereal bowl. The sugary flakes glistened against the pearly white milk. I made a decision: I would not be alone. That afternoon—no matter what I risked in the doing—I would take up again with Miss Zora.

And that's exactly what I did. Nearly every day after school, Miss Zora's cottage once again became my haven, my safe place. She gave me free rein to have all the fun I wanted.

She taught me how to cook red beans and rice and meatless chili. Sometimes we went to the pond to check for avocets, but we never did see any. We located plenty of nests, though, belonging to sundry other birds. Yes, spring unfurled all around us, and not just in my dreams. I asked

Miss Zora questions about sex, and she answered me frankly, although some of her explanations were like staring into muddy water: "In a few years you will start your period. Once a month for almost the rest of your life, you will lay an egg. But you won't ever see it. It stays inside you until you fall in love and have sex with some good-looking fellow and he helps that egg to grow. Then a baby is born."

Amazing news to me. I said, "Mike Mikulski at school says girls get pregnant when they French-kiss. He says the end of the boy's tongue falls off and the girl swallows the tongue bit and that's what stays in her belly and becomes a baby."

When Miss Zora finished laughing she said, "Lord God, child, you're funny. No. That's not how it happens."

Come April, it was warm enough to swim again. I decided to learn how to dive. L.J., like Hank, could leap from the board and touch his toes, spin in the air, and all sorts of things. He and Phoebe went swimming together when Mama wasn't home—like when she went grocery shopping or to a parent-teacher conference at one of our schools. Sometimes they made out in the pool.

L.J., he had a good heart: he knew I didn't steal that money and he offered to teach me how to dive. He suggested we first try a jackknife because it looked "aces" but was not real difficult.

Easy for him to say. My body did not know how to flow. It held no grace. I excelled at only one kind of dive—the belly flop.

But what I lacked in style I made up for in stubbornness. I would follow L.J.'s instructions, concentrating, practicing, listening. However, every time I left the board and rose into the air, my body would twist and get tangled in itself.

When I hit the water, sometimes the sting was so bad I'd stay at the bottom of the pool, trying to get over the hurt. L.J.'s and Phoebe's laughter would echo down through the depths, wounding me further.

During this time, a boy and his daddy stayed at The Travelers for about a whole month. Mr. Roberts and his son, Jeff, were mourning the loss of Mrs. Roberts, who had died of breast cancer. When Mr. Roberts said, "Cancer stole my wife from her son," Mama said, "God certainly knows how to inflict pain," and Mr. Roberts said, "Amen!"

Jeff was nine—two months older than me—and should have been in school, but his daddy said his mama's death had been so traumatic for the boy that Jeff was taking the rest of the year off. The two of them were slowly making their way from Sarasota to Atlanta. "We're going to throw ourselves on the mercy of that fair city—capital of the South," his daddy explained to Mama one afternoon when we were sitting at the concrete picnic table under the blue aluminum umbrella by the pool. "But my son and I are going to indulge in some R and R before we jump back into the thick of life."

I'd never met another kid with a dead parent. I thought we would be immediate pals. But as Mr. Roberts went on telling Mama about how he knew someone who lived in Atlanta who was going to try to get him a job at the airport fueling planes—evidently that's what the friend did for a living—I said to Jeff, "My daddy has been dead eight months. It's creepy, not having him around."

"So what if your daddy is dead?" Jeff said. "Who

cares?" Then he shoved me, and Mr. Roberts snapped, "Straighten up and fly right, boy."

One other thing we had in common is that Jeff liked the pool, too. That's where we got to know each other, where he tried to act tough, telling me he never thought about his mother. I figured he was lying. And even though I gave him the benefit of the doubt about his feelings for his mama, he proved to have a bad temper. But I proved I knew what to do with it.

The motel was near to empty because it was a Wednesday, so there weren't any weekend travelers clogging up the place. The weather was gorgeous—mid-eighties, sapphire skies. Earlier, during a math quiz in school, when my mind kept wandering and the teacher kept saying, "Remember, there are no second chances in arithmetic. Each problem has one—and only one—correct answer," I decided not to visit Miss Zora's that day, and hit the pool instead. As soon as I came home, I changed into my swimsuit and braided my hair into two Indian-maiden braids. I had the pool all to myself, which left me free to practice my various water talents without anybody laughing at me. I was concentrating on holding my breath underwater while performing a handstand—L.J. said holding your breath underwater was good for your lungs. According to Phoebe and L.J., my handstands were about the best they'd seen anybody do. The secret was in my pointed toes.

So there I was, headfirst in that chlorine-drenched water, my eyes open and stinging, and I began to walk around on my hands, which is more difficult than it might sound. My feet, which of course were above the water, felt disconnected from me, and I was thinking how funny it would be if I were in a horror show and my legs suddenly took off in the opposite direction of my in-the-water parts, when I bumped into Jeff. He had sneaked into the pool and intentionally blocked my way. I came up sputtering. He sneered at me and said girls couldn't do anything right.

"Let's see *you* do a handstand!"

"Handstands are for sissies!"

"No they ain't! You're the sissy."

"Only crackers say 'ain't'!"

" 'Ain't' is in the dictionary, stupid!"

I turned my back to him and swam to the other side of the pool. I didn't want to talk to him, some boy who didn't make sense. But he followed right behind me. I started to spin around and yell at him not to bother me anymore, when he reached over, grabbed one of my braids, and yanked as hard as he could.

"Ouch!" I shouted, and the next thing I knew, Jeff was dunking me. The little weasel. I dug my nails into his arms, wrestled free, gulped oxygen.

He taunted, "Who's the sissy now?"

"Don't dunk me again."

"You don't scare me. You're a girl. Girls aren't worth mud." And he spit in the pool.

I raced through my options. Mama would probably have a fit if I whipped him, so I really had only one choice and that was to ignore him. I got out of the water and walked over to the slide—it had a fast left curve that I loved. When no one was watching, I'd shoot down headfirst, despite a sign at the foot of the ladder saying NO HEADFIRST SLIDING. But I played it safe with Jeff around because I knew a tattletale when I saw one. I slid down on my butt, and when I hit the water with a loud splash, Jeff called me Moby Dick.

I started to say, "Sticks and stones can break my bones but words—" when he dunked me again and this time held me under longer than before. When I came to the surface, I screamed, "I'm warning you. One more time and I'll have to slug you. Leave me alone!"

"You couldn't beat me up even if both my hands were tied behind my back. Take this, carrot-top!" He grabbed my braids and tugged hard.

"That hurt!" I yelled.

Then he dunked me for the third time. We fought underwater like a couple of crocs. He was trying to stop me from coming up; maybe he was trying to kill me. His face was white but red around the edges, and there was some gnashing of teeth.

A righteous anger boiled through me. I didn't deserve to be called names or have my braids yanked or be dunked and drowned. I came out of the water swinging. "I warned you, you asshole!" Then I punched him hard, landing a right hook into his eye.

His cocky smirk gave way to shock, then pain. "You hit me, you hit me!" He burst into tears.

My daddy's voice trumpeted across the sky: "The Devil ain't nothing but a sissy in wolf's clothes."

Jeff held a hand to his eye and, like a half-blind old man, wobbled out of the pool, using the stairs and handrail. Between his tears, as he ran away, he said, "I'm going to tell my daddy!"

I felt pretty good after that. I swam for a while longer, practiced my underwater somersault—my reverse spin was a little wobbly—and thought about L.J.'s perfect diving technique. "Visualize the dive, Bird," L.J. had told me. "See it in your head as you jump." I closed my eyes and envisioned myself pulling off a flawless jackknife: My body, arrow straight, springs from the board, lifts up, up, up. The skin and fat and heavy bones of my body fly away. In the air, I am a graceful being—winged, light.

With my hopes and confidence high, I got out of the pool, walked over to the diving board, and climbed the ladder. The sun shone brightly and cast jeweled shadows across the water. I stood still and calm, shoulders back, dripping wet. *Visualize the dive.* I did. I did. One, two, three, step, up, into the air, high and free—the entire world was blue. My legs were straight, my toes pointed. I touched my feet—the folded knife. Then I unhinged my body—the flashing, dangerous knife. This was it, the perfect dive, the moment you feel you are flying. The ladder sliced past my eyes. Close, awfully close. Why was I facing the ladder? Before I could twist away, my chin slammed into the board.

My head snapped back, and pain seared through my jaw. Like a chunk of concrete, I dropped to the bottom of the pool. The crystal-clear water grew murky, black, and cold. I lay crumpled—a fleshy sack of bones. I tried to breathe and took in water. I felt my mind spiral to the surface, saw it hover in the bright air, watching, whispering, "No," to the black stuff seeping into my veins. "Swim, Bird. You have to swim."

I tried to move my legs. A warm current pushed at the cold. An invisible hand grabbed my heart, lifted me through the crushing water. I broke the surface. Oxygen rushed down my throat. I felt the hand fly away, thought I heard the rush of wings. Something flowed down my chin. Bright red blood.

I swam to the side of the pool and, belly down, clambered out. I ran to the trailer, crying, blood dripping down my neck. I flung open the door and stumbled in. Mama turned around from the stove. She said, "Goddamn it, Bird, what have you done now?"

"I, I, I fell at the pool. Hit my jaw really hard."

Mama sat me down at the kitchen table and put a washrag on the wound, told me to hold it firm. "Press hard, Bird. I know it hurts, but the pressure will stop the bleeding."

She went into the bathroom and came out with a box of gauze bandages, scissors, tape. "I told you to be careful over there. You are so careless and clumsy.

"Let me see," she said. "Lucky you're so hardheaded. Otherwise, you'd have a cracked skull."

She poked at the cut, and I flinched. "This one is going to need a butterfly bandage."

"Butterfly bandage?" I asked. In my mind's eye, I saw myself walking around The Travelers with a butterfly stuck to my chin, working its wings.

"It's a certain kind of bandage. Helps close the wound so the skin can knit. If it doesn't work, we'll have to take you to get stitches and—"

"We can't afford that." I finished her sentence.

She told me to stand by the sink and hold my head over it. I did, and she poured peroxide into my split skin. The medicine flowed in a cold, ticklish stream.

Then Mama sat me back down at the kitchen table and went about trying to fix me with that white tape. "The dive, Mama, except for me hitting the board, was my best one yet."

"Bird, I don't want you on that diving board when there's nobody there to supervise you," she ordered.

I thought about protesting and then decided it would be in my best interests to keep quiet. But I did say, "You know, Mama, it felt like somebody put their arms around me and lifted me out of the water."

"Nonsense. Your body does those sorts of things when it's in shock. You mind doesn't work right—imagines all kinds of stuff—so your body takes over."

"Oh. Too bad." I pictured an angel wrapping her wings around me and ferrying me into the air.

As soon as Mama was finished fixing me, I looked at myself in the bathroom mirror. The bandage really did resemble a crisp white butterfly. "I will take very good care of you," I whispered.

When I came out of the bathroom, I asked Mama, who was dicing an onion, how she learned to fix cuts.

"I told you, Bird, that a long time ago, way before I met your father, I went to nursing school. But my first husband didn't want me improving myself. Said I belonged at home. So I quit."

She slammed down the knife and stared straight ahead, out the living room window, but I couldn't say what she was actually gazing at. "Jesus," she said, "that was a wasted lifetime ago."

Then she swung her gaze to me. "What are you looking at?"

"N-n-n-nothing."

She sat me down on the couch with two Bufferins, a glass of water, and my math book. "Sit there and do your homework. The Bufferins should make you feel better."

I tried to add up long rows of numbers, but my chin throbbed and I found myself gingerly touching my bandage, over and over.

Mama's potato-and-onion stew was simmering on the stove, and she was relaxing at the kitchen table, having a cigarette and a beer, when there was a firm knock at the trailer door. Mama arched an eyebrow, obviously irritated at the intrusion. She set her cigarette in the round-bottomed tin ashtray and opened the door. "Mr. Roberts, what a surprise."

Oh, shit. This was trouble. I dropped my number two pencil into the spine of my math book. *Dear Jesus, make me invisible.* With all my might, I wished that I'd dissolve into a handful of crumbs and sift into the space between the couch cushions. If Jesus could turn water into wine, I reasoned, He could stuff me into the far corners of this scratchy hunk of furniture.

"I hate to be the bearer of bad news, Mrs. Jackson, but I have no choice. Jeff, come here. You remember my son, don't you, Mrs. Jackson? Well, ma'am, I'd like for you to take a look at what your daughter did to him."

"My, that's quite a shiner. Bird, get over here."

Goddamn it. One more unanswered prayer. Sheepishly, I got off the couch, then cowered behind Mama so I couldn't be seen.

"Mr. Roberts, hold on. It's good you're here. Bird, get out from behind me. Sir, I'd like you to take a look at what your son did to my little girl."

I came out of hiding, not believing what just tumbled from Mama's lips. A polite defiance lit her face and, like a family disease, it spread to mine. I took a gander at Jeff Roberts. Mama was right, it was quite a shiner. Jeff met my eyes once and then glared at his shoes. He knew he'd lost. Big time.

"I'm so sorry, Mrs. Jackson. I had no idea. Do I need to pay the doctor bill? Is she all right?"

"No need, Mr. Roberts. I took care of her. She's fine. I think that eye of his, though, could use some ice."

"Of course. I'm sorry to have bothered you. Jeff, say you're sorry."

I gazed at him from my pious perch.

"Sorry," he growled, and stuffed his fists into his pants pockets.

"Children, they are always up to something," Mr. Roberts said weakly, and he managed a rubber smile. Then he grabbed his son by the shoulders and marched him out of our yard. I heard him say, "What did I tell you about hitting girls!"

Mama slammed the door, and we both started giggling. Mama said, " 'Well, ma'am, I'd like for you to take a look at what your daughter did to him.' "

We howled with laughter, and Mama went on mimicking Mr. Roberts. " 'I hate to be the bearer of bad news.' 'Do I need to pay the doctor bill?' " Then she called him a stuffed shirt.

I said, "That Jeff will think twice before messing with me again."

But even through our laughter, I was having a serious thought: This was so much fun. Mama had taken up for me. We were behaving like buddies. Why couldn't Mama be on my side more often?

As our giggles slowly eased off, Mama tossed her hair out of her eyes and said, "You shouldn't be hitting people, Bird."

"I know, Mama. But he deserved it. He kept dunking me and pulling my braids. I warned him. Three times!"

Mama nodded, but I could see our good time was ending. Her face hardened. The tough years of her life lined up in anxious rows of wrinkles and knots. "Okay. Now go finish your homework."

I settled back into the couch and stared at the gibberish of my math book. Mama said to no one in particular, "I didn't like that man from the moment he walked into the office."

Instead of scribbling rows of numbers, I drew doodles—big sweeping circles—and thought about what I'd last read in the Bible, how Esther was good and just and some fellow named Haman who was full of evil wreaked havoc all over the place. Seemed he didn't like Jews, especially someone named Mordecai. So Esther and the king solved the whole damn problem by sending Haman to the gallows.

That's what Mama and I had done to Jeff. I wrote in big block letters, TO THE GALLOWS. But beside it I wrote, FORGIVENESS? I mulled over those eleven letters for a few minutes but then scratched them out. Forgiveness was too complicated. That's what was good about a wrathful God: simplicity. You were good or evil. Cursed or blessed.

I looked at Mama. She was spinning the ashtray, lost in thought. We'd had a breakthrough. In the face of accusation, she had stuck by me, even lied for me. But then a chill clamped down on my bones as I realized what was wrong with a wrathful God. He could change His mind at whim, justifying His swift, crafty moves with rules He made up as He went along, rules that changed without warning. Sending floods. Cursing brothers. Painting rainbows.

"How's that homework coming?" Mama asked as she slapped a hand on the ashtray to halt its spin.

"I'm almost finished," I lied. Then I drew a picture of God. I bore down hard, nearly ripped the paper. A circle, a planet, dark and dense. Yes, a black hole. Not a speck of light. Sucks you in. Never lets you out.

THE NEXT DAY at school, children gathered around to admire my butterfly bandage. I decided to expand Mama's fib. Not only did I suffer my wound in a fight with a boy, I'd given him a black eye and busted his lip.

Mary Louise Alvarez, a prissy girl whose daddy had a lot of money, so she was always wearing the very latest in fine cotton and ribbons, said, "You white trash people fight constantly."

I looked at her, with all her starched clothes that matched—a white cotton blouse with a blue lace collar, and a blue plaid pleated skirt—and I said, "Yeah. And rich folks like you ain't never going to get through the gates of heaven because God hates snobs."

As soon as I got home from school, I visited Miss Zora. Took Old Sam with me. I don't think he got much attention at home, because nearly every afternoon he was waiting for me outside the trailer. The two of us walked the back way, through the field, to Miss Zora's, and she seemed pleased to see us. I told her all about the fight and the dive, except I told her the truth, even admitted I was scared to get back on that diving board.

Miss Zora fixed us a pot of blackberry tea and she laughed a raspy full-throated laugh when I told her what Mama had said to Mr. Roberts.

We sat outside to catch the afternoon light. Old Sam curled up by my feet. I asked her why she had a sock tied around her neck, and she said, "To keep away the sore throat that's been chasing me."

"Oh."

"About that diving business," Miss Zora said, and she reached over and squeezed my arm. "My mama, who was a very smart woman, taught me that the only way to conquer fear is to pick it up and stare it in the face."

I leaned over and pulled a sticker out of Old Sam's fur. "What do you mean?"

"Miss Avocet, do you like to dive?"

"Yes, ma'am. Makes me feel, I don't know, as if I don't have any troubles. From the second I step off that board to when I come up out of the water and breathe air, things are fine right then."

"Come over here. Let me see your chin in this good light."

Miss Zora tilted my head and studied me. She made noises as if she were a squirrel foraging for nuts and finding exactly what she wanted. "Your mama did a fine job. You're going to be healed in no time flat. Now, you might not want my advice, but I'm going to give it to you anyhow, and it won't cost you a dime. Try it again, Miss Avocet. Get back on that board and dive right past your fear. Otherwise, it will grow bigger and bigger every day until finally when you look in the mirror you won't see Avocet Abigail Jackson. You'll be looking at some other little girl, someone who has lost her way."

THAT NIGHT, PHOEBE didn't come home for supper, and Mama said she was going to have to do something about my sister's rebellious behavior. Mama stood at the stove, watched our boiling-bag dinners boil, sipped Early Times out of a coffee mug. Then she said, "Phoebe's not like us, Bird. There is many a day I can't believe that girl came from my womb."

I kept my mouth shut, didn't like the game—Mama playing Phoebe and me against each other. I was smart enough to know that there wouldn't ever be any winners in a game based on mean-heartedness. I picked up my English book and pretended to read.

Using a pair of tongs, Mama plucked the boiling bags from the water and set them on the counter. "I found out today why Louis takes up for your friend," she said. She turned off the stove. "Seems she helped him out when he was in a financial bind—actually loaned him money—and then did something to scare off the people who put him in the bind. He thinks she threw a spell on them. I think they went away because they got what they wanted. Anyhow, seems there's more to Miss Zora than we know." She put two pieces of bread in the toaster. "Go wash your hands."

I shot into the bathroom like a streak of lightning. I didn't know if Mama's words about Miss Zora were well intended or not. And her mood was too shaky for me to find out. "Please, God, make Mama stop drinking, at least for tonight," I said to the mirror. I turned on the faucet, let the hot water burn me all the way up to my elbows.

"What are you doing in there?" Mama yelled. "Your supper is getting cold. Get your ass out here and eat."

When I came out of the bathroom, supper was on the table, served on avocado-green plastic plates Mama had scrounged out of the garbage. We were having creamed chipped beef over toast. I hated boiling-bag suppers, but the worst was the creamed chipped beef. It tasted like salted cardboard wrapped in pus sauce.

I poked at the food. Mama could see I didn't care for it. "Eat!" she ordered. Then she got up and poured herself another whiskey.

"What do you think about your high-and-mighty sister staying away from us?" she asked as she sat back down.

"Don't know."

"Well, let me ask you this. What about Miss Zora? Maybe we ought to invite her over. You spend so much goddamn time with her, anyway. Shit, you act like you love her more than you love me. Do you, Bird?"

"No, ma'am."

"No, ma'am, what?"

"No, ma'am, I don't love her more."

Mama gulped her liquor, wiped her mouth on her paper napkin, and said, "What's wrong? Why aren't you eating? You too good for this food?"

"No, ma'am."

"Then what's the problem? Tell me, Bird. Listen, you start acting like your big sister, looking down your nose at everything I try to do, thinking you're too good to live with me, you're going to find yourself out on the street.

Maybe your wonderful Miss Zora will take you in. But don't count on it."

I stared at my plate and said, "There's nothing wrong, Mama."

"The hell there isn't!" she shouted. She grabbed my plate, threw it across the room, shoved back her chair, and stood. She chugged the rest of the liquor, slammed down the mug, and said, "You've had this one coming for a long time, little girl." She grabbed me by my hair and pulled me into the bedroom.

"No, Mama, please, I'm sorry, I'm sorry." I looked at Mama straight on. *Face your fear.* "I didn't do anything wrong, Mama. The food is good. I swear. Let's just go back and finish supper."

She tugged at my shirt. "Get this goddamn thing off. Now!" We struggled and twisted as I fought to stay clothed. She called me a bitch, grabbed the front of the shirt at the neckline, then ripped it off.

Embarrassed and scared, I covered my chest. I didn't want her looking at my two bare mounds where titties would eventually grow.

She slapped me across the face. I did not see it coming.

"You're no damn good!" She reached for Phoebe's wide hip-hugger belt hanging from a nail on the back of the bedroom door. "Take off what's left of that ridiculous blouse. It's too tight for you, anyway, you fat bitch. Look in the mirror. Do as I say. This is one beating you're going to watch."

I did as I was told. Rage careened through me, kept me steady, kept my fear alive and bouncing. This anger was permanent. No amount of baptismal water was going to snuff it out.

Mama raised her arm and swung the belt. It whizzed through the air like a striking snake. I heard myself grunt as the leather bit into my skin. My skin felt as if I'd been bee-stung, then knife-slashed. Before my grunt could grow into a scream, I felt something else, something cold and hard, nearly a fist. *My God, she's beating me with the buckle end; she ain't holding anything back.*

"Stop, Mama. Stop!"

I watched myself mouth the words, heard my voice mushroom, felt it stain the trailer's dark, paneled walls. The air grew misty with blood. One blow after another, endless, as I saw my face cave in and the butterfly bandage work its stiff wings.

"Holler all you want," Mama snarled as the belt tore into me. "It won't do any good, Bird, because there's no one close enough to hear. You're nothing but a lying sack of shit. It's no wonder your father is dead. He couldn't stand the rotten likes of you. He'd be alive today if it weren't for you!"

I spun around, and the belt buckle caught me beside the eye. "No, Mama! I did not kill my daddy! I did not! I did not! I did not!"

Mama dropped the belt to her side. She shut her eyes. The energy seemed to ooze right out of her. "Stay away from me, Bird. Just stay away. Listen here. See if you can't get one goddamn thing right. I'm going to go for a long drive. When I come back, you'd better have thought of a way to make up for all the suffering you've caused. If you can't do that, if you can't appreciate what I can give you, then get your fat ass out of this trailer and don't ever come back."

She dropped the belt on the floor and walked out of the

room. I collapsed in the corner, stayed there, shivering. I heard her grab her car keys, heard the front door open and close.

As I huddled in the darkness, I saw the future: In minutes, the Plymouth would crank and I'd listen as she backed out onto the drive. I would stand and glance over my shoulder, looking at my back in the mirror's reflection. I would see blood mixed with strings of flesh. I would put on clothes—two heavy sweaters—one to soak up the blood, the other to keep me warm. I'd slip on my tennis shoes. I'd raid the change jar Mama kept in the kitchen cabinet behind the salt and flour. Yes, I would rise up out of that corner. And I would disappear.

I LEFT THE Travelers Motel and headed south on Nebraska Avenue, toward town. It was a clear night, and I was glad that there were plenty of stars. I had considered crossing the road and seeing if the door was unlocked at the Triumphant Church but then I thought, *Who are you fooling? God has forsaken the likes of you.* Then I thought I might cross the road and buy a piece of pie at the truck stop. Maybe I could catch a ride with a trucker to Somewhere, U.S.A.

But I did not. There seemed to be too much road between me and May Ellen's. I wasn't moving too fast because my back hurt real bad. Better, I decided, just to walk a straight line.

I saw a lot of sights. Homeless people. I had to step over one. A black man with an Afro bigger than my face asked me for change. I gave him a quarter, and he said, "God bless you, baby." Women wearing spike heels and short skirts hung on the street corners and stared into the night, their faces painted with such hopelessness that they reminded me of my daddy. In my mind, I saw his suicide face, him gazing upon the black waters of Moccasin Branch and finding no peace. *Don't think about him,* I told myself. *Just keep walking.* I hurried by Nebraska Avenue Gun and Pawn, then Camp Nebraska, a travel-trailer park with small cabins and a split-log sign painted in ribbons of green, yellow, red. I passed neon-lit storefronts bragging that they had live models. To my way of thinking, that was a helluva lot better than dead ones. A blaze of lights polished the distance. I imagined a cemetery of fallen stars. *How pretty,* I thought. *That's where I need to be—wherever that glow is.*

I looked at the street sign: Lotus Avenue. Then I gazed again at that faraway glow, stepped off the curb, started to cross over, but those distant lights held my attention too well. I walked into the path of oncoming traffic. The world turned into a blur. Horns honked, Mama's hate played in my ears, a red Pontiac swerved. The driver, a man who looked so clean he probably worked in one of those new glass skyscrapers that were rising amid the ruins of downtown, yelled, "Watch where you're going, you little fool!"

Tears welled; I stumbled, but finally reached the other side. I squatted on the sidewalk and covered my eyes. Goddamn it! *Bitter is the girl who is forsaken,* I thought.

Bitter is the girl who is tired of being a little fool. A voice filled my head, a voice unlike the one that had whispered comforting words to me these past few months: "Don't you wish you were dead!"

I pounded my knees. "No! No! No!" I cried. I didn't want to be like my daddy. Was that why Mama beat me? Because he and I shared an evil streak? Someone drove by in a Mustang and threw a beer can. It landed at my feet.

"Assholes!" I yelled. A night bird started singing. A white Buick drove by. Latin rhythms from its stereo mingled with the night bird's song. I stood up—my back felt on fire—and kicked the beer can. What in the hell was I going to do? I couldn't spend the night on the street corner, feeling sorry for myself. I looked behind me. Did I want to turn around and go home? When Mama got back to the trailer, she'd be drunk and tired. She'd go to bed. She wouldn't hurt me anymore, not tonight. But no, I had to go on, had to see what was ahead of me. What lived in the beauty and glare? I did not want to die.

So I walked on, but for how long I do not know. Time had been shattered by something strong, something that could crush you with its hate. I fixed my gaze on the haloed distance, and when I arrived, I discovered not fallen stars but red and white marquee lightbulbs that spelled, in no uncertain terms, Diamond Lil's Saloon.

The only saloon I knew about was the one on "Gunsmoke," run by that nice lady Miss Kitty. She was decent, always gave Matt Dillon and Doc good advice. Maybe Diamond Lil was Tampa's answer to Miss Kitty.

Parked in front of the saloon was an angled row of Harley Davidsons. Lined up as they were, the motorcycles looked like a dinosaur's backbone. And then I thought,

Wouldn't it be wonderful if these bikes suddenly turned into horses? All saloons had horses out front. And the bikers—I could see them barreling out of the saloon wearing cowboy hats and six-guns. They'd be yelling things like "Yippy-ti-yi-o!"

I looked away from the Harleys and to that impressive sign. I cracked my knuckles, tried to ignore the pain in my back, wondered if I had the courage to go in. Kids weren't allowed in saloons, not even on "Gunsmoke." But if Diamond Lil was anything at all like Miss Kitty, she wouldn't be cruel to me, wouldn't have it in her. I told the voice inside me that had wished me dead to go to hell. I had to believe in possibilities.

Clicking the nickels in my pocket, I walked toward the door. I read the instructions nailed to the wall next to the entry: NO MINORS. NO FIGHTING. NO SPITTING. NO BYOB.

"I promise not to fight or spit." There wasn't anything I could do about being a minor, and I didn't know what BYOB meant. Maybe I could sneak in and locate Diamond Lil before anybody threw me out.

I slapped a gnat off my arm. The door opened. Juke music spilled into the cool air. I jumped into the bushes that edged the building.

"Okay, man, very good. We'll catch you next time."

A big fella with a long, blond, curly beard and his hair in a ponytail stood on the walkway by the door, looked up at the sky, and took a deep breath as though he was trying to inhale the stars. Then he stepped over to the bushes, unzipped his pants, pulled out his turtle, and started to pee.

Oh my God! I was scared and furious in equal doses. What gave him the right to pee in public? Weren't there bathrooms in Diamond Lil's? I looked at his splatter and realized it was forming a stream that was flowing directly toward my tennis shoes. I tried to move away without making a sound but stepped on a stick, and it cracked like a firework. I eyed the flowing stream. Time was running out. I had to do something, so I muttered, "Stop that right now."

"Jesus fucking Christ!" the man said. He backed away from the bushes. His eyes were wide, as if he were expecting a talking bear to leap out. He put his turtle back in his pants and zipped up, but never quit watching the bushes. He rested his hands on his hips, whistled low and long between his teeth. Then he reached over and parted the branches.

There wasn't anything else for me to do. I looked at him straight on and said, "Hey. You're not supposed to pee in public."

He chuckled, stroked his beard. "Well, hey yourself. But let me tell you, little lady, where I pee is my own damn business. The bigger question is, what are you doing?"

"Nothing."

"I'd say hiding in the bushes by a strip joint ain't nothing."

"Strip joint?"

"Yeah. Where ladies take off their clothes and—never mind."

"You mean like ribbon dancing?"

"I guess you could call it that." He spit on the ground and said, "I've got to give up chewing tobacco. Turns my teeth brown." He grinned for me. "See?"

"Yes."

"You here looking for somebody?"

"No."

"Then what, pray tell, are you doing in the bushes outside a pussy house?"

Reading this man was difficult because of all that hair on his face. His eyes reminded me of my daddy's. Blue and, by turns, kind and thunderhead-wild. He wore a black Daytona Beach Bike Week T-shirt. He was tattooed. There was an anchor on his right forearm, and on his left biceps there appeared to be a hula girl. I pointed at it. "Can I see that?"

"What? This?" He looked at his arm. "Yeah, sure." He rolled his sleeve over his bulging arm muscle. It *was* a hula girl. Bare-breasted.

"Lookie here," he said. He flexed his biceps. Up, down, up, down, up, down, and damn if that grass-skirted lady didn't shimmy! I touched his arm where the hula skirt shook.

"I'm running away from home," I said.

He let her shimmy two more times, then rolled his sleeve down. "Why's that?"

"My mama. She hates me."

He felt around by his ear and pulled out two toothpicks, the sort you get in restaurants—individually wrapped. "Want one?"

"Yes." I took it from him. He smelled like exhaust and salt. I tore away the cellophane, stuck the pick under my tongue. The point was sharp. I was glad this was round and not one of those flat types. I hated the flat ones. They set my teeth on edge.

He rolled his toothpick from the side of his mouth to the front and back again, didn't say anything. Neither did I. But I huffed, as I was getting tired of standing in the bushes. He took the toothpick out of his mouth and pointed it toward the row of motorcycles. "See that bike over there? Third one in, '58 panhead? I know grown men who'd cry like babies to own one of them. She's a sweet piece of steel, legend in her own time. Spent all my IRS money and emptied my bank account to buy her. She's all I own. 'Cept for the clothes on my back. Yep." He stared at the sky. Hitched up his pants. "My name is Al. Big Al. Want to go for a ride?"

I stepped out of the bushes. "I ain't never rode on one before."

He turned away and started toward his motorcycle. "I'm guessing that's a yes," he said over his shoulder, and I thought, *Man, he's so big he could be a wrestler.*

"Hey, wait up," I said. "My name is Bird."

"Nice to meet you, Bird."

I ran over to him. "I think my daddy had a bike like yours. Won it on a bet."

"Sounds like a lucky man." He tossed me a helmet. "I've got three rules, sweet thing: hang on, no screaming."

"What's the third one?"

"No screaming, again. It counts twice."

THAT NIGHT, WE chased the stars. Big Al would point to a constellation, and then he'd aim the Harley in its direction. I hung on tight and stared at the sky as best I could. The rumble and roar of the bike was far more intense than a ride in Daddy's white Impala, and the wind rushing over me was so cold and pure that I thought I heard it whispering the true name of heaven.

We rode fast and long. Sometimes Big Al leaned into a curve as if he was thinking about swallowing up a piece of the road, but then he brought her straight again and I could feel the vibration in his back muscles. He was laughing, kicking up stardust and laughing.

We rode past the skyscrapers of downtown, past the hotel-turned-school with its Hershey-kissed domes, past the government check office, straight down the worn-out spine of Kennedy Boulevard, and then over the Howard Franklin Bridge. I'd never been on the Howard Frankenstein, as most folks called it, but I'd heard a lot of bitching. I guess this wasn't the best bridge in the world, but it was the main link between Tampa and St. Petersburg—stretching over Tampa Bay like a long gray tongue—so it bore a lot of traffic. Maybe it was because I was on a motorcycle, but I enjoyed riding across the bridge.

Night birds appeared suddenly, flashing past like ghosts in the headlight's glare. Moonlight shimmered on the water's surface as if it were its own being, wholly separate from its source, not a reflection but a golden animal riding the everlasting swells of the bay.

As we rose to the bridge's crest, Big Al pointed to the left. There she was: the moon—full and round and radiant—resting low in the sky as if her fullness were weighing her down, as if she were too pregnant to journey from the horizon and claim her place in the dizzy crown of night.

Big Al took the first exit off the bridge and then sped down a winding, narrow dirt road that led to a mangrove lagoon fed by the bay. He slowed as we bumped along, and then he nestled the bike into a grove of wax myrtles. He shut down the ignition and helped me off the bike. I winced—my back was hurting bad—but he didn't notice because he was busy trying to help me get that helmet off my head. He set the helmets on his seat, and I fiddled with my hair, which must have looked like hell.

"Where are we?"

Big Al looked around. "From the looks of it, planet Earth."

"You gonna hurt me?"

Big Al made a screwy face, as if I'd wounded him. He walked down to the water's edge and sat down. In a voice so soft I was compelled to follow it, he said, "I don't know who you are or where you came from or who puts notions in your brain, but I don't hurt people. I don't. You got that?"

"Don't be mad. I had to ask." Fiddler crabs popped in and out of their holes and scurried, hither dither, all around us. I wasn't sure if we were scaring these tiny crabs or if this was how they always behaved.

"What are you doing, standing there? The crabs ain't gonna hurt you, either."

"I know that," I said as I sat down beside him. "You don't have to tell me."

He patted my back and I jerked away.

"What's wrong with you?"

"My mama beat me with a belt tonight."

"Jesus." He shook his head. "I'm sorry. She do that to your chin?"

"No." I touched the bandage. "That's from something else."

"What about your eye?"

I hugged my knees to my chest. "Yeah, that was her."

"Goddamn. Life sometimes sure does suck."

"Yep."

Then we were quiet. We stared at the sky. Mullet jumped. Birds fussed. The moon slowly rose.

A quick, light shower drifted over us. Big Al leaned back on his elbows. " 'Till rising and gliding out I wander'd off by myself, / In the mystical moist night-air, and from time to time, / Look'd up in perfect silence at the stars.' "

"Did you just make that up?"

He laughed. "Shit no. I can't make up words like that. Walt Whitman, 1865. I've memorized a slew of his poems."

"Why?"

"*Why?* I don't know *why.* I guess, I guess because I sort of think like him. I mean, I'm not as smart or anything. But when I look at the world—not cities, but water and sky, birds and trees—I'm real moved by its beauty. So was Walt. Thing is, he knew how to string words together in such a way that the perfect moment—the millisecond you realize you're connected to all this wild living mess—was captured for eternity. He flash-froze the world as he saw it into poems. Sort of like a photograph, but with words. Me, I can't write verse. But I can ride my bike. And it will take me to a perfect moment every time."

"I'm not sure I know what a perfect moment is."

He sat up and searched through his jacket pockets until he came up with a pack of Winstons and a matchbook. He struck a match across the heel of his boot and lit his cigarette. He took a deep drag and then asked, "You get beat a lot?"

"Some." I fidgeted with my shoelace. "It's gotten worse since my daddy died. Can't ever seem to please my mama.

I just keep doing bad things. Can't stop myself. And then she beats me, see, to make me better."

"Hold on there a second." Big Al cupped the cigarette in his huge paw of a hand. "My old man used to beat me unconscious. And I thought I deserved it because that's what the bastard told me. I hated myself for a good long time. Drank too much. Slept with too many women and didn't treat a single one of them the way a woman ought to be treated. Couldn't barely hold down a job. Then one night—I'd gotten the shit kicked out of me in a roadhouse down in the 'Glades. Jane's. That's the name of a bar, can you believe it? Like it was some sweet juke joint, but believe me, it was not. Don't be fooled by a name. But that's not my point. My point is, I'd been left for dead outside of Jane's, back past the bathrooms, down by the swamp. Skeeters were all over me. Hoped I'd soon be 'gator meat because that was a damn sight better than being skeeter meat. I lay there, and between my busted lips I whispered, 'Come on, 'gator, I want to mother-fucking die.' "

Big Al paused, reached over, gently touched my butterfly bandage. "Pay attention now, 'cause this here is the important part. I laid there, 'bout near dead, hoping the angels would come for me soon, when suddenly it hit me. My old man had lied. I wasn't bad. I didn't deserve those beatings. Somewhere along the way, my daddy's soul had been poisoned, and he sprayed all that shit from here to frigging eternity. I had a choice to make. I could pick up what was left of me, scrape off his shit, and find something good about myself, or I could wallow in the filth and die. Walt Whitman wrote, 'The scent of these arm-pits aroma finer than prayer.' Well, if all I've got that's good is my armpit aroma, I'll take it and be glad. But I won't ever again believe a son-of-a-bitch who tells me I'm no good."

The anger that strengthened my bones as Mama whipped me with Phoebe's belt rushed through my arms, legs, blood, teeth, battered veins. A tidal wave. A hot white blast. I stood up, pulled off my sweaters, and unbuttoned my shirt. Big Al's mouth fell open—he couldn't believe what he was seeing—and I thought, *You son-of-a-bitch.*

"Look! Look! Look!" I shrieked. I held my shirt in front of me so Big Al couldn't see my bare, flat titties, and turned my back to him. "That there. All across my back. You and your pretty words! Well, big shot, what have you and Mr. Walt Whitman got to say about my hurt skin!"

Big Al whispered, "Oh my God, little girl. You been beat to pulp."

I faced him, keeping my shirt pressed to my chest. "Nobody cares. My sister, she stays away from home as much as she possibly can. My brother is grown up and far away. My daddy is ten feet under. I screamed tonight. Screamed so loud I must have woke the dead. But nobody came. What do you do, mister, when you beg loud and long for help but there ain't nobody listening?"

Big Al looked away from me, out to the water. "Put your shirt back on, sweetheart." He sucked air through his teeth and then said, "That brother of yours. Can you go live with him?"

I eased my shirt back on and caught my breath as the cotton stuck to my slashed back. "I don't think so. He's—" I tried to pinpoint the exact words but could not. Maybe like Big Al, I wasn't any Walt Whitman and never would be. "He's busy," I said, falling miserably short of the truth about my family, unable to explain I was a burden to my mama and she hated me because of it, and I didn't want to turn to spoiled goods in the eyes of my brother, which is what would happen if I lived with him.

"But see here"—I pulled one of the sweaters on—"I don't want to leave my mama. She couldn't get on by herself. She needs me. And I don't want to go to no orphanage or live with some strange family. I just want things to be better. Mama and me. But better."

"Why you running away, then?"

"I don't know. Please don't ask me stuff I don't know." I looked at the ground. There weren't any fiddler crabs in sight. *They must be hiding from us,* I thought.

"Have you done this before?"

"No. I've wanted to, but didn't."

"Well, maybe this will be your mama's wake-up call." Big Al stood and slapped the dirt off his pants. He started down a footpath that cut to our right through the wax myrtle grove. I hesitated, not sure what to do, but then ran and caught up with him. When he heard me coming, he stopped and turned, with his finger to his lips to signal quiet. We followed the twisting path, which led us to another branch of the lagoon, and I tried to step softly but didn't succeed. It seemed everywhere I went I was destined to cause noise and trouble.

Big Al rubbed his thumb against my cheekbone and then nodded toward the water. Wading on the lagoon's far side, ankle deep, was a small flock of birds with long, upturned bills, stilt necks, white feathers edged in black.

My, oh my, I knew what they were! I remembered the picture of them I'd studied in the bird book at school. I thought about how they were almost shot out and how Miss Zora and I had trooped to the pond in hopes of spying them there. She had told me they lived mainly in Texas or Mexico. But she'd also said that creatures with wings could end up most anywhere.

How odd, I thought, that this night I would find my avocets. They were pretty birds, nothing run-of-the-mill about them, not with those bills aimed in the wrong direction. But what had appeared wrong and upside down was not. The avocets swept their bills back and forth through the water, sipping food. I thought, *These birds are hanging in there, surviving the curveballs.* I put my hand in Big Al's, and he squeezed it. Just the way daddy used to do.

I watched my avocets and heard their call. *Weep! Weep!* And I wondered how I was ever going to go home. How could I ever walk softly enough to please my mama? What act could I commit that would be so sweet it would wash away her sadness? What information did I need? What prayer wasn't I praying? How would I turn Mama and me into good women? Who would help me?

IT WAS NEAR to midnight when Big Al brought me home. He asked if I wanted to be dropped off on Nebraska Avenue rather than at the motel, and I said, "Nope, I'm tired of hiding things."

He parked the Harley right in front of the trailer, helped me off the bike and with the helmet, then held my head to his chest and whispered, "You're a good kid. Don't listen to anybody who says otherwise. Now, how are you going to get inside without a ruckus starting up?"

I pulled away from him. "She ain't here," I said, and pointed to where the Plymouth was usually parked. "I wonder where she went."

"Probably driving around, trying to cool down. Just watch, she'll walk in that trailer in a little while and she'll be all better. Want me to come in? Make sure there aren't any surprises?"

I shook my head no and thought about those avocets wading in calm water. "I'll be okay," I said. But I was afraid for my new friend to leave because I didn't know if I'd ever see him again. I reached up and we hugged once more. I could tell he was taking care not to touch my belt welts. Then he knelt down and kissed my cheek. It was a soft, sweet kiss. The kind parents are supposed to give their children.

"Promise me you'll stay away from Diamond Lil's," he said.

"Cross my heart and hope to die." We shook on it. "Am I ever going to see you again?"

He looked me in the eye and said, "I'll be around."

I believed him.

Big Al got on his Harley and kick-started it. Over the bike's loose, gurgling roar he said, "Good night, sunshine!"

Then he sped away.

I stood in the road and watched the darkness take him. But I held on to his voice: "Good night, sunshine!" The only other person who ever called me sunshine was my daddy—my faraway, untouchable daddy.

WITH BIG AL'S advice and Walt Whitman's poetry ringing in my ears, I walked up the trailer steps and opened the door. Phoebe was sitting at the kitchen table, fretting over her math book.

"Where have y'all been?" she asked, not bothering to hide her worry and obviously believing Mama was walking in behind me.

I slammed the door, went and got a Co'-Cola out of the refrigerator. "I've been running away with a biker man. Don't know where Mama is."

Phoebe looked as if I were babbling in tongues. "What are you talking about? And what happened to your hair? It looks awful."

Standing beside Phoebe, in the dim glare of the overhead light, as a roach slowly promenaded across our kitchen table, I started laughing and could not stop. My laughter brought tears and shortness of breath. Phoebe kept asking what was so funny. Her face danced back and forth between confusion and amusement. But I could not answer her. My mind was a jumbled mess: Poor Phoebe commenting on my windblown hair, poor Mama wandering the night, poor me wishing Mama were dead. I slammed my Co'-Cola on the kitchen table, which made that cockroach move faster. My laughter slowed to something akin to hiccups. I took off my two sweaters and lifted my shirt. "Please, Phoebe, go get Miss Zora. I think I'm hurt bad."

MISS ZORA CLUCKED and cooed all over me. I lay belly-down on the couch, and she slathered my wounds with a homemade salve that smelled sweet and charred.

Phoebe ran her hand through my hair and asked, "What's in that stuff?"

"Oh, nothing special. Pine bark, aloe, ground lamb's ear—don't worry, that's a plant."

"How do you know it works?" asked my doubting sister.

Miss Zora paused from me for a second and said firmly, "Because my grandmama said so. And I've never found anything she said not to be of the utmost truth. Would you please cut those gauze bandages into strips?"

"Yes, ma'am," Phoebe said. "Then what?"

"Just set them here by me, that'll suit us fine. And when you're finished, would you put some water on to boil? I'll brew us some tea. We'll get this little girl feeling good in no time."

Phoebe said, "Yes, ma'am," but I thought it looked as if fear had pulled down a waxy shade over her eyes.

I said, "Phoebe, don't worry. So what if Mama comes home and catches Miss Zora here? It don't matter anymore."

"Listen, ladies, do not get worked up about me and your mama," Miss Zora said. "If I'm here when she comes home, I'll know how to deal with it. I've been around the block a few times."

I imagined Miss Zora giving Mama what-for and Mama fitfully wringing her hands and experiencing one of those fundamental changes of heart I'd heard TV preachers spout off about.

Phoebe began cutting the bandages. "I just don't want any more fighting," she said.

Miss Zora rubbed the salve into my back. "From the look of things, something is going to have to give. Your mama must be in a world of trouble."

Phoebe and I didn't say anything. But Phoebe paled. Just the thought of Mama's many troubles was enough to make us both sick to our stomachs.

Once my "dressing was set," as Miss Zora put it—which sounded to me as if she'd just stuffed a turkey—I sat up. Phoebe got our pillows off the bed, plumped them as she situated them on the couch, and said for me to stay still and rest.

"Thank you, Sister."

Then the three of us settled down to elderberry tea. I let the steam waft over my face. I was prepared for Miss Zora to start asking nosy questions about Mama, but she did not. Instead, she nosed into Phoebe's business. Did Phoebe want to go to college? What did she want to become? What was her favorite color? What sort of man did she want to marry?

At the last question I gleefully screamed, "L.J.! L.J.!"

"Bird," Phoebe protested, "I'm not going to marry L.J."

"Who's L.J.?" asked Miss Zora.

Phoebe giggled and stared into her tea.

"Mr. Louis Ippolito Junior himself!" I announced.

Miss Zora said, "Mmm, mmm, mmm! He is one good-looking boy. He can stop traffic, the way he's built."

"I seen them smooching."

Miss Zora patted my leg. "Sweetheart, be careful about snooping on your big sister. Because when it comes time for you to start seeing boys, I have a hunch Phoebe's memory is going to be clear and exact. You just might end up getting a taste of your own medicine."

"I'm never going to have a boyfriend," I said. Jesus didn't count, as He had jilted me. "Boys are nasty."

Phoebe said, "Yeah, right."

"Child, I want to be around when you start changing your tune," Miss Zora said, and then she asked, "Is that a radio over there?"

"Yes, ma'am," Phoebe answered.

"I'd love some music. How about y'all?" Miss Zora walked over to the kitchen counter where the radio was and clicked it on. She twirled the dial, seemed to know exactly what station she wanted.

"Your favorite hits from the forties, fifties, and today," crooned the DJ.

Miss Zora turned to us, a smile stretching across her leathery face as if she'd just stumbled upon a brilliant idea. "I think we ought to have a sock hop," she said.

"A sock what?" I asked.

"A dance," Phoebe explained. "They used to do it a long time ago. Dance in their socks."

"It wasn't that long ago," Miss Zora said.

"Rock Around the Clock" suddenly blared through the

room. Miss Zora kicked off her old canvas shoes and said, "Come on, Phoebe, let's dance."

"I don't know how to dance to that."

"Well, I'll teach you. If you're seeing boys, you've got to know how to dance. Hurry. Before the song is over."

Miss Zora pushed the coffee table out of the way. Phoebe stood, but she crossed her arms and legs as if she wasn't about to let anybody loosen her up.

"Look here, it's all in the footwork," Miss Zora said. In her baggy dungarees and a plaid work shirt—she was not one for fancy clothes—she proceeded to teach my sister something that looked an awful lot like the jitterbug.

Miss Zora was light on her feet. There was talent in her body. Even a fool could see that. I remembered the photo of her in front of her house with her husband and baby Moses. She'd been a pretty woman in her time. I bet she and her husband used to dance together on that wide, windy front porch. I bet they were happy.

Phoebe reluctantly followed Miss Zora's lead, and before long, a smile tripped over my sister's face. I cheered them on: "Yeah, go!"

Pretty soon, my feet were keeping time. Miss Zora spun Phoebe around as if my sister were one of those porcelain-skinned dolls hidden in a jeweled music box.

"Y'all could win a dance contest!" I crowed.

They kept on through the next three songs. Phoebe was taking her dancing lesson as seriously as she took the rest of her life, but still, she was having fun. I could see that. Her shoulders weren't hunched, and that brow of hers unfurrowed into a smooth high forehead fitting for a girl her age.

After the fourth song, Phoebe set out a bowl of potato chips, and we started drinking Co'-Colas instead of hot tea.

Miss Zora was sweating up a storm. "Lord God," she said, "I haven't moved that quickly in a good ten years. I think I'm going to faint!"

But right then Chubby Checker came on with "Hey, Let's Twist."

"No, you can't sit this one out," I said. I got up from the couch, grabbed her hands, and pulled. Miss Zora groaned. "Dance!" I said. "Please dance!"

The three of us, in the living room of that cramped trailer, did the twist so good we would have turned heads had there been anyone watching. If we'd been on "American Bandstand," Mr. Dick Clark himself would have rushed over to us, stuck that big microphone in our faces, and asked questions. The music and the joy in that room were pure enough that for a few minutes, I forgot about my hurt back and our lost mama.

Phoebe twisted all the way to the floor, and Miss Zora said, "Girl, you can twist!"

During a slow song—something from the forties—Miss Zora taught Phoebe the box step. I watched closely because, despite my pronouncements of disgust for boys, privately I understood that such dancing knowledge might prove helpful to me one day. Phoebe said, "I wish people still danced like this. It's so romantic."

I looked out the front window to the empty space where Mama's Plymouth should have been, and then turned to Phoebe and Miss Zora and said, "I've got a good idea. Let's have a slumber party. We can bring in the covers off our bed—Miss Zora, you can use Mama's pillow—and we'll sleep in the living room."

Phoebe opened her mouth, and I'm near positive she was going to object for fear of Mama coming home, but Miss Zora got there first. "What an excellent idea, Miss Avocet. And just in time, too, because I'm pooped!"

She squeezed Phoebe's shoulders and asked me, "How's your back feeling?" She walked over to the radio and flipped it off.

"Please, no! Can we keep the radio on?" I pleaded.

Miss Zora looked at Phoebe, who just shrugged, then she looked at me.

"Please?"

"Well, I guess we can keep it on real low. Background music for our sleep."

I traveled such a far distance that night—from suffering the brunt of Mama's unbridled rage and receiving the worst beating of my life to stumbling upon that cemetery of fallen stars at Diamond Lil's to the strange joy of meeting Big Al to the thrill of riding on his Harley and the awe-inspiring sight of my avocets to the comforting and idle chatter of us three souls—Miss Zora, Phoebe, and me—lying on the living room floor, trying to find comfort in a world bent on spinning out of control.

And so it was time to sleep. Miss Zora was in the middle, Phoebe was nearest to the kitchen, and I was tucked in next to the couch. I stayed flat on my belly, as my back was too tender for me to do otherwise.

Miss Zora talked us into Sandman Land. She told us about fishing for her and her family's supper down there in Ochopee. "Mullet, reds, grouper. We ate like royalty back then," she said.

As she spoke, I listened beyond her words, trying to detect the sound of the Plymouth turning off Nebraska Avenue and then Mama traveling under the oaks to her parking place in front of the trailer. I thought about Big Al and his poetry and how he looked when the night swallowed him up. He looked eternal, as if that Harley and those stars and the fat moon rising above the mossy branches were a part of my life forever. I rested my hand in Miss Zora's and made a giant wish. Maybe Big Al would bring Mama home. He'd find her Plymouth parked outside a church or a bar or a dive motel and he'd sense that the car was my mama's and he'd go in and get her. And just because she'd met a good man who carried her to her children and who lifted a corner of this jagged world off her shoulders, she would change. In the evening's first dream, I saw her and Big Al sitting in an all-night diner, drinking coffee, smoking cigarettes, talking—sweetly, gently, sweetly.

THAT NIGHT, TO help remind me that I wasn't alone, I kept my legs pressed against Miss Zora's. Part of my brain stayed awake, alert for the sound of Mama's car. Big Al and Mama and the diner drifted into the shadows, allowing nightmares to nibble at my heart. They went like this: I'm standing in front of Mama. She's sitting on the couch, gazing at me as if she loves me. She reaches for my hand, grabs my shirt. Her face explodes. She turns into a ghoul. Toothless, her fingers sprouting razor blades, she sings, "You're a little lump of coal," as she slashes my face.

I must have made noises as I struggled because at some point Miss Zora kissed my cheek and said, "There, there, baby, everything is okay."

Her words carried me beyond the bad dream, floated me out of the trailer and into the field, where, disturbed by neither nightmares nor dreams, I rested. The grasses rustled, sounding like windblown lullabies. The moon warmed me with her buttery light, and eventually a choir of dragonflies swept me up in a hundred gauzy wings, guided me back to the trailer and into a new dream. I thought maybe Big Al and my mama were still hashing things out in that diner. But no. It was Miss Zora, her voice mingled with my mama's.

What a strange dream! A dream without pictures and only snatches of conversation:

"What are you doing here?"

"I'm here to talk to you. To let you know I'm your friend, and to say I think you need help."

"You don't know anything about me!"

". . . a mother raising good children."

". . . out of my yard. What do you want?"

". . . about yourself, your pain."

"Dear God, I almost killed my baby tonight. What's wrong with me? . . . Phoebe . . . brush. I need help."

"What about you . . ."

". . . a horrible life . . . always feeling guilty, worthless. My father was so violent . . ."

". . . find a way to let go of the past . . ."

"Tell me about your husband, Zora. What was he like?"

". . . as if it was yesterday."

"She loves you so much . . . horribly jealous of the two of you."

". . . little girl loves her mother. Nobody can take that love away but you."

The dream was a beautiful quilt, stitched with Mama and Miss Zora's words, pieced together by my many wishes. *How nice for Mama and Miss Zora to make friends! How very, very nice,* I was thinking as I floated awake on Mama's voice: "The children deserve a good home, a decent mother."

I opened my eyes and reached for Miss Zora. There were no soft tunes whirling out of the radio, and Miss Zora was gone. I sat up and looked around. Phoebe was dead to the world, her arm flung over her eyes to guard against the sun that fell in bars all across us. My back ached and felt tight, as if Mama had not beat open my skin with that belt but had stretched it so taut it had split. I scrambled up, looked out the window that faced the road. The Plymouth was back, parked like a giant blue moth in front of the trailer. I tiptoed past Phoebe and peeked out the side window.

Oh my God, Miss Zora and Mama *were* talking to each other! Maybe I hadn't been dreaming. Miss Zora was listening, looking down at Mama, who was sitting on the concrete steps, smoking, spilling words and tears. I watched as Mama stood and walked over to the garage. She stared at the trash Mr. Ippolito insisted on keeping. Miss Zora followed her. They were speaking softly. I couldn't hear a thing. Then all my hopes crashed down around me because Mama raised her voice. I heard the words "Bird" and "temper," and then she went back to a near whisper. *She's probably telling Miss Zora how bad I am,* I thought, *and Miss Zora is going to believe her and then won't be my friend anymore.*

I walked away from the window. "Phoebe, wake up!" I whispered. "Phoebe!" I shook her with my foot.

She groaned, rubbed her eyes. "What is it?"

"It's Mama. She's back. And she's talking to Miss Zora. This is bad, Phoebe. I had a dream that they were in the yard, talking like a couple of friends. But it ain't true. She's out there saying all kinds of mean things about me! I just know it!" Then I couldn't go on because those wretched tears started falling.

"Bird, maybe they're simply talking, like, about themselves. The world doesn't revolve around you." Phoebe threw off the covers. She got up and peered out the window. I grabbed hold of the end of her T-shirt.

"What do you think?"

"I don't know. At least Mama's not screaming at her. I wonder if we ought to go out there." Phoebe chewed on her fingernails, attempted to eavesdrop. "Can you hear what they're saying?"

"No. If they'd come back over this way, I could."

"Well, watching them isn't doing us any good. Go put on some clean clothes, Bird. I'll straighten the living room. At least she won't be able to yell at us for that."

I moved slowly out of and into my clothes because my back hurt and because I couldn't think straight. My body was a sack of rage, and there wasn't anything I could do with it, I had nowhere to dump it. I wanted Mama to quit telling lies to my friend. I wanted to believe in my dream. I wanted Mama to come in the trailer and not leave me again. I wanted her to get back in that Plymouth and never return. I loved her and feared her, pitied her and hated her. How could that be? Love, hate, fear, pity, all in the same heartbeat?

Phoebe came into the bedroom, her arms loaded down with sheets and blankets. She stacked them on the bed. I studied her face, trying to see if she was as upset as I was. But Phoebe had learned long ago how to hide her thoughts. Mama accused her of being unfeeling. But that wasn't so. She'd simply buried them deep, deep down so Mama couldn't use Phoebe's emotions against her.

"Bird, what if I fix some pancakes? You can help."

I looked in the mirror. My butterfly bandage was tattered and dirty. I ran my finger along my right eye socket. A dark, purple bruise shaped like a belt buckle framed my eye. I straightened my shoulders and pulled my T-shirt away from my back. "Can I stir the batter?"

"Sure. I'll even let you try to flip some over if you promise not to burn yourself."

"Okay." I imagined myself flipping pancakes into the air. But then I realized the ceiling was too low. The pancakes would get stuck up there; it would make an awful mess.

From where we stood in the kitchen, we could not see Mama or Miss Zora, but we kept looking toward the window anyway. My first two pancakes fell apart. Phoebe said I turned them over too soon. I got it right after that.

We ate at the kitchen table. I picked up the Log Cabin syrup and drenched my pancakes. Phoebe used only a squirt. As usual, she was watching her figure. We talked quietly, hoping to catch a phrase or two of the conversation going on outside.

"You know, Bird, I think they're getting along. Looked

to me like they were having a real serious conversation. And Miss Zora is your friend. She's not going to turn against you. I don't think you need to worry."

"I sure hope not." I sponged up syrup with a wedge of pancake, shoveled it into my mouth. The mixture was sickeningly sweet, just the way I liked it. "In my dream, Mama was talking as if she was so sorry for beating me," I said with my mouth full. "She wanted help so she'd behave better."

Phoebe made a doubting Thomas face. "I don't know what to tell you, Bird. We've got to wait and see."

Then Mama's voice rang out clearly. "Thank you, Zora. I mean it. Thank you. I'll get back with you by this evening."

Miss Zora's reply was lost in the sudden chatter of a blue jay.

I looked at the door, watched the knob turn, and held on, knuckle-white tight, to my fork. The door swung open.

Mama walked in, red-eyed from crying and maybe from booze, maybe from no sleep. She dropped her pocketbook on the floor, walked toward me. I tried to back away. Didn't want that sting, that pounding against my bones. Mama swooped down. I shut my eyes and braced for the impact of her open palm, her fist. She was so close I smelled her: sweat, cigarettes, coffee, booze, regret. Then the blow came, but it was different. A few seconds passed before I understood what had happened. Mama had pressed her lips to my cheek and kissed me.

I opened my eyes. Mama was moving away, descending on Phoebe, kissed her, too. Then she walked to the sink and hung on to it. After about a ten-count, she opened the cupboard and reached for the bottle of Early Times but then stopped. She turned and walked to the refrigerator, got out three RC's, set them on the counter, and with the bottle opener in hand, she said, her voice trembling, "Girls, I did a lot of thinking last night."

She opened the RC's and handed us ours. She pulled out a chair and sat, took a sip. "Phoebe, will you get my cigarettes out of my pocketbook for me?"

Phoebe reached for Mama's purse and handed it to her.

"How are you, Bird?" Mama asked, and she seemed to be struggling to hold her face together. It was as if all the beatings she'd ever suffered and all the ones she'd dished out were conspiring against her, forcing her bones off their hinges, causing her to shake and rattle as if she were nothing but a creaking skeleton of a mother.

"I'm fine," I said.

She looked past me, through me, and a sad smile began to steady her face. She opened her pocketbook, rummaged through it, came up with her cigarettes and that lighter Daddy had given her back in the grove, the one with the lady skiing in a kerosene sea. Mama lit a Salem, took a couple of slow drags, finally spoke. "I don't want to scare the two of you. I've done enough of that. But I've got to talk straight, and goddamn it, it's not easy."

She planted her elbows on the table, laced her fingers, balanced the cigarette between two knuckles. I stared at my plate and heard her say, "There is something wrong with me. You two look at me when I'm talking to you."

I turned to her. Hair fell in my eyes. I thought I heard that blackbird cackling. But that wasn't possible. My brother had killed it. He'd made it go away.

"Something has happened inside me," Mama went on. "Bird, beating you the way I did last night, honey, when I came to my senses, I realized what a god-awful thing I'd done." She picked up her RC, took a quick sip, then set the bottle back down, all without ever letting go of her cigarette. "It's as if that beating back in the grove, and your daddy dying, and me worrying so much about money and where our next meal is going to come from, and this hard fear in my head that keeps whispering that if I'm not tough with you, then you'll become like me—a person without a future—all that's balled up inside me like a cancer. It is eating me alive. Are you paying attention?"

"Yes, ma'am."

"I drink too much, I know. I should not hit either one of you, ever. I know that, too. But I can't stop myself. I want to do right, but something snaps. I turn into my father and then into my husband, and I do to you what they did to me. And it's not right. It's not right." She put her hands to her face, the cigarette was terribly close to burning her, and she moaned.

I patted her arm. "Mama, it's okay. Phoebe and me will help. We'll be better so you won't get so angry." I looked at Phoebe. Her eyes were saucer round. I thought of the Devil's box and wanted to shout, "Cry, damn it, cry!"

Mama stubbed out her cigarette, lit another. "Phoebe," she said, "you're older. You're going to understand what I'm saying better than your sister. So listen very carefully because Bird is going to need you. You're going to have to explain my words to her far down the road. I have got to get help. See, I think I beat you because I was beat. I yell and call you names because that's how it's been for me my whole damn life, people hurling filthy names at me."

I stared again into my pancakes and syrup. I saw that blackbird descending through the ceiling. My stomach churned. I willed the bird back to its grave, and then I spoke my mind. "Does this mean I'm going to grow up and beat my children?"

"No, Bird," Mama said sadly, "because I'm sending you away."

"No, no, no, no!" I began to scream.

"Listen, child, listen to me! For once in your life, listen! I can't get well—I can't stop drinking or being too rough on you girls, I can't find a way to stop hating myself—unless I am alone for a while. I need to concentrate solely on myself. This is the hardest thing I have ever done. But—this is the God's-honest truth—I'm doing it because I love you."

"But I don't want to go away," I wailed.

Mama reached for Phoebe's hand, then mine. "Zora has agreed to take you to south Florida with her. She has people down there, roots. I was wrong about her. She is a good woman. We talked for a long time. I don't know how somebody gets that wise in a lifetime. When I came home, she was outside waiting for me. And that made me mad. But I guess I didn't have much fight left in me, because when I told her to leave and she wouldn't, I caved in and listened. After all, she did come over and take care of you."

I looked at Phoebe, and she looked back. With all my heart, I knew we were thinking the same thing: It wasn't a dream, I'd heard the real thing. Mama let go of our hands, gingerly touched her broken nose as if it hurt, and then started again: "Before I knew it, I was telling Zora my whole life story. We talked it all through, about what was best for you girls and what was best for me. She said she'd do anything to help us get through this bad time. And that's when we came up with our plan. She is going to raise you for as long as needed. I'm going to stay here and get help. I'm going to try to get my health back. And when I do, I'll come for you. I'll come find my babies. Please, don't fight me on this. I can't take it."

I felt that familiar falling, falling, falling, coming to pieces in the middle of a hard blue sky.

Mama said, "Come here, let me hold you."

The three of us huddled, cried, tried to push away the evil that had soured our family's blood for generations. I dug my nails into Mama's arm and into Phoebe's waist. *Hang on, hang on,* I said to myself.

FOR THE NEXT two days I stayed close to my mama. She washed all of our clothes—Phoebe's and mine. She folded and refolded our skirts, shorts, shirts—most of them she'd sewn herself—lingering over them as if each scrap of cloth contained soul-saving memories. Finally, when she couldn't put it off any longer, she packed every stitch of clothing we owned in that old black suitcase we'd brought with us from the grove.

Decisions were made: Miss Zora would take the Plymouth and leave Mama her old truck. Mama insisted on this, said she'd feel better if we were in our own car. Miss Zora's belongings, including the bones, would not fit in the Plymouth, so Mama and she decided to rent a small U-Haul trailer. Money details were worked out in private.

Mama worried about my back, but when the time came for the bandages to be changed, she called on Miss Zora.

The day before we were to leave, Mama sat on the couch, sipping iced tea that I don't think was spiked, looking lost, and I thought maybe she was going to change her mind about sending us away. I sat on the floor, by her feet, sifting through my treasure chest of spring. She said, "Life can be so damn rough. I want yours to be better. You and Phoebe deserve that—a chance at a happy life." Then she pressed her hands to her head as if she were trying not to explode.

Even though I loved my Miss Zora, I did not want to be with her at the expense of Mama. Why couldn't we all be friends together? I looked at Mama and said, "Please, let me and Phoebe stay. You'll heal faster with Miss Zora's help. We'll be good. We won't get in the way."

"No, Bird, I told you already—this is something I've got to do alone."

I asked her to call Hank and tell him what was happening. She said she needed to wait a few days, didn't want him arguing with her.

Mama rubbed her forehead—she had the shakes bad—and said the county offered free counseling to poor women like her. She was going to work hard, do everything those doctors ordered. When the anger and sickness was out of her, she would come and get us. "Maybe by then your big brother will be finished with school and he'll move back down here and we'll be together, like a real family."

"Yes, Mama," I said as I balanced a broken bird egg in my hand, "that's probably how it will be."

OUR LAST MEAL in the trailer was hot dogs, coleslaw, and potato chips. We sat at the kitchen table and tried to make small talk. But when you can't imagine the future and the past is too awful to mention, words tend to stick in the back of your throat. And when you do think of something to say, it usually comes out wrong.

But I tried. I slathered a bun with mayonnaise and said the first chatty thing that came to mind. "I sure am going to miss the pool." Phoebe kicked me under the table.

Mama didn't respond, just sipped ice water and smoked. Sister got a second helping of coleslaw—that's all she was eating. The sound of our chewing grew gigantic. Somebody had to say something. Even bruising words were better than this pounding silence. So I piped up again. "Are you gonna come visit us?"

"Bird, I can't make any plans right now. There are too many things to think about." She drummed the lip of her glass and then, as if her brain were a tape recorder, she erased her answer. "Of course I'll visit you."

Phoebe, lost in thought, stirred her tea about ten times. She waved a fly off the table, pushed away her plate, and asked, "Have you told Mr. Ippolito?"

Mama grabbed her cigarettes, tried to tap one out, but the pack was empty. "Your boyfriend did it for me. Don't worry, I'm not mad." She twisted the empty pack until it resembled a corkscrew. "Actually, Louis has been real good about it. He said that Miss Zora would take great care of you. He said he was there for me if I needed him."

"That's good," I said.

"Yeah, I guess. Phoebe, get me that pack of Salems on the kitchen counter. Bird, are you done eating?"

"Almost."

Phoebe handed Mama the Salems. She lit one, took a deep drag, flicked an ash, opened her mouth to speak, hesitated, took another drag, and then said in a voice so soft it didn't seem like hers, "I know this may sound crazy, but I'd like for you two to do me a favor. Would you mind if I brushed your hair? I'd really love that."

Phoebe and I stole glances. Then my sister spoke for us. "Sure, Mama."

We sat outside on the concrete steps. To a stranger, our actions would have seemed ordinary. But maybe that's why families are important: what's humdrum to an onlooker is an outright miracle to a couple of sisters.

Mama did Phoebe first, then me. The only sounds: the soft untangling of our hair, the satisfying songs of birds that had lived another day.

I faced the field, the setting sun casting it in gold, as Mama brushed far more than a hundred strokes. I closed my eyes. Mama began humming some long-lost tune, and it shook free a memory in me. I saw myself when I was a very small child, maybe three. Mama and I were sitting on the porch swing together. She was running her hands across the back of my head, stroking me, singing a nursery rhyme.

A fresh wind, full of the scents of the field, blew through my hair. I put my hand on Mama's, the one that held the brush, the same brush she had used to beat Phoebe, and my heart filled with sad amazement—without a doubt, there was a time when I was not afraid of my mama. Or her hands.

The next morning, after we were packed and as Mama and Miss Zora made sure the trailer was properly hooked to the Plymouth, Phoebe said she had something to do. She tossed her long black braid over her shoulder and headed to the pool. We all knew she was meeting L.J.

I thought about following her and showing off. Maybe try one last dive, face my fear. But no, deep, deep down, I knew I'd already done that. In fact, I was facing my fear even as Mama and Miss Zora chatted about gas prices and mileage. I pressed my face against the hood of the Plymouth, tried to think of a way to change the course of this terrible event. *Please, dear Jesus,* I prayed, *bless my mama with an immediate healing.*

A cold nose nudged my leg. Old Sam come to see me off. I hugged him, told him I'd miss him.

I heard Miss Zora say, "I think I'll check my cottage one last time for anything I might have forgotten."

Mama looked in the direction of the pool. "Yes, I should go through the trailer once more, too. Make sure the girls have everything."

Before Miss Zora walked away, she caught my eye; her meaning was clear: You are loved.

I followed Mama inside. She didn't look for items we might have missed, as she said. No, she sat at the kitchen table and stared at the wall. So I took my seat on the couch, the shadows of those jalousie windows falling across us like a pile of timbers. We did not speak, just let the stifling heat wash over us. And unlike the uneasy silence that marred our last supper together, it felt good, secure, being that quiet, sitting that still. Words would have been dangerous, they might have busted us loose.

Within the hour, Phoebe returned, half a silver heart hanging from a chain around her neck. She said L.J. was wearing the other half and that he promised to visit her over summer vacation. Mama walked to the sink and turned on the faucet. She waved her cigarette under the water and then threw it in the trash.

"Phoebe, I know I've been rough sometimes about you and boys. I'm sorry. I was wrong. That L.J., he's a fine young man."

Phoebe nodded and clutched the half-heart to her chest. Then she broke down—convulsing, heaving tears. I saw the Devil turning the key in his box and Phoebe's tears flying right out of his hot hands. Mama hurried over to her, held her, and said, "Sweetheart, please forget the bad names I called you."

I went back outside. Old Sam evidently didn't understand good-bye because he stood in the road in front of the trailer, wagging his tail, ready to play. I called to him, "How about one last walk?"

We wandered all over the field, going where Old Sam's nose led us, pausing for him to pee on nearly every blade of grass. I picked a rich girl's lily, tucked it behind my ear, and thought, *Maybe by the time we get back to the trailer, Mama will have changed her mind and God will have answered my prayer and miraculously healed her.* Then the three of us—no, the four, Miss Zora was part of our family—would live happily ever after.

The shadow of a large bird darkened Old Sam and me and that billowing field. I crouched in the grass. Fear wrapped itself around my ankles, and I tumbled into the past. It was all there—the kittens in the grove and the blackbird who stole my voice and the dark blue revolver in my daddy's dough-white hands and Mama's crushed face limp against my brother's shoulder. I remembered that Devil boy on top of me, taunting, "This is what girls want."

I grabbed a stone, stood up, and threw it at the moving shadow. "No it's not, you son-of-a-bitch!" I screamed. "We just want to be free of the likes of you."

The shadow rippled across the stiff reeds, then spiraled out of sight. *Goddamn it,* I thought, *there ain't no simple answers.* Mama's life was sad and mean and it had been for years. But still, wasn't Mama doing something great, something huge? Wasn't it a miracle, in and of itself, that she decided our grief and violence needed to end? I looked at the sky, raised my arms above my head, imagined myself walking across the clouds, riding the wind. But to where, to where? I didn't know. I lowered my arms and gazed across the field. It would not be easy for any of us, I realized, this stepping out of my family's barbed-wire circle.

We turned around, Old Sam and I. Lost in thought, I wound my way home through the broken dreams of my parents. Mama and Miss Zora were standing by the trailer steps, talking like a couple of old friends. Adults were confusing, the way they could hate one day and love the next. Phoebe came out of the trailer, the granny bag Mama had made her for Christmas slung over her shoulder. I walked up to them and said, "Miss Zora, we gonna go to your home?"

"Yes, little girl. We're going to open its windows and air it out and get started with a whole new life. And your mama is, too. And when she's ready, she'll join us. I know she will."

"How about your daughter? We gonna make up with her?"

Miss Zora took off her straw hat and planted it firmly on my head. "We just might. We'll see how things go."

Mama gave Miss Zora some money and said she'd send her a check every month.

Miss Zora handed her the keys to her truck. "Be sure you ease the clutch slowly," she said. Then she hugged my mama. "I am proud of you. This is a strong act, baby. We all might just find our way to a peaceful and happy place because you're being so brave. I will take good care of them. You know that." Miss Zora kissed my mama smack on the lips, which surprised us all, and then she said, "We're counting on you to get well."

"I'll do my best," Mama said unsteadily. "I promise."

Mama turned to Phoebe and hugged her. They started whispering good-byes.

I walked out to the Plymouth and opened the back door. My treasure chest of spring was on the seat. I pulled it out and held it close—bird bones, dried lizards, fallen nests, my Gideon Bible. Then I went back over to Mama. She had her arm around Phoebe but no one was talking. Just tear-wet eyes all around.

"This here, Mama, is all I've got. My treasures. I want you to have them. Take care of them."

Mama spied that little pine chest that Daddy had made with his own two hands so that I would have a safe place to stash my heart's desires, and a tired smile creased her face. She took it from me and said, "Thank you, sweetheart. You are a rare bird. I'm going to miss you."

She hugged me and kissed my forehead. She held on tight. I felt her blood in my veins, felt the goodness that was buried there, deep-rooted goodness that wanted to shoot toward the sun. Just like the grasses and wildflowers of the field—bright, green, tender, if given a chance.

"I'm sorry," my mama whispered. "I'm so sorry."

I pressed myself against her. She smelled like the old days—talcum powder and orange blossoms. "I forgive you," I said, "I really do."

"Oh, baby, oh, baby, this is too hard." Mama pulled away, tears rolled down her cheeks.

"Don't go away from me," I said. I put her hands to my face and held them there. I wanted to remember her fingers, her palms, her knuckles, touching my skin so gently. I wanted to forget all about the sound a fist makes when it slams into flesh.

Then I heard Miss Zora. She cleared her throat. She said, "I might be wrong, sweet ladies, but I think it's time."

"All right, Bird. Everything is okay. You heard Zora. Be a good girl." Slowly, I let go of Mama, and as I did, I felt the invisible cord rip—the cord that ties together children and parents.

Mama handed Miss Zora the keys, and the three of us—Miss Zora, Phoebe, and I—slid into the front seat of that angel's-wing-blue Plymouth. Our voices rose, mingled, hung like blossoms in the spring air:

"Good-bye!"

"Good-bye!"

"Good-bye!"

"See you soon!"

"I love you!"

"I love you, too!"

"Good-bye!"

Miss Zora turned the key in the ignition. The Plymouth roared to life. We moved slowly forward. I stared out the window at Mama. She looked small and not at all scary, standing in front of that broken-down trailer.

I waved at my mama and held her in my heart. I didn't know if I would ever see her again. Maybe she would get the help she needed. Or maybe she would sit in that trailer and drink herself to death. Or maybe she would soar. I could not know those things, the alphabet of our infinite blue future. But at that exact moment—before time marched on, before all the clocks in all the world pushed us into the next moment, as Mama stood alone under the oaks, waving good-bye—I knew she loved me. And I knew she wasn't completely shattered. Somewhere inside her a tendril of strength remained, or else she never could have unlatched that ancient cage door, she never could have stared at the dark wall of her life and said, "Enough."

Miss Zora inched the car down the shady drive of The Travelers Motel. Mama grew smaller and smaller, and when we turned the corner, she fell out of sight.

We drove past the office, then paused before pulling out onto Nebraska Avenue. We were going to head south on Highway 41, after all. I thought that Miss Zora's house in Ochopee might be on 41, and if so, we weren't going far from Mama at all, just to a different neighborhood on the same stretch of road. I turned around in my seat, hoping to see Mama, hoping she had walked down toward the office to get one last glimpse of us.

But no. No one was there. No people, no squirrels, no Mr.

Ippolito singing opera, no good sons, no birds chirping. The motel seemed devoutly empty. I faced forward.

Miss Zora stared dead ahead into the traffic. A Harley roared in the far distance. A semi's air brakes squealed to a halt over at May Ellen's. Miss Zora tapped the steering wheel. "Last chance," she said. "Do we stay? Or do we go?"

I looked into her calm, brown eyes and saw no hint of violence, no spirit that was mean. I slipped my hand into Phoebe's and hooked my arm around Miss Zora's.

"Let's go," I said.

And we flew.

"Evocative . . . There's no denying Connie May Fowler's talent and the breadth of her imagination."
—*The New York Times*

RIVER OF HIDDEN DREAMS

Connie May Fowler

Forty-something Sadie Hunter is a loner. But more than that, she is afraid of not being alone. Ever since her mother and Native American grandmother died together when she was a child, Sadie hasn't let anyone get too close. Not even Carlos, a passionate Cuban who sees the rich soul that Sadie tries to hide from herself. And although she tries to fight it, she half suspects that with Carlos's help, she could find the truth of her past, and it could set her free.